# DIRTY BORN: A DARK MAFIA ROMANCE

(MICHELI MAFIA) BOOK 4

ZOE BETH GELLER

KINKY INK PUBLISHING

Dirty Born
A Dark Mafia Romance
The Dirty Series: Micheli Mafia Book 4

Copyright © 2021 by Zoe Beth Geller
Kinky Ink Publishing
All rights reserved.
Cover Design by Shepard Designs
Edited by Partners in Crime
Proofreading by Sandra Sjoquist

No part of this book may be reproduced or transmitted in any form or by any means, electronic or mechanical, including photocopying, recording or by any information storage and retrieval system without the written permission of the author, except for the use of brief quotations in reviews.

This is a work of fiction. Names, characters, places, and incidents are either products of the author's imagination or are used fictitiously. Any resemblance to actual persons, living or dead, events, or locales is entirely coincidental. The author acknowledges the trademarked status and trademark owners of various products referenced in this work of fiction, which have been used without their permission. The publication/use of these trademarks is not authorized nor sponsored by the trademark owners. This e-book is licensed for your personal use only. This e-book may not be resold or given away to other people. If you enjoy this story of hot and steamy romance, please refer your friends so that they can download their own copy.

You can also visit me on Facebook and Amazon.

Please visit my website at zoegellerauthor.com

# DEDICATION

Dedicated to my Aunt Rose, cousins, and good friend, Diane, in Italy. I can't wait to see you again. Every trip over the ocean leads me to new adventures and I'll cherish them forever. I live for adventure and my aunt makes every trip special by giving me new sights to explore.

# PLAYLIST

## Playlist

Don't Go Yet (Camila Cabello)
Summer of Love (Shawn Mendes & Tainy)
Bad Habits (Ed Sheeran)
Circles (Post Malone)
Blinding Lights (The Weednd)
Lost (Maron 5)
Run (OneRepublic)
Killing Strangers (Marilyn Manson)

# FREE BOOK

A FREE taste of Bratva Mafia
Https://geni.us/BratvaBride
Bratva's Bride

# GLOSSARY

*Italiano*
*andiamo – here we go*
*buona notte – good night*
*Capisci- you understand*
*ciao – hello*
*consigliere – advisor*
*diletto – darling*
*famiglia – family*
*Fantastico! – Fantastic!*
*grazie – thank you*
*Guardia di Finanza- financial investigations of Italy*
*il mio amore – my love*
*niente – nothing*
*Oddio! – Oh God!*
*principessa – princess*
*polizia – police*
*Prendere due piccioni con una fava-* I'll kill two pigeons with one stone
*rosso – red*

*saluti* – greetings, usually a toast

*signorina* – miss

*scusi* – sorry

**1**

---

## MASSIMO

**T**WO AND A HALF MONTHS BEFORE DANTE *AND JULIET'S WEDDING DISASTER...*

"DARLING, why don't we go for a nice drive today? The sun is out, and it's such a beautiful winter day. It's the perfect time to take your McLaren through Tuscany. Let's go to Siena," Lia says, rolling over and taking the sheet and plush micro-suede blanket with her to face me.

Her enthusiasm is enticing, almost tempting.

"Lia, you know I don't have time," I growl, throwing back the duvet lying over the bed. A designer suggested this linen duvet with a green and white paisley print to go with the eggshell-painted walls.

Supposedly, everything goes with the neutral colors except Lia. Don't get me wrong. She's attractive, with long, dark, silky hair, but there's something behind her cold eyes that has me sleeping with one eye open.

I find it off-putting the way she's always trying to take up more of my time. It's no secret she has worked the jet-set circuit for years, looking desperately for a sugar daddy. If I cared more for myself, I wouldn't touch her. Instead, I compromise and make sure I always use a condom when I fuck her.

Rumor has it her family had money until their accountant embezzled most of it. With that bit of misfortune, it's no wonder she has to leech off of people in order to travel in the same circle as her friends. I never should have hooked up with her, but a lonely night of drinking left my guard down. She's easy on the eyes, but everything else about her is work.

I stand and walk buck naked toward the shower, one of the many renovations I've done to the house. I want to keep as much of the original house as possible. However, I draw the line in the bathroom, opting for the most expensive modern faucets, cabinets, and tiles on the market.

I could invite her to shower with me, but I don't. Poor girl has no clue I'm not the nicest of guys around, and we have no future.

She, of all people, should know most women come with an expiration date, a date that rolls around quicker than the stamp on a carton of fresh milk. They are for my amusement and only when I want it.

I step into the tepid water, and the shower head releases water like rainfall over my head. I drown Lia out as I lean into the water and wash my thick hair with scented products. Thankfully, I'm not going bald in my twenties like my dad.

As I stare at the marble walls around me, the drive to Siena sounds inviting. I love fresh country air. I imagine wood burning in fireplaces and backyards as I drive through the smaller towns in Tuscany. I would have to go alone if I wanted to relax. However, reality kicks in when I grab my towel to dry off.

Unfortunately, I can't take today off. I have to make a trip down to Florence. Tommaso has stuff for me to do, and I need to swing by my office to get some work done secretly. It's not easy being me, but I manage it with aplomb.

I would have made a great secret agent with my James Bond-like life. I'm a billionaire and have enough to never work, but I need to watch my grandfather's back, and he needs my help with diplomacy, log shipments, and logistics. It's all getting more and more complicated as the years pass.

Besides, my home has eight bedrooms, five bathrooms, and a statue and mural predating Caesar. This multi-billion-euro mansion is just one of many homes I own. Normally, the amount I've spent on this home in the country would be considered gauche by most working Europeans—maybe even most people. However, someone has to be at the top of this mountain. It might as well be me.

Recently, with the number of jobs I'm juggling, taking on more than a decent fuck when I want it is all I can handle. Lia should know by now I don't partake in two-way relationships. My way is the only way. That's how I like it. That's how it's going to be. I'm in control.

It doesn't help me knowing my grandfather wants me to get married. It's not like I'm desperate to find someone. I don't need a wife. I'm not at the age where marriage is a concern. I'm not old. Maybe he's afraid he'll die before I give him heirs. I'm up for some kink, not kids. Fuck no on the kids.

I'm selfish. I like coming and going as I please. I always make decisions, take care of crews and shipments, and attend business meetings. Being the one in charge allows me to fix details I might have missed or ones that didn't work out well. That way, no one gets hurt unless they deserve it.

My goal in life is simple. It's self-preservation, but not at the cost of my family, the one I was born into[ and pledge my loyalty to. My family of brothers will always come first.

Before shaving, I wrap the plush Hilton cotton towel around my waist. I don't need to look manicured, but I don't like scruff unless the job calls for it. Getting a good lather in my cup, I check my reflection in the mirror.

My curly hair comes from my mother, but the jet-back color is a misnomer. My face is wider than a typical Italian, it's an attribute I attribute to recessive genes from a distant relative, but it's unclear as I don't have many photos. I smear the fluffy paste on my chin and cheeks, take a deep breath, and pick up the barber blade I use. As luck would have it, the first swipe over my chin lightly nicks my face.

"Fuck," I mutter.

I stop the bleeding with a piece of tissue paper and get back at it as Lia walks into the room. Because I'm looking in the mirror, I notice she's wearing my thousand-euro Armani shirt to ward off the morning chill. Her perky breasts are inviting me to touch them.

"Everything okay in here?" she asks, moving behind me and wrapping her arms around my waist.

I bristle at her touch and wish she wouldn't get so close. Sexy time is over. I'm in my own head, and there's no room for her in it. The switch has been flipped. I'm in work mode, and I have a ton of shit I need to get done.

"Lia, I think we need a break," I turn and notice she looks surprised.

"What? You can't be serious." She plays it off, but it has to hurt to be rejected. Ironically, I know because I get that from my own father when he looks at me.

Lia runs her hand up my chest and tugs at my thick, dark chest hair. I knock her arm away, and she huffs before storming out of the bathroom, yelling in Italian. I catch a glimpse of pillows flying through the air.

What the fuck?

I enter the bedroom and grab her by the arm, "What the fuck are you doing?"

"You are an asshole. I like you, but I can tell you're just using me."

"Lia, you've been with every man I know with over a million euros in his bank account. If you think I want more than a quick fuck from you, you've overestimated your importance. Men like me don't have time for relationships or someone as used as you. You look good now, but what will you look like after five more years of taking cock and doing coke? I'll give you a cursory answer. You'll be washed up on harder drugs to fill the hole in your soul. You whore yourself out trying to maintain an unsustainable standard of living. Give it up. Get out before it's too late." I walk to my dresser, open a door, and throw euros on the bed. "That should give you money to get an apartment outside the city."

She picks up an expensive vase on my dresser and throws it at my head. I wrestle her to the bed, and I find it's turned me on. Swiping a condom from the nightstand, I tear it open with my teeth, quickly cover my engorged cock, and fuck her.

She moans as she pretends to fend me off, but her nails dig into my back from the pleasure I give her, and she knows she's powerless in any attempt to stop me because she wants it to, not even caring that she didn't come.

I shed the condom when I'm done, dropping it into the

nearest trash container. I'm thankful my housekeeper picks up after me.

I clean up quickly and decide on regular street clothes for the day ahead of me. That idea of a car ride into the country is looking better and better.

MY FATHER IS one person I can't read to my satisfaction. Maybe it's best I don't know what he's thinking. I guess nothing I do is ever good enough as there is contempt in his eyes that I've never understood. I'll never meet his expectations like my younger brother, Cosimo, who is in medical school. It's competitive to get in, and fortunately, I know people in the right places. I've never let on that I had anything to do with his acceptance letter.

My family launders money through our gelato store which is on the only bridge not destroyed in WWII, the Ponte Vecchio. This is why I told Sal Micheli the truth about my mother working at the gelato store when we met on at the warehouse shortly after Tommaso hired me. It's smart to stick as close to the truth as possible. It reduces the chances of making a mistake that could be fatal.

Locals know we're important in a scary way, and it's also why we have little competition on the bridge. Papa doesn't mind being connected. He's happy to be married to Mama and helps her because he's Italian, and she's the daughter of the number one man in Albania. Not the perfect setup as we like to stick to our own except for making alliances through marriage, and Papa didn't bring much to the table.

Would I be part of a mafia family if I had a choice?

Maybe not. However, I tend to be a night owl and like putting puzzles together. I'm good with numbers, making me an asset to any business. When it comes to my grandfather and the older generation back in Albania, I'm beloved. I used to go back home every summer as a child. Now, I'm too busy running things with other lieutenants, and I love living in Italy.

Tensions have been mounting with our important money man, Argon, who's out of control with his power. He's encroaching on the Micheli turf, and our Albanian leaders didn't sanction it. He wanted to move more coke and use Sal's bars, but he wasn't smart about it. He lets his men blatantly do deals in front of Sal, which is disrespectful, and in doing so, puts us on their radar. I don't want to get in a pissing contest, nor do I want to give another family a reason to escalate this into an all-out war.

I came up with this bright idea we could move more drugs and guns if we didn't have to worry about the government looking over our shoulders all the time. What better way to ensure our deliveries than to throw the Guardia di Finanza off us and onto someone else?

It doesn't mean I have to give the Michelis up. But when I get a call, there might be a tail on our drugs, and the Michelis' warehouse is empty, it makes a good diversion. I view it as a good business decision. Once I get more of a handle on their operation, I could totally fuck them up from the inside, but for now, I just want to protect my own interests and gather intel. In the meantime, I lay low, watching the situation.

Italy has stepped up the penalties for what we do and has increased its crackdowns on organized crime. I need to have as many diversions as possible. It's added insurance for the day it might save our necks. What if our largest shipment of coke is about to be discovered? I can't lose the money or the coke. The street value is high because it's a commodity with a demand we struggle to meet. If there is a disruption in the supply chain, it's not good for business.

Tommaso doesn't need to know my family history, nor does the Micheli family. I need to protect my family's interests and determine how much damage Argon and his men have done. The streets have been noticeably quiet around Sal's bar, and it makes me uneasy.

Every day that passes without the Michelis' sending a message makes me wonder what they are planning. Dante is a thinker, and he's biding his time in which to make a definitive decision on his next step. In my line of work, the waiting is more nerve-wracking than if he just took Argon out ourselves.

## 2

―――――

## VALENTINA

"Valentina, time for dinner." Papa's voice ricochets off the cashmere-tinted walls, which gives light to the vast interior of the house. I don't have to be beside him to know he's grumbling, "Don't make us wait." It's not like this is the first time he demanded family dinner be kept. I'm twenty-three, I know the drill. However, tonight we're eating earlier than usual as it's football season, which is soccer to the rest of the world.

The breathtaking sunset over the Tyrrhenian Sea never gets old. I'm in my family's fortress, standing on the balcony outside my bedroom, and from this vantage point, near the top of the mountain, no one else in Palermo can see what I see. In one direction, newly furrowed land waiting to be cultivated for agriculture, and in the other, a mix of green landscape and tiled roofs with the bright sea as a backdrop.

My great-granddad made sure he built this place on the highest elevation so no one else could build above us. Now, I know it was due to his pride and need for power. We retain much of the empire he built by keeping local officials on the payroll. Papa's no different when it comes to pride and power. He runs Sicily and his family, especially me, his only daughter.

To say he keeps me on a short leash is an understatement. If I don't get off this island soon, I'm afraid I'll go crazy.

The only thing keeping me sane now is knowing there is a huge gala coming up, and I have a new gown to wear, a champagne dress made specifically for me by Stella McCarthy. It's been altered to cling to my figure. The annual event is being held at the Borghese Museum of Art.

I'm looking forward to viewing the art collection. I can't deny I'll enjoy getting attention from the paparazzi, as I don't have anyone else giving me the attention I crave.

My focus is drawn back to the water and the freedom I see in the unpredictable waves. Tempted by the freedom outside our fortress and yet, confined within these stark and sterile walls, I'm mocked at every turn.

In moments like this, I fantasize about what I might be doing if I wasn't under the constant scrutiny of bodyguards and Papa's keen and vengeful eyes.

I want to rebel. I do. I'm tired of this twenty thousand square foot gilded cage and all of the servants needed to maintain it. God forbid my mother break a nail or miss an appointment at the salon. She is a good cook when she's in the mood, which isn't often.

I'm jealous that my best friend, Laura, has so much more freedom and even gets to choose her husband. Her father is only an underboss, so she doesn't have the bank account and finery I do. However, she has the ability to move about and go places with her fiancé.

There is a price I pay for all the expensive things Papa pays for in order to placate me. I didn't need a degree in psychiatry to figure this out when I was twelve. Instead of doing what the other kids did, I had to go home, and there would be another bribe.

Laura is engaged to Marco, a man who works under her father, so I know it won't be long before I will be, too. In fact, I'm surprised Papa hasn't already arranged something.

With our large breasts and curvaceous hips, I'm the same size as Laura, but our days of sharing a wardrobe ended when I went off to college. The days of dressing chic to go to the movies or a concert in Rome are infrequent. We're not kids anymore, even though we are young. We tend to mature faster in our world.

I will admit I love the Jonas Brothers, and who can resist Adam Levine? Sure, I also love Italian pop culture, but everyone follows American trends. For the past twenty years, English has been taught in our schools, so many Italians, including myself, speak it perfectly.

In Rome, everyone wants to be so cosmopolitan. Even Germans who visit there would rather not speak their native tongue. I find it strange. Ironic that, with all of these cultural changes, not much has changed for women. Antiquated laws still govern our lives, and women still struggle for success in the business world dominated by men.

Once the sun dips below the horizon, I go inside and descend the marble staircase, my pink kitten heels clicking on each step. I make sure to hold on to the mahogany banister as these steps are endless and treacherous. There is an elevator, but I can always use the exercise.

The smell of fresh seafood greets my pert nose, and my stomach grumbles in anticipation. Mama had the chef cook my favorite dinner tonight, and I hope it isn't to buffer bad news.

Our dining room table seats up to twenty guests and sits atop Italian tile the color of chocolate pudding. The Versace china with the matching red velvet tablecloth and gold cloth napkins give the impression my mother has excellent taste, but an interior designer picked out everything.

She pretends it's all her doing, but her friends know she paid the most sought-after decorating firm in Italy to redecorate the house, the dining room being her most recent upgrade.

"About time," Giovi says as I make my appearance. My brother looks a lot like Papa. They are both tall, and their broad shoulders carry the stature of their positions. Giovi is a made man, and at the young age of thirty, Papa is grooming him in the business.

"Shut up," I quip, taking my seat beside him.

"Basta, you're both too old for such nonsense," Papa speaks as he pours the wine, and we fall silent.

The guards don't bark as much as Papa, but then again, everything is routine. Get in the car, get out, go here, go there. I want to go away and run my own practice and call my own shots. But I'd have to go where no one knows my lineage. Even though it's for my own safety, I abhor the idea of being some made man's wife. I'll always have to walk a step behind him. I pray he will treat me well because I have no say in the matter.

I should be grateful for what I have, but I can only imagine all the bad things my family does to make the amount of money it takes to live our fancy lifestyle with our own jet and numerous properties.

A famous crime boss in New York once said he never trusted a man who didn't serve time. For Sicilians, it's the same attitude towards those who aren't made men. The soldiers know few of them will move up the ranks with its limited positions. The greed of those who run the organization wants the lion's share of the money. Our influence and power extend well past our small island, and the 'family' grows larger each year.

I've seen Giovi become more mature when he's not out fucking off with his friends. Papa is giving him more responsibility, and he has to pass the tests because there won't be anyone left in the family to run the business if something should happen to Papa.

When the leader dies unexpectedly, there is usually a power grab. Internal fighting transpires, and maybe another boss of one of the families will rise to power. In reality, one never knows how it will unfold. Depending on the situation, there can be a smooth transition to power. This is why Papa is grooming Giovi, not so much for today, but for the future. One day this will all belong to my brother, who must lead the Sicilians. Which means Papa probably won't be here anymore.

The damp air blowing through the open windows has a chill to it, and soon the shutters will be closed for the night.

I place a cloth napkin in my lap and lament that I still live at home even after graduating from Oxford. Many would say it's a blessing and not a curse, as life could be worse.

"What's the matter, Valentina? Your nose is out of joint again. It's nothing new. Sit, eat." Papa fills his plate, and the food is passed around.

"Luciano, please." Mama pleads with him to be nice. She of all people should know it's not in his psyche to behave any better.

Her hair is black that it looks like a dark blue. Her eyes are dark, too, giving her an exotic Mesopotamian look.

"It's fine, Mama." I offer her some solace as she can only do so much. I swallow my resentment for Papa and a mouthful of the antipasti.

Our wine glasses are refilled with only the best Chianti. There is no need to save money or drink the less expensive red table wine most Italians drink daily.

"Papa, did you think about my business plan?"

"Yes, and no, there's no way you can see patients here. Everyone knows you. It would be a security nightmare."

I scoff, "What if I got plastic surgery and saw clients online? It's the wave of the future. Better yet, dress up with wigs."

"I want pictures of that. You should have gone into art. That you can do in a room like Rapunzel," Giovi mocks me.

I turn my nose at the suggestion and deliver a nice slap to his upper arm. We are close. He's just not mature enough to see the rest of his life filled with social complications as I do.

No man on the island dares to date me, and I'm desperate to get laid. No doubt Papa will have me married off to a lieutenant, probably a Sicilian, as a way to keep me close to home where he can secure my safety.

Believe me, if Papa weren't getting something out of my marriage, he wouldn't have all these guards around me and restrict my life so severely. I'm valued. I'm not sure about being loved. Maybe that's why I'm closest to Giovi.

I long for one more solo flight of freedom before then. Just one, as a woman with an appetite for lovemaking I want a man to worship my body like he cares for me—not the family fortune. I don't want to be traded like a commodity. However, it looks like my dreams will die a long, agonizing death.

"You can help your mother with the gala we're going to next month. Charity work is what your role is, and don't forget it." His stern gray eyes meet mine as the table is cleared for the next course.

It's clear I've hit his limit on any talk of change around here and turn my attention to Mama. We discuss a mother-daughter day at the salon, getting manicures and updos for the big event, as my brother makes another wisecrack.

As a high schooler in Switzerland boarding schools, I didn't have to ask for permission and could hobnob with socialites, including the princess of India, Priyanka Ramen. Those are fond memories, and we still stay in touch. Her father is a business mogul only she's allowed to voice her opinions and strives to obtain more rights for women.

Ironically, Italy could use more women's rights, as well.

Giovi agrees to watch the football game with Papa tonight. I know it's the most popular sport, but I don't enjoy it.

I spend as much time on the beach as possible to escape the house. Each day, the walls remind me Papa has enemies, and the longer I remain here, the more suffocating it all becomes.

No price can be put on freedom. Even with none, I yearn for my days at college when life wasn't so serious. A taste of a different life has given me an obsession to get it back.

Unfortunately, I'm the only woman who wants to change my family's traditions.

*There must be a way to outsmart these guards.*

**3**

---

# MASSIMO

I'm in a newer version of my old Mercedes heading into Prato when I receive a call from a guard at the house. He's telling me after I left, following a heated argument with Lia, she decided to throw a bottle of red wine at a rare mural painted on the ceiling by none other than the one and only Michelangelo Merisi da Caravaggio. Currently, an entire floor at the Uffizi is dedicated to his work. How dare she try to ruin my prized possession? Has she no regard for culture?

As history goes, I make poor choices regarding women, something I have in common with Caravaggio. His life was a rags-to-riches story and ended with a dual over a female prostitute. The woman belonged to Ranuccio Tomassoni, the gangster he killed in the duel, and the family got their revenge years later when the bill came due for killing Ranuccio. Knowing the gangster history that took place under this mural, anyone who knows me can understand why I immediately fell in love with the house. I had to have it at any cost.

On the other hand, my mother is not a fan of Caravaggio's work. Like most, she prefers Michelangelo, the 'famed' artist of Florence and the Vatican, because he made everyone perfect. You cannot say the same about Caravaggio, who painted people as flawed and real, which caused a stir in the day.

As for Lia, she was apprehended by my staff, received a few kicks and a black eye for her insolence, and was banned from the property. I never knew she had that much anger in her, but now that I do, I will take whatever measures necessary to protect myself and my sanctuary. Lia got off easy because if I were there, she would have received a punishment she'd remember every time she sat down.

It's the rainy season, and after a week of nonstop drizzle, I wish I had the day off to enjoy the break in the weather. Instead, I find myself pulling up to the warehouse to meet Tommaso. He has a laundry list of things to do because they are beneath me. He gets pissed when I'm late or doesn't show, but my family comes first. I try to schedule my work around him, but life isn't predictable or perfect, and I don't know how long I can keep up this charade.

I met Marchello Micheli, and we bonded immediately over our common interest in high-end sneakers. It's refreshing when one of the top families shows up in person and gets to know their crew. There is no egotistical machismo about him, and I wonder if that's from his upbringing. My own mother had plenty of practice slapping me upside the head every time I mouthed off to her. In the end, I learned manners.

"Tommaso," I greet the man in his late fifties, overweight but with a big heart for a man who runs the trucks and organizes the staffing needed to keep things moving.

Tonight, we're moving trucks full of cocaine and pills. The pills are actually heroin made to look like OxyContins.

We do this because the penalty for trafficking in heroin is stiffer than getting caught with Oxy. It's ingenious, really.

"Massimo, we have a shipment coming, and I would like you to go to the port in Livorno tonight and make sure there aren't any problems. I don't like to leave things to chance," he explains.

"No problem." I nod in agreement. Cocaine has never gone out of style and is still popular all over Europe. Because it comes from as far away as South America, many things can go wrong getting it past custom inspectors and opportunists out to hijack the load between point A to point B. It wouldn't be the first time the shipper double-crossed us and slipped it to someone else, claiming it was confiscated at the port. I know this because it happens to all of us sooner or later.

Because people lie. Especially in this business. Penalties are harsh for us on the street and in prison.

"So, how was your weekend?"

"Great, no complaints— except for a pissed-off girl-friend, all is well." I grimace at the thought of Lia.

"Yeah, girlfriends are the downfall of many a man. Be careful," he chuckles, and his belly jiggles under a t-shirt he has clearly outgrown.

"You've been married forever. What's the secret?"

"Ah, I guess when you meet the right one, you know. It helps when they're your friend and lover. Y'know—the one you want to go home to at the end of the day. But on the other hand, what do I know? Maybe I got lucky." The smile reaches his heavily hooded eyes, and I know then that, even though he complains his wife won't let him drink too much, I think he enjoys that she still pays attention to what he does and gives him shit about it. It means she cares.

I would love to have someone like that in my life, but in

this business, it's easier if we don't get too attached to people. My job is my life, and both can get messy.

"I'll remember that," I reply, opening my car door and getting in.

"Nice car, good ride?"

"Yes, I'll be on the docks tonight when the shipment arrives," I assure him.

"Thank you." He taps the car hood for luck as I back out.

The cover of darkness is ideal for drug smuggling, but it would be better if it didn't rain because driving on poorly marked highways is treacherous at best. The drugs are wrapped and hidden in the bottom of cans packed with pineapple. The cans must be opened, and the drugs repackaged before moving them along the supply chain.

I stop at a tabacchi where sundries are sold to buy nicotine gum. I've been trying to quit smoking for years. While sipping an espresso, I notice an advert on the counter for a large fundraiser in Rome at the end of the week to raise money for restorations at the museum. My interest is piqued, and I'm free of Lia, so I make a mental note to go. These events typically draw people with money and influence, which may be an opportunity to mix business with pleasure.

With so much history in Italy, there is always something to restore. Stick a shovel in the ground, and you're bound to hit some antiquity. The new subway terminal for the Colosseum has dragged on for fifteen years because a work stoppage is called every time a relic is found, no matter how small. I understand the government wants everything salvaged, but there's a point when you need to press on in the name of progress.

My second phone vibrates; ah, family.

"Hello, Grandfather." I slip inside my car for privacy. I

ignore the ugly stares and gesticulations of those waiting impatiently for my parking spot.

Horns honk as I put my car in gear and head downtown to see my mother.

"I want you to check out our Sicilian friends. Word has it they will be in Rome this weekend for some museum event. Don De Luca has been shipping in more cocaine than he's selling us, and it's part of our joint venture. He might be skimming. We're also light on the weapons."

"I'm on it. Do you have proof?"

"We're working on one of his informants as we speak. He'll crack. This might be a way into the oligarchy. I want that before I die," Grandpa states.

I know how important it is for him to have a seat at the table with the others who run the international underworld syndicate referred to as The Twelve.

"Got it. I'll be there. Do I approach him?"

"You can tell him we know he's cheated us and there is a price. He won't give up his seat at the table, but he might be persuaded to share it if you know what I mean. Until then, we can use him for access. I'll think about it. Plan to kill his son as a warning for stealing. How is your mother?"

"Sure, I'll wait for your word. As for Mama, I'm on my way to visit her now."

"Enjoy your time with her." He hangs up.

I find his words are cryptic even for an old man.

I pull into a reserved spot near our ice cream shop. It's one of many businesses we own and launder money through. Plus, we deal drugs out the back, packed under pints of gelato or boxes of waffle cones right under the unsuspecting noses of the authorities.

"Mama." I hug her and her cheeks before she returns to a huge mixer filled with lemon gelato. "You work too hard," I say, and I mean it. I can't remember a day when I haven't seen her break her back to make everything from scratch.

Even though she comes from one of the most successful Albanian criminal families, she wants her independence, and I admire her for it. As always, she's dressed for work in the kitchen, wearing a smock over a faded house dress and sensible no-skid sneakers.

One would never suspect she has riches at her disposal. Her hair is under a shower cap to keep it out of the food, but she no longer tries to cover the gray. I notice dark circles under her eyes and worry she and Papa are not getting along.

"It's a normal day," she says, wiping her brow with the back of her hand.

"What's up?"

"What? You've been out. I hate you being near the Michelis," she chastises me.

"Mama, it's part of the job. It's a brilliant plan. It's always good to have an inside track when we're encroaching on their territory."

"Shit, it's dangerous as hell. I don't know what I'd do if something happened to you. You could be taken for a mole. Well," she scoffs, "you really are one. I raised you better. You're too important for such nonsense. Look at what your grandfather has built. It will all be yours one day."

"Yeah, like when I'm too old to enjoy that kind of money. I mean, grandfather won't give up the reins for a long time, and then there is your brother who might take over. Besides, I love living in Italy."

"True, but you can be head of the family in Italy, and my brother can take over things in Albania."

I shrug. I'm young, too young to be that powerful, and

I'm still learning from Grandfather. I'm smart enough to know there are a million ways to get things done.

"Grandpa has many years left, and I'm fine where I am. He has already given me much of my inheritance, and I love it here. Besides, I can't be that far from you."

She lets out a huff. She loves my house, just not the history, and is worried some bad karma will befall me.

"I'm fine, really. You look tired. What is it?"

"I'm fine. Didn't sleep last night. Go say 'hi' to your father."

I go outside and find him sitting at one of the bistro tables on the sidewalk.

"Papa."

"Oh, hi Massimo, nice to see you. How's that gig going for you?"

"Fine, have to drive to the port tonight to check on things. How are things here?"

"Good, business is good."

I pull up a chair, and we sit quietly, watching the locals and a few tourists pass by. It's the slow season, and I know he's keeping an eye on the illegals we have working the streets.

"How is Cosimo?"

I haven't seen my brother in a month.

"Fine, fine. Busy with school. He's making good grades. I'm glad he'll have a normal life one day."

Another slight. I should be used to it. I wish I knew what his beef is with me. For as long as I can remember, he's given me mixed signals, and our relationship has grown more distant over the years.

Does he resent my grandfather and I being close? Papa forgets that I create my opportunities, and Grandpa rewards that.

My father is Italian, not Albanian, and has zero interest in working for the family other than manning the street and helping Mama do her part in laundering money through the shop. He's not motivated by money or power, and as long as he has enough to live comfortably, he's content.

Mama has taken a lot of flack over the years because she did not marry an Albanian. Grandpa is known to throw the most punches in the family, which will never change. He can't be bothered with anyone of no use to him. His life is consumed by work. I know I'm just like him in that respect and maybe that's why we get along so well.

Cosimo isn't street-savvy. In his teens, I thought he might turn to the family, but he got involved in school and wanted to become a doctor. We used to be close as we were only three years apart in age. However, our lives are in different directions now.

"Tell Cosi I said hi." Tapping my father on the shoulder, I stand to leave. "Gotta go."

"Ciao," he replies. "And Massimo., be careful," he says after a pause.

"Always, Papa."

That's as good as it gets between us. He blows hot and cold. I don't get it. Mama says that's just him, but, in my eyes, Cosimo is his favorite son.

I head to my car as it's time for me to meet up with my best friend, Savio, for a quick lunch. He's of Italian and Albanian heritage, just like me, and we grew up on the same block. He's my right-hand man who makes a good living. He's one person I trust. He has always had my back in my darkest hours. And I've had a few over the years.

The first happened when I delivered a tiny envelope to a man in jail because Grandpa asked me to do it. He knew the man couldn't beat an incriminating rap. Grandpa told me to tell the man we promised we would take care of his family and with one unallowed grasp of his hand, I slid him a tiny packet. I told the stranger we'd take care of his family, and he ripped the brown envelope open, downing the pills inside without hesitation.

I snuck the pills in through a seam I ripped in my suit jacket. Then I re-sewed it making it undetectable by security.

It had to be done, but nothing can prepare one for that moment when a family member has to prove his loyalty. The man had two young daughters I heard, but he took those pills like they were vitamins. I sat in shock as I realized my family asked me to send him a death sentence. That moment of realization that he was going to commit suicide and he'll never get to say goodbye to his family had a profound effect on me. His kids will grow up without him.

I was much younger then, coming to grips with the darkest moment of my youth and my soul. Savio was there for me.

After a late lunch together, we catch up, and I mention the gala. I ask him to keep his schedule open, considering the trip to Rome, possibly Sicily. He agrees before heading off to meet up with a girl he recently met.

I return home to nap in preparation for a long night. As I drive, I contemplate my trip to Rome. Having a quick getaway's never a bad idea, so I think I'll take the jet. My instinct for survival was ingrained early on by a military-style upbringing with Grandpa. It has saved my ass more than once.

**4**

———

**VALENTINA**

Dinner drags on, and after we break, I can walk down by the water's edge. By the light of the moon, I pull my jacket closer standing against the wind as two men escort me, scanning the horizon for intruders.

I think it's ridiculous. We haven't had an issue in years, and there is nothing to gain by taking me hostage. My father has always made it clear he does not negotiate with kidnappers. And if they come for us, he'll make it worse for them. It doesn't need to be said.

The path from the house dead ends at the beach, so my kidnappers better have a boat, a very fast boat. Not only do we have our own speedboats, but we also have a high wall to prevent unwanted entry and tons of cameras watching every inch of the property. I'm told there are one hundred cameras in all, enough to make me feel like I'm being watched like a prisoner.

Why would anyone want to date me, let alone marry me? I'm an average woman. I don't turn heads when I walk in the room like Laura or Priyanka. Laura has the freedom to marry for love. Pry is changing the world. They aren't bound by the same rules that are imposed on me. Nonetheless, I'd love to have a man that's mine out of choice, someone I can build a life with, and maybe I can make a contribution to the world. I'll find a way to use my degree and my mind.

I want to experience courtship and romance and find love. I want to get lost in it, but that won't happen if Papa arranges a marriage for me. Thank god Federico doesn't have a son as he would have been a fitting match.

The underboss, Federico Gambino, is like an uncle to me. He's one of Papa's longest supporters. His grown daughter is a piece of work which makes me wonder about him. Last year his daughter, Ignazio, resurfaced out of nowhere. I don't trust her.

I wonder if Papa realizes she's trouble. She's much older than me, so we never hang out when she comes around. Mama remembers her as an overly spoiled child who always got her way. Then, in her early adult years, she abruptly went abroad without explanation. Just disappeared. Everyone stopped asking about her. Supposedly she slipped in and out of Sicily occasionally, but it was all hush-hush.

Ignazio is hiding something. Even our dog, Bianca, growls when she walks into the room. As they say, animals know people.

Italian women have their superstitions. No one is into this more than Nonna, my grandmother, who lives with us as well. She's in her eighties and spends most of her time watching TV in her room. She's hard of hearing and refuses to wear her hearing aids, so I must repeat everything I say, but I love her. How she put up with my dad for so many years is the question of the millennia.

My only boyfriend was when I attended Oxford for a degree in psychology. Crushing on the men in popular boy bands is the closest I can get to a boyfriend nowadays. My boy band posters remind me of my youth. I leave the posters on my bedroom walls to piss Papa off.

He hates everything about American culture. My teenage years spent at an exclusive boarding school in Switzerland were sublime. And in a way, sending me away backfired on Papa as I resented coming home.

It didn't take long for me to understand boarding school and college were cost-effective and meant to keep me safe. I never went on social media, and for a time, my life wasn't all about being the little principessa.

My brother Giovi went to summer camps near home. He will fill Papa's shoes, not me. Italy is still a man's world, and it's as frustrating as my non-existent sex life.

Papa likes everyone to keep a low profile, but Giovi can have all the women he wants and hangs out with the boss's sons until after the bars close. There isn't much to do in Sicily besides shopping, tourism, fishing, and thieving.

We used to bring in fish to export, like tuna and anchovies. Over the years, our boats became outdated, and one has to go out further to where the fish live, but our small boats aren't equipped for that. Therefore, Italy can't sustain local demands. With all the hills and Mount Etna, this is still a beautiful place. Nothing can take away from the beauty of the sea and the picturesque sunsets the tourists visit annually.

AFTER A REFRESHING but windy walk on the beach, I return home, change into my favorite pajamas, and video call Laura.

"Laura, what are you doing?"

Her face is covered in something green when she answers, and her hair is wrapped in a towel.

"It's a new mask with mud. It's the best thing for my skin. You should try it."

"No thanks," I dismiss the idea as I see it cracking on her face. "You need to wash it off. Now."

"Two more minutes." She glances at her designer watch. "What's up?"

The woman takes her skincare seriously. She's engaged and has nothing to worry about.

"I'm bored."

"See, I told you all those fancy degrees you have are useless. You could have gone clubbing with me when I was single had you spent more time here," she teases.

"Tell me about it." I sigh in agreement.

"Well, I'm going out with Marco tonight for the opening of a new movie." Her wicked grin tells me it involves sex.

She's lucky, her intended has his own apartment, and she's in love with the man she's marrying.

It's not like I can date a man in public. No one can know much about me. There is no social media and no routines that can't be moved around unpredictably.

It's times like this I'm happy for the year I had with Rudy in Switzerland, or else, I'd still be a virgin. Imagine how hard it is to go without physical attention from a man. I'm dying on a vine, my youth is slipping away, and yet, I don't know what's worse– being alone or married to someone I might despise. Either side of the coin is enough to drive me mad.

"No word yet?" she asks.

"No, I might as well be locked in a vault." I sit on my bed with an unopened book in front of me and turn the TV on to distract myself. "I'm climbing the walls being alone. You're so lucky." I sigh.

"When is your brother settling down?"

"No idea."

"We have to plan a day together. You need to get out."

"True. I'm looking forward to the gala at the Borghese Museum in Rome."

"You and your art," Laura says. I'm sure she remembers me lagging behind the rest of the class on our first field trip to a museum.

"Well, promise me you won't get lost this time. I don't want to go looking for you again." She reminds me of our past as I watch her stand in front of her dresser where her phone is propped up. She puts a dainty diamond necklace around her neck.

"I won't get lost. You'll never let me forget that, will you? Besides, there will be too many people there to be alone. I wish we could sneak out. I need room to breathe. I can only hope I get lost in the conversation and paintings. It will be a good turnout. Mama and I finished hand-addressing the envelopes for the largest donors weeks ago."

"You do have great handwriting. Calligraphy is a lost art. I'm glad you're able to use your gifts."

She grabs the phone, and I see the inside of her room as she gathers her purse and light coat off the bed.

"You're so pretty," I say. For a second, I wish I was Laura, confident and flawless in everything she wears.

"I gotta go. Talk tomorrow?"

"Yes, let's plan to shop and maybe get our nails done," I suggest.

"Hang in there. You never know when you'll meet the right guy. Hell, it could be you getting married next."

I can only manage a wan smile. It's doubtful I'll meet

any man my father approves of. He will be the one to find me a husband. It's just not his priority right now.

I'm looking forward to the gala in Rome. Not only do I want to see the art, but I also want to check out the eye candy. Finding someone suitable to have an intelligent conversation with would be nice, but it would be tough to give my guards the slip. At the very least, I hope we stay overnight so I can walk around the Coliseum and see what new items they've unearthed before we head home.

"Gotta go. Ciao," she replies as she blows me kisses, and I blow a kiss back.

Ciao indeed. I'm caged like a goddamn bird while she enjoys a hot date and the latest American blockbuster. It's not fun being the principessa because I sit on the sidelines watching everyone else live their life.

**5**

## MASSIMO

I drive an hour to the port and chat with the men on the docks. I check for myself to make sure the work is done correctly. Then I leave, moving to a higher up the mountain to watch the trucks pull out. I marvel at the irony of how we all commit the same crimes.

Each outfit is like the other only the designer labels are different. Like the men in the mafia who look different but commit the same crimes. Albanians, Italians... the same routines are repeated over and over again just like anywhere else in the world. No doubt possible surprises lurk behind every face and every shipment. Not to mention new players who are suspicious of you, and we are leery of them until we earn each other's trust. And even when we work with men for years, it sometimes doesn't go far. The business acumen we learn on the streets is more valuable.

I'm sure there's more bad shit I couldn't possibly be aware of as this is a dangerous business. One where the rules are the rules and perception isn't always the reality. Tragedy may befall a person who didn't deserve the consequences they received. Like life, it's not always fair.

Collateral. There's always collateral damage. It's why my grandmother isn't here today, and Grandpa keeps a low profile. She didn't know she was taking a bullet for him, but it happened nonetheless. True love? Possibly. It's tragic all the same. Grandpa never remarried. I assume he's encouraging me to get married so I don't grow old alone. I'm young, still making my way in the world. As the youngest lieutenant, no one dares breathe a word of favoritism.

It's only a matter of time before jealousy over rank or money gets in the way of the 'family.' I surmise it's more likely someone gets greedy, and a chain of events unfolds. One can never predict the damage their actions caused until restitution has been made—or taken.

That's when bad shit happens. We don't kill over debts from gamblers. They are worth more to us alive than dead. It's another matter altogether when one of our own steals or someone in another family is stealing from everyone. I don't know why Don De Luca of the Cosa Nostra would want to steal from our pipeline to Eastern Europe. We're the only family with contacts in Belarus, and it's used to get supplies into Russia. Lies are lies, and it's only a matter of time before they are uncovered.

All Syndicates have a code of silence and brotherhood, but we've adapted to working with many of foreign countries. The world went Global, and so did we. Still, I'm insane to be infiltrating the Michelis., It's not unheard of as there are moles everywhere. How else would we own so many politicians?

Here, in Italy, we bribe them with information we have on them or entrap them in something so we get what we want. In other countries, the elected officials are essentially their own mafia as they control channels to the outside world. People know they exist but can't say much because they can make your life miserable in your own community, like in Russia.

It's two in the morning, and I should go to my shithole of an apartment in downtown Florence. It's in a rough area where many Chinese and Nigerians live, mostly illegals. I use it during the week as it helps with my double life. It's next to empty and provides a great cover for me. My mansion in Fiesole is reserved for days I can take off and not jeopardize the fact that I'm Massimo Rizzo to the Italian mafia, even though my real last name is Romano.

I have a trusted housekeeper, Mrs. Koroveshi, who is in her sixties. Samira comes daily to clean, cook and oversee my large property. Her auburn hair shows more gray with each passing year, but, to me, she never changes. Her husband was a loyal boss and passed away three years ago. She's not one to talk about her work. In fact, I love her like I loved my own grandmother and consider her family.

I pay her enough never to complain, even though she never asks for a raise. I like to make sure she's happy and well taken care of as she lives alone, traveling to me daily. I also have soldiers who keep a low profile on the property, so I don't worry when I'm not here. It's always a plus to have outer buildings so they can bunk and take shelter from the weather. I remember those days, as brief as they were, and a bit of comfort goes a long way on the night shift in winter.

I pull my wool trench coat around me as the wind whips around the mountainside. Fuck, it's getting cold. It makes going to Rome all that more appealing. Hopefully, the city won't have a deluge of rain for the event.

The trucks are on the road, and my task is completed. I turn towards my car and take in the luminescent face of the moon giving me light on this cloudless night. Inside my vehicle, I crank up the heater for the seat.

I've decided to take the easy route to Rome, flying out of here and possibly staying overnight. I don't care for the commercialization of the city, but I love walking through the ruins. As a donor to the arts, I have special access to the Colosseum. It would be a shame not to use it.

My sources texted me earlier. They have seen the list of VIPs, and the De Luca family is on it so I will combine business with pleasure. In essence, *Prendere due piccioni con una fava.* I'll kill two pigeons with one stone. I'll view the art and take care of the family business.

I'd love to have my own bed tonight, but given the time, and the fact I need to pack, I'll swing by my mansion and enjoy the comfort of my own bed.

I check in with Tommaso and tell him I'll be out of town for a few days for family and nod to the guards walking my grounds as I put my gun in the clip before attaching it to my belt. My coat will cover it.

I love the Berettas. Italians make so many incredible and beautiful items. We have famous designers who create top-selling clothing, cars, and handguns. The only thing Italy hasn't given me is love, which is ironic. Italian men are known to be good lovers and unfaithful to their wives. But Italy, like Paris, is made for love and making love. I don't make love. I just love to fuck.

THE SHEETS on my bed are crisp and smell slightly of lavender. I pull the blankets up and hear the wind howl around the house. Unusual as this weather is more suited for the dead of winter. February is wind and rain. The climate isn't as predictable anymore.

The wind lulls me to sleep, and it's such a great sleep I

don't want to get up. I'm having a dream, a pretty girl who's by the ocean and waving at me. I want to know more but my eyes open and I'm staring at the blank wall in my bedroom. I'm alone, and the dream ends. Poof. Gone.

I'm sure it's Grandpa putting the thought in my head. Sure, I've dated pretty women, but they are all a bit touched in the head at times. Maybe I like women a bit crazy. I've never thought about it before.

I shower and dress, having already texted the pilot to be at the airport. I transfer him money through an app on my phone. Wearing only my bathrobe, I open the false bottom of my desk drawer and grab a filled magazine clip.

I press a small button inside my large closet, and the wall slides back. It used to be a hall closet I had covered, and now, I have a safe only I know about. Reaching in, I grab a stack of euros. No doubt I'll have to procure a ticket with a nice donation and use a fake passport for the hotel check-in. Never hurts to be vigilant.

I pack my polycarbonate carry-on luggage. On second thought, I head to the huge armoire near the bed and pull out a standard-sized umbrella. It never hurts to be prepared, and it will easily fit inside my long coat.

I flick through my dress shirts and pants picking out a dark blue suit for traveling and place items inside my shiny luggage. My local tailor had a tuxedo delivered to my favorite hotel near the Colosseum since I booked the room in advance.

I dress for the day pulling my trench coat off the coat stand as I head out the door. Good to go.

I'M LET out on an opposite the street from the museum. I exit the Mercedes limo and stand on the sidewalk waiting for Savio.

I figured he needed a break as well. His life is mundane, and the money for the trip is nothing to me. He took the train down, and he's booked in a room adjoining mine.

I glance around looking for him, and I'm caught off guard by a woman in a long, slinky dress. I notice how it clings to her curves judging from her turnabout after she exits a black SUV. She's joined by her parents and a man who might be her brother as he looks so much like his father with his dark hair and olive complexion. I can't help but crack my lips into a grin when I notice her curvy buttocks and ample breasts on display. Her dress is low cut in front which doesn't distract from her beauty. She is a sight to behold and takes my breath away.

Her breasts jet out like firm round clouds I would love to squeeze. I can only imagine what lies underneath her shimmering dress because there is no room for undergarments. What I wouldn't do to slip that dress up and...

"What's up? You okay?" Savio asks, joining me at the worst time imaginable as it takes seconds away from admiring her beauty from afar.

"Hold on," I impatiently respond with a scowl as I notice she has a female companion with her. She is a young woman who is pretty in her own right, and yet she pales in comparison. The two girls exchange a short sentence or two and smile as they wait for the woman who must be Emelia De Luca. I've seen her picture on some charity pamphlets for the event. She's a chairperson on the committee.

She picks up her daughter's dress in a motherly fashion. No doubt it's instinctual. The material escapes the rough concrete as they walk to the red carpet for pictures. I wonder if she's married, but see no evidence she's taken.

Savio gives me grief over having the best-fitted tux. One I picked as it paired with my favorite gold Bvlgari cufflinks nestled around black onyx. We both wear Italian leather dress shoes. What self-respecting Italian wouldn't?

"Do you know her?" Savio asks, following where my eyes are fixated.

"Not yet, but I will." I crack a wicked smile knowing I've discovered Don De Luca's hidden gem, the daughter he keeps hidden. His weak link, even if he is void of emotion. I know she has to mean more to him because his eyes give it away when she's not looking at him.

I did my homework on the family before I left home. The Don of Sicily himself is here. He's rarely seen but revered.

My impish grin of excitement implies I'm up to no good. Savio takes me in with a long breath. He knows I'm headed for trouble as I rarely show this side to anyone other than him.

My interest is piqued. I can't wait to enter the museum and learn more about the mysterious woman.

"Well, just don't land in jail, that won't go over well in any of our circles, and it would piss off your grandfather," he says.

"Don't I know it? He's on me to get married. As if I want a wife hanging around all the time nitpicking the hours I keep for work and expressing her jealousy by breaking shit when she's pissed."

"Another one? Again? Don't tell me Lia got dumped."

I shrug as we cross the street as the humidity rises. My hands remain in my pockets, and I use them to close my trench coat around me. Rain is imminent.

"I can't stop women from falling in love with me. I treat them like crap. I don't lead them on."

He chuckles.

"Okay, I tease them, maybe. But it's only for the sexual tension. They like it."

"Must be that big dick and wad of euros that talk for you," he snickers. "Can't say I blame them. I wouldn't mind a woman putting me up, but then again, I'd lose face with all the guys. That just doesn't happen here unless it's an elderly woman who needs attention and is willing to pay for the privilege. And you know 'that' guy won't be advertising it."

"Well, let's just say I'm here for work, but I might get some pleasure out of this event other than the art I love while inflicting some pain."

"If she takes your attention away from the art you love so much, then I think you might have met your match."

We flip our passes to the attendant as we walk through the entrance. The umbrella sets off the security alarm, but once I show security what it is and walk through again, I receive an all-clear.

We slip in alongside women in extravagant gowns worthy of the MET in America with cameras flashing everywhere.

No fucking way do we want our ugly mugs on the news and in tabloids. A reporter shouts out names, but they mean nothing to me as the little principessa walks with confidence and an aura of superiority I would expect from her father's upbringing. Her shoulders are straight, proud. Her statuesque figure is showing off her gown as it shimmers in all the right places making my cock jump to life. I can't remember the last time just observing a woman made me this excited.

I tear my eyes away from her and her friend enjoying

their minute of fame before slipping into the museum. The night gives a different aura to the art and sculptures as classical music greets us and the chandeliers glisten.

The number of participants is limited, the air moves freely, and it leaves room for us to move about. It's a treat to be here without hoards of tourists who dress in flip-flops and shorts. Tonight, everyone is dressed to impress.

This is a group of elite and wealthy families, and I wonder why I didn't receive an invitation, but I do keep a low profile. Still, I have friends in high places and others in influential ones who never said a word. I surmise they might not want competition on tonight of all nights. Then again, maybe I'm too well known by the powers behind this soiree.

I refused to check my coat with the umbrella telling them I was not sure how long I'll stay. Savio and I snag Dom Perignon as it floats by on trays like clouds wisping by, only it's carried by well-trained staff who walk stiffly and don't say a word.

Next comes the antipasti of little snacks for such occasions. The last time I attended a fundraiser was a larger affair for one of the newer hospital wings. We made a large donation in exchange for a commissioner's vote we needed on another project. We build elaborate, million-euro apartments and office buildings. We received the zoning changes we needed. Tit for tat is how it goes. It was a revered coup as we rarely outbid the Italians.

All favors have strings attached. We're not in the business of goodwill or being good Samaritans. Right now, the only tits I'm interested in are the blonde's as she just entered the room. I can't deny the fact all eyes are on her. The old crystal chandeliers in the main room give a warm glow to her exposed skin. I hate how she's showing off her large breasts noting how they remain in place without the use of a bra.

My cheek twitches when I notice a tattooed man in the room paying too much attention to her, and I want to beat the shit out of him for being so forward.

Savio distracts me with chit-chat as he urges me to walk about the room. He mentions my mother has missed some work while I've been away living my double life.

"That's odd. I just saw her, and she said nothing, but I noticed she seems tired and pale."

"You may want to look into it."

Given Grandpa's cryptic message, I'm not liking how this is shaping up. I wonder if there's something wrong with Mama. I might be the last to know, which wouldn't surprise me as she always goes out of her way to make my life as carefree as possible. Maybe it's to compensate me for my father's disdain.

Walking into a smaller room of portraits, the museum orchestra becomes faint and more serene, similar to a lazy summer breeze. Classical music is fitting and provides an inviting backdrop as everyone makes their rounds of introductions, sees old friends, and sometimes observes the artwork and sculptures. For many, this is society's annual winter event. I find it ironic as most can't recite from memory the artists whose artwork adorns the walls.

I pass by men who look like me, dressed well for the occasion and gathering in small groups. I wouldn't be surprised if they had guns in their cars outside. It's the vibe I pick up, and it takes a mafia man to know one in most circumstances. I work more in the shadows, and Rome isn't my territory. It's customary for those who are higher up in the family to keep a low profile.

We pass by strangers, and Savio overhears a younger

man without much couth mentioning the name Valentina. My ears perk up. Supposedly, she will go for a high price, higher than anyone he knows can afford to pay.

Valentina, there are no works of art here with that name, and none of the art is being sold. There are very strict penalties if art is forged or sold illegally. We take our heritage seriously.

"I wonder whom he is speaking about," I murmur rubbing my hand over my smooth chin as a long curl drops to the middle of my forehead. Damn, the humidity.

"What the hell is that about?" Savio hands me another champagne and we blend in.

"No clue. Maybe we can find out." I use an outstretched hand as our cue to continue to circulate in a clockwise direction while taking note of the exits and the number of stiff men in the room because we're not the only connected people here.

Hell, today some of the elected officials even have bodyguards due to the bombs that took out a road and killed a judge and other innocent people years ago. One was Rosario Livatino. He denounced the mafia and is earning sainthood for his plight to clean up Sicily.

The canapés are making the rounds with the servers who move as cardboard cutouts wearing white gloves and lacking a sense of humor as I make a crack about a woman fussing over the food.

"I'm picking up an odd vibe. How did you get these tickets?" Savio asks, "This is clearly not our scene. Well, not entirely," he muses.

"I got them from a fence. Apparently, it's a closed circuit."

"Hm. Now might be a good time to ask ourselves 'why.'"

Savio is only stating the obvious. I'm not used to

listening to the word 'no' because, in my life, everything is obtainable. Everything.

"There she is," I mumble taking in the goddess with blonde hair piled upon her head similar to a style a movie star would wear. She makes moving on heels as high as stilts an effortless feat.

"The woman in the champagne-colored dress? The one that's clinging to her like a second skin?"

"Mm," I reply.

"Yummy," he mumbles.

Two men pass before us as my dark eyes zero in on my girl. "That's De Luca's daughter. This must be a place they are auctioning off their daughters. What an ingenious ruse," one of the strangers says.

"She must be the catch of the night," Savio murmurs to me.

"Watch it, Savio. She's quite the woman with family ties to an unfortunate man who screwed the wrong mafia family."

My phone vibrates. I pull it out of my coat pocket and glance at the text.

"We have work to do. We need to get to it. It's going to be a long night," I say slipping the phone back in my pocket.

# 6

## VALENTINA

Mama says we, the De Luca family, must make a statement at the upcoming gala, so in preparation for this, my dress arrived weeks ago. I'm glad Papa agreed to Laura going with us because it wouldn't be nearly as much fun without her.

As promised, we're spending today shopping for her dress and getting facials together. Walking along the cobblestone streets lined with designer stores, we search shop after shop for the perfect dress. We're about to give up when we stumble across a boutique off the beaten path. It's here that Laura finds the perfect dress by Marchesa, with a nude tulle base and red flower design overlay. The long sleeves are perfect for Rome this time of year, the bottom of the gown blossoms into yards of fabric at her feet, and the cinched waist shows off her enviable figure.

Like a bridesmaid at a wedding, I pull the dress at the bottom to show off the flowers in the fabric because it will trail behind her as she walks.

"You look good enough to be on the red carpet at the American movie awards," I exclaim.

The tulle creates the illusion of nudity, but her skin is covered. It's captivating. No doubt, all eyes will be on her.

"I don't want to be around when your father gets this credit card bill," I mumble as she hands over the black card her father gave her last year on her twenty-fourth birthday.

"It's a once-in-a-lifetime event. Your parents never let me go before, and my parents never get invited to these swanky events. They are not A-listers like yours."

"I'll give you that, but honestly, it's my father's large donations that open doors," I state what we both already know.

"Besides, this is just a prelude to the wedding dress I want. He may as well get used to the taste of my spending," she says. The associate hands her a zippered bag with the dress and a handle bag with the shoes and matching clutch inside.

"I'm sure you'll make that back from cash gifts at the wedding." I mean, this is Sicily, and the mafia still carries on the tradition of huge weddings. Every member of 'the family' knows they need to pay homage to my father, even if the bride is only a friend to his daughter. To not give an envelope full of cash to the newlyweds would call their loyalty into question.

We find our tail, I mean guard, Ridolfo, outside, standing guard. Even though we consider him a third wheel, he comes in handy when we have too many shopping bags to carry.

"I'm starving."

"We should head home," Ridolfo grumbles, looking at his watch.

He's intimidating with his six-foot frame. His bulging muscles strain against his ill-fitting blazer. He wears a wedding ring, but I have no idea if he has a family. The man has never shared one detail of his personal life.

"Just forty more minutes, please," I beg.

"You're pushing it, but considering we're close to home, I will allow it."

"Thank you," I chirp as we dip into the next café before he has time to change his mind.

This area of Sicily is home to vineyards covering the landscape and the crops coming in this time of year. Marsala wine is one of our more successful exports, olive oil another. Like most Italians who can still afford it, my family keeps a barrel of olive oil in the cellar.

We also have an extensive wine collection. When we have a party, he serves the most expensive wine to the guests he wants to impress, like local judges or councilmen. Giovi told me the entire collection is worth over a million euros, minimum.

I ask the server to bring the chef's freshest seafood dish without bothering to look at the menu. I don't care what it costs. I want the best. He returns with fresh clams and grilled calamari with an antipasto. Laura and I share tasting everything while Ridolfo sits at the table behind us and drinks an espresso to blend in.

The locals are well aware of Mafiosos. When Francis Ford Coppola was filming *The Godfather* in Sicily, he was adamant about finding the perfect spot for each scene. Even though the story was based on a family in Palermo, the scenes were shot on the other side of the island.

After lunch, Ridolfo checks the street and rooftops for anything suspicious as he holds the door open for us. I almost wish something dangerous and exciting would happen to break up the monotony. The only time my panties get wet is when I'm laughing too hard at Laura's funny one-liners.

She's always had a great sense of humor, and she totally gets me. The best is when we make fun of my bodyguards and exaggerate how they walk and talk. When we were teenagers, we'd stay up late eating tiramisu out of glass cups and watching American TV shows dubbed in Italian.

We eventually graduated from the *Ninja* obstacle course competition and the dating show with a rose. Laura is more vested in these dating shows than I am. All that love-at-first-sight nonsense is hardly believable. Plus, my brain gets tired from listening to English, and my eyes get tired from reading subtitles in Italian. Italy is on a big push to make everyone learn English. Even the buses and trains announce the stops and safety information in both languages.

The last time I checked, I live in Italy. I-T-A-L-Y. I love the Italian language. It's spoken much faster and makes more sense. Ironically, it's a romantic language, but I can live with that. Maybe one day God will surprise me. Mama tells me to pray and still drags me to church. Early on, Giovi and I saw the hypocrisy of all that church stuff. However, we go to church every Sunday, as all good Catholics do.

THE FOLLOWING two weeks pass quickly. Then the big day arrives, and Mama takes me and Laura to an exclusive day spa. With all the commotion, you would think we were getting ready for a wedding. Between glasses of Prosecco, we enjoy the Jacuzzi and sauna before heading to private rooms for a relaxing massage.

The following day, we returned to have our hair and nails done. I like Laura's updo so much that I get something similar. There are so many style options with long hair. My hair is so blonde; it's almost white. I can thank my Viking ancestors for that DNA.

Changing into Lululemon leggings and hoodies, Laura and I join my parents and brother in the family limo for a ride to the airport.

THANKFULLY, the private jet has a fully stocked bar, and I find a bottle of French champagne to open. Papa gives me a look of disapproval, but he knows a glass or two of bubbly will help to calm my nerves. I've been on planes all my life, but for whatever reason, I'm still a nervous flyer, especially on small jets.

My brother had no interest in coming, but Papa forced him into it. I don't know what's up with Giovi lately. I thought he would want to tag along and check out all the pretty women. They are all suitable for marriage, and he needs to start thinking about producing an heir.

Laura and I stake out a spot in the back, away from the others.

"Marco is so jealous," she whispers, slipping her phone into her purse.

"Well, have you set the date?"

"He's waiting for a promotion, but honestly, I can't wait. I don't care about it. We can rent something and make do with what we have."

"He wants to take care of you. That's sweet." I wonder who I'll find, if anyone. I've given up on finding a man at any of these affairs Papa takes me to. These things are disguised as social events, but arranged marriages don't drop out of the air. I begin to suspect I might be on display soon.

The corners of Laura's mouth curl, and instinct tells me she's thinking of her man. I long to have the same cat-who-ate-the-canary smile when I fall head over heels in love. I want to marry for love like Laura, but I don't think it's in the cards for me.

Papa and Giovi are in what appears to be an intense conversation. Mama intervenes, and it is quiet, except for the hum of the jet engines. I wonder what is happening, but I know better than to ask. I've been taught to be seen and not heard. But it doesn't stop me from wanting to know just the same.

After a smooth landing, we exit the aircraft and carefully make our way down the steep steps with the help of our bodyguards holding our hands.

Two black Escalades wait to take us to the hotel. Both come with a set of bodyguards dressed for the affair later, which tells me my leash is still attached, albeit invisibly.

The five-star hotel we're staying in is near the museum. Laura and I squeal with excitement when we open the double doors to our own suite to use for getting ready for the event.

As soon as I'm dressed, I go next door to model the silky dress for Papa. I'm nervous about going without a bra and panties. I have to because the dress has a deep V cut in the back and the front is a nude mesh so fine it resembles bare skin. I'm using a special tape to keep my boobs in place. The fabric is sparkly and shimmers with my curvy butt when I move.

Daddy would die if he knew I didn't have panties on. His eyes furrow at me as he lets out a gruff 'hm' that sounds more like a cough.

He looks at Mama. "You expect her to get a suitable husband dressed like a goddamn stripper?"

"She has nothing else to change into." Mama defends my choice knowing I don't want to dress like a nun.

"Papa, let me live a little. Sheesh."

He waves his hand in the air, dismissing the discussion. His phone rings, and I can tell it's Uncle Federico on the other end. Good, that takes the focus off me, which is what I was counting on. Papa is being distracted with work and bigger problems. Federico is Papa's underboss of the highest rank.

It's a long ride to the museum, and by the time we arrive, the humidity has caused a few tendrils of hair to fall out of my chignon. No matter how much hairspray I use, it will turn curly in this humidity.

It's too dark to see the gardens, so maybe I can talk Papa into coming back in the spring.

We pose for pictures on the red carpet, just like movie stars. This is extremely satisfying as cameras flash as we briefly pause and continue. I grab Laura's hand when we exit the area, and we're like two teenagers seeing our first boy band.

While Laura and I make our way around the room looking at art, I notice a man and stop abruptly. I almost spill my champagne but save myself the embarrassment. The last thing I need is to appear to be sloshed.

"What's up with him?" I ask Laura.

"Holy Mother of God." She makes the sign of the cross over her chest. "That's one gorgeous specimen of a man. He looks Italian and so fine in his tux. I'm horny just looking at him and wish Marco was here."

"Who is he?"

"Hell, if I know, but I like what I see. The way his tux is tailored, I can tell he has a body built for sin if I ever saw one."

His dark hair is thick and curly. His dark eyes are the kind to hold secrets. I wonder if Papa knows him. He has someone with him, a friend or brother, judging by their body language when they talk. Eye contact and facing each other says a lot in the criminal world.

I check for a ring on his finger, knowing it's useless. Men can always take a ring off. Normally, Italian men don't have to sneak around. Cheating is part of the culture and not something they necessarily keep secret.

I notice there is a spark missing from his eyes and it reminds me of my own. So much of me has been chipped away that I have nothing left to lose. I live in a void of emotion. My parents have not hugged me since I was a child, and now, I am not attached to a man. I'm in the gray zone, each day like the last. Empty.

We continue to walk, and as I turn to avoid him, our eyes meet. A shiver goes down my spine. I can't break away from the darkness in his eyes.

Laura whispers, "Don't look now, but the devil is in the room."

7

———

## MASSIMO

"Alright," Savio concedes. "I'll walk around and see what I can find out."

"I'll do the same," I say, nodding and heading in the direction of my goddess. Just before I reach her, a woman approaches visibly excitedly, whispering something in her ear. They both look at a gentleman across the room, but I can tell he's no gentleman. With scars across his knuckles, his hands belong to a boxer, not a businessman.

Stepping behind a large Baroque vase filled with enough flowers to hide me, I'm close enough to hear what's being said without being seen.

"He's so handsome. Maybe that will be the one," says her companion, who is shorter and possibly younger.

"Hm, well, I'm not impressed." My new obsession says this with a firm tone. She has common sense. Good girl.

She also has eyes the color of a blue Tiffany box, unusual for an Italian but not impossible with our history of mixed ancestry.

"This dress is too damn tight. I didn't eat all day, and

now I'm starving. Can you grab me a plate of the shortbread with tuna caviar and dill mousse? I could eat that all night."

*Indeed. I'm thinking there might be something off the menu that I'd like to eat all night, as well.*

Her friend leaves and returns with a small plate of hors d'oeuvres and another glass of champagne.

Using this as an opportunity to make my move, I step out from behind the flowers and walk toward her. With the skill of a pickpocket, I bump into her causing her champagne to splash on my coat.

"I'm so sorry." She blushes and fumbles with a napkin, dabbing my coat. It's a black coat. The wet spot can't be seen anyway. I just wanted to meet her, and the bump-into-move works every time. It's the first thing we learn on the street about stealing items of value. And she looks valuable, priceless in fact.

"Would you like another drink? Perhaps something other than champagne?" I offer as she stands up, giving up on my soiled coat.

"I'm fine, thank you. Who are you?" I ask, noticing her glass is tipping and that her champagne is about to spill. I wonder if she's had too much to drink.

I don't want to scare her off, and I need to make sure this looks accidental—like a chance meeting. It's unlikely but still possible, someone in her famiglia might recognize me.

I need to meet with her father soon. His son is my target, and he's in a corner with his mother according to Savio, who's keeping tabs on him.

Standing this close, I can feel the tension radiating off of her hot body. I can't imagine what she has to be tense about, but my balls tighten as I gaze at her full, beautiful breasts. I long to grab them with both hands, bury my face in them to smell her, and lick her sensitive, alabaster skin. My teeth would nip at her nipples before I suck on each one before reaching between her legs to find she's wet and ready for me.

"Valentina," she says, extending her hand. "I'm not used to these affairs. You?"

"Not at all. But I do love art and beautiful women, and you are by far the most beautiful in the room." I take her hand in mine and kiss it.

"Really? I don't picture you as the romantic type."

"And what do you picture?"

"Moody, broody, dark. . ."

"Sounds like you are describing my daily moods," I tease, but I'm impressed. She might not be as naïve as she looks. "And you? Your moods?"

"Hm, happy when I'm pushing my parents' buttons. I think I've perfected the art." She gives me a hint of a smile and this damn coat is warm all of a sudden. I want to take it off, but I need to wear it.

I'm drawn to her and suppress a smile. My balls fill with cum just waiting to fill her up.

"Nice to meet you. . ." She stops mid-sentence, not knowing my name.

"I didn't say. Remember, I'm broody and moody," I point out, pulling my hand away.

The handshake ends quickly as her touch sends chills up my spine, my cock is hard. I'm relieved my coat covers the desire manifesting in my pants.

"Valentina, such a nice name. Sicilian?"

"Yes, how did you know?" She plays it cool, but I see an awareness in her eyes signaling to me her mind is turning. I wish I had more time to figure out what she's preoccupied with.

"Lucky guess. I've only been to Sicily once, as a child.

But I'd love to go back and check out the Greek amphitheater. I hear it's a sight to behold, like you."

She blushes. Judging from the pink glow, she doesn't wear much makeup.

"I took in a concert there this summer. Definitely worth the trip. You are from around here?"

Clever girl, getting information on me.

"Yes, somewhat, more central Italy, but I travel."

"I'd love to travel to—oh, no. Here comes Papa."

I turn to see her overbearing father walking towards us. He is beginning to lose his hair, along with his waistline. I peg him to be in his mid-fifties. Valentina must get her mother's eyes because her father's are as gray as our winter clouds.

"Valentina, where is Laura? She was told not to leave your side."

Realizing he had interrupted our conversation, he looked me over with such scrutiny; I believe a rectal exam would be less intrusive.

"Excuse us," he says. Taking her by the hand, he lures her away. By his dismissive tone, he doesn't care to see me again.

I wonder why he feels threatened. Or, more importantly, what has him on edge? He's walking by himself through the crowd.

Savio appears out of nowhere. "Yes, that's them, alright. The De Lucas. You're here on business, aren't you? And you needed backup. That's why I'm here."

"Time will tell, but my goal is to make a business arrangement one way or another."

"You might want to know there is a private auction going on in the basement, and your girl is one of the young women going to the highest bidder. And get this, the creepy dude with the tattoos over there is rumored to be enamored with her."

Fuck, fuck, fuck.

"I need to get down there now and speak to her father."

"First, we must steal a special key card to get in."

Damn.

"Which I already obtained." He smiles and slides it into my coat pocket while grabbing another treat off a nearby tray.

I grab another champagne and toss it back like a shot.

"What? Where is it?" Mr. Creepy Tattoo Man cries out in a panic, checking his pockets and the floor around him. Clearly, he's lost something.

"Hm, his key card, I presume." I send a knowing look to Savio.

"I had to even the playing field," he says, washing his food down with a swig of champagne, "and he had the jump on you. You can't say I'm not a good wingman. You can thank me with my holiday bonus."

I chuckle. Savio does not mince words, but I know he means no disrespect. Unless he is disloyal, there is not much I'd punish him for; that's how tight we are. At this level, men like him are hard to find.

"Go get your girl. I'll run interference here. Follow the hallway blocked off with the red theater rope.

"Wish me luck."

"You were born lucky," Savio says with a smirk.

8
───────

# VALENTINA

"What do you mean, the devil?" I'm alarmed, as any woman would be. I liked the handsome stranger who wasn't upset when I spilled champagne on his expensive tux.

"I mean, he's dangerous. I've seen that conceited look before. It screams arrogance. He's not for you or me. Let someone else have him. He can eat their soul instead."

"He doesn't look menacing to me." I have no idea what he means by 'type.' Massimo has danger written all over him, too, with his chiseled jaw, dark olive skin, and the way he challenges anyone not to notice him. "I might like the aura of mystery about him," I add just to goad him.

The stranger next to me is the most handsome man I've ever seen. Sure, his confidence level could be reigned in a bit, as no man should be confident to the point of being smug.

So why do I want to learn more about him? And why is it slick between my legs? With no underwear on, the wetness has only one place to go as it oozes down my inner thighs.

"Exactly, that mystery is meant to be locked in a box, along with his hatchet."

"You're joking. Is there something you're not telling me?"

I grab another tasty morsel off a passing tray. I'm flustered as hell, and my face is warm as the temperature in the room just went nuclear.

"I just know things, that's all," he says as Papa barrels down on us.

Papa interrupts us, and my thoughts are interrupted by jailer number one, previously known as Mama, showing up. Sadly, at some point today, she stopped being a mother and became more of a guard herself. Her unusual neurotic behavior, combined with the three arguing and whispering on the jet, makes me wonder if something is afoot.

The handsome man at my side is nowhere to be seen.

My family keeps me in the dark about everything, and I'm beginning to resent it, especially when they tell me how to live my life now and in the future.

"Stop eating those." Mama scolds me as I attempt to snag more food. "People will think you're hungry."

"I am. Besides, this champagne will make me woozy on an empty stomach."

What can be better than an extravagant evening with my best friend and the fantastic food coming by as if it's transported on a magic carpet? The champagne is light and exquisite as the flavor lingers on my tongue and pairs nicely with the fancy finger foods. I can't get enough of it or the mystery man who makes my body tingle. I sneak another look his way, but he's gone.

Mama's voice pierces my thoughts. "Act like a grow-up, Valentina. I swear, we indulged you too much as a child. You should have been engaged to be married instead of attending that overpriced college you insisted on. You're lucky your father saw your point and agreed it was good for business. An education makes you more attractive, and school was cheaper than paying for round-the-clock bodyguards."

"I'm a grown-up, and I don't drink much," I reply. I eat another crostini with ricotta and quail eggs before chasing it with more bubbly.

"Oh, my," Laura moans. It's as if she's having an orgasm as she slips the toasted bread with honeyed figs and goat cheese mousse past her lips.

Mama turns on her heel and can't escape the spectacle fast enough. Laura and I exchange a mischievous grin.

"Well played, Laura."

"Um, really, it was by accident, but seriously, your mother needs to pull that stick out of her ass." She speaks so softly that not even a bug planted in our boobs would pick up the words.

"The mystery man is gone," I murmur.

"It's for the best." She slips her arm through mine, and we head off to take in more art.

Even though she's in the family, Laura can't show outright disrespect for my mother without it reflecting poorly on her father. It wouldn't be pretty; not even splitting his fingers by Papa's goons would get him off the hook.

"Why is the tattooed man staring at me?" I ask.

"I don't know. What I do know is he's an enforcer. I'd be careful around him. I hope he isn't going to be your match."

"What do you mean?"

"Haven't you figured it out yet? Your family is looking to marry you off tonight. Time is running out. You're getting older. School is over, and you've run out of options."

"Not if I run away."

"Like you could," she jokes.

She's only telling me what I already know. I've never had enough room to run anywhere besides the beach. No one is meeting me there to rescue me from a world of preconceived notions, where I am obligated to be a model housewife or be slaughtered in effigy to pay for the sins of my father.

"Shit." She's right. My destiny is set in stone. There is no escaping the fact I'll be married within the year.

"I should have put it together sooner. It's the only reason I was allowed to wear this fancy dress, and I suppose you're here to keep me calm while my father takes one of his calculated risks."

"It makes sense." She shrugs her shoulder, but we're in agreement.

How foolish of me to think I was special. Maybe that's why Papa loved me from a distance, knowing this day would come.

I was foolish to think he loved me as much as Giovi. In this world, sons are the future kings. Daughters are the pawns on the chessboard.

"I wonder what he's gaining out of my match."

"No clue. Normally you'd be promised to a Sicilian to keep the bloodline. There are others here, I suppose. I don't know them all. Tattoo Man visits your father's restaurant from time to time."

She's referring to the restaurant that's used to launder money, and we have stores selling lottery tickets, taking bets, and collecting protection money.

"Let's just sit here," I suggest, finding an empty bench in the main room.

I'm beginning to think the mysterious man disappeared down a roped-off section. Earlier, I saw a shadow heading that way. Maybe he's an art thief, chuckling at the irony. If I love anything as much as freedom, it is art.

My freedom, such as it is, is running out and I long to breathe fresh air in the garden. Looking around, I check the doors and the security in the room. I wonder if I could slip out without anyone noticing.

Suddenly, the man with the tattoos is shouting and carrying on as if his pants are on fire. I wonder what his problem is.

**9**

---

# MASSIMO

I make my way into the secret room used for dirty deals as the auctioneer rattles off numbers to match the women who are under the pretense of a gala upstairs. I walk into this blindly, and I hate not being prepared. The man commanding the room is going through the women quicker than a collection of Di Vinci drawings at a Sotheby's auction.

To avoid a paper trail or mistaken identity, the men in attendance are looking at a large screen TV showing pictures of the women while security cameras affixed to the walls keep an eye on everything. These old walls have been painted over countless times during the 119 years of the museum's existence.

I'm impressed at the level of ingenuity but still find this repulsive. How can men sell their daughters? Whatever happened to simply arranging a marriage? Families did that for centuries to build wealth and form alliances.

Daughters are considered the little princesses of the family, but if this is what they are groomed for, it's seriously fucked up. Believe me, I know. I have fucked up more men and women over the years than I care to admit.

Some would consider me a hypocrite because my grandfather takes part in human trafficking, but this is treating family like livestock, to be sold to the highest bidder. My grandfather trafficks in strangers, not family. Not that it's right, but one would think family would be more compassionate.

Auctioning off the daughters of Dons pisses me off and goes against even my questionable moral code of ethics. Women and children should be off limits when it comes to this shit. Some women volunteer for it, but Valentina didn't impress me as a complicit mafia princess. I noticed her eyeing the exits, but does she know what's happening here tonight?

Doubtful.

A name is announced, and the bidding continues with men nodding their heads to make a bid.

The man with the neck tattoos stumbles into the room, out of breath but here, nonetheless. By the way he stared at Valentino upstairs, I know he has his sights on her. The man is bad news. He looks like a professional killer, but didn't give away his profession to anyone other than Savio and me because we have so much in common, we can read each other.

I find Luciano De Luca and his son, Giovi, sitting together and take a seat behind them. When I tap Luciano on the shoulder, he flicks my hand away like I'm nothing.

I lean in to hiss in his ear. "I know all too well who you are, and you're stealing from my grandfather, charging us for products we never receive. We're short on the coke and guns you shipped us. You know the punishment for that."

Turning around abruptly, he shouts, "Who the hell are

you to tell me anything? Do you know who I am?" He's drawing unwanted attention from those around us and smiles politely to give the impression he's got it under control.

I know for a fact he contracts out all his killings, which tells me either he can't stand the sight of blood, or he's above doing the deed himself now that he's reached 'untouchable' status by mafia standards.

The way he hands out money and medical supplies in Sicily is the textbook way to buy the hearts and minds of civilians so they won't rat him out. That's how it's been done since the 1800s when the mafia started in Sicily.

Valentina's name is announced, coming up faster than I anticipated.

"I was just notified of the discrepancy. One of my lieutenants has disappeared, and we discovered the issues ourselves. It's not me. I need time to find out who has sticky fingers."

"Everyone lies when their life is on the line."

"I know that, too. I assure you this is not the case. I need time."

"Your time ran out days ago. I will bid on your daughter, and I will win." My voice is calm, void of emotion, a business deal just like any other.

"I will not sell her to an Albanian. She needs to be in Sicily, where I can see her and make sure she's taken care of and safe," Luciano argues.

"I can do all that and more."

I see the tattooed man nodding. Fuck, the bidding is fast, and this fucking prick Luciano is purposely procrastinating, trying to throw me off my game.

I'm done with his pompous ass. Looking at the auctioneer, I nod.

I'm acknowledged, and Tattoo Man shoots me his look of displeasure. By the looks of him, he's served time in prison, and he's not a fitting husband for Valentina.

I don't have time to question why I care. I only know once she's in our family, we will have a working relationship with her family and a shot at getting into the oligarchy. And her family will be spared, for now.

I'm not going about it the way my grandfather asked, but it will work just the same. We both understand unforeseen events transpire, and I adapt quickly to my circumstances.

There is no time to lose as someone else bids and the price increases.

I nod again.

"Your daughter for your son's life," I whisper. "Final offer."

I stand, and before I can take a step, he is beside me. Squaring his shoulders, he tugs his vest down and buttons his tuxedo dinner jacket closed.

Waiting to see if anyone can outbid me, I say, "When we expose you, you are out of the oligarchy," and with that I see no one in the room nodding.

"End it now," I demand to end future excuses. I'm done negotiating, and he knows it.

He nods to the auctioneer to accept the bid and raises my hand to declare me the winner.

All eyes are on us as the bidding stops.

Luciano and I agree on a price palpable to him. It's enough to make things right with us, and he'll have plenty of euros to line his pockets. He knows if he fucks up again, his family will be dead.

Applause erupts in the otherwise silent room. A faint whisper of "it's the highest bid ever made" buzzes around the room. I'm relieved to have beat out all the competition salivating over the gorgeous picture of my future bride.

"Is that what you are after? Access to the oligarchy?" Luciano asks as his gray eyes meet mine for the first time.

"Partially."

"If I turn my seat over to you, questions would be raised and an inspection demanded of all of our dealings, yours and mine."

"It could also prove to be deadly if you don't comply." My voice is low but no less commanding, and I smile at the men in the room as we lower our arms.

"Are we even?" he asks to close out our negotiations.

"Not by a long shot. But the money from the auction should make you right with my family, you made some money, and Valentina will have a life of luxury. But if there are more problems, there will be consequences."

He turns, and we shake hands. His are as cold and lifeless as a dead fish.

I must say, it's a weird way to meet my future father-in-law.

"I assume you'll muscle into my decisions and information from the twelve," he says, the quiver in his voice giving away his nervousness.

"Perhaps, but it's a small price to pay in order to spare your only son's life, isn't it?"

"He has nothing to do with it," he barks as if to warn me off his son; a few men look our way.

"We're done here," I say, handing him a card. "My attorney will work with yours, and we'll put this to bed before midnight. Otherwise, you and Giovi won't see another sunrise."

He pauses like a mouse standing in a glue trap, guaranteeing death. He understands the painful process in which his son would have died: slowly, tortured, and without Luciano's fix, his wife's future is in jeopardy as well as his daughter's.

Human nature predicts he will take the path that guarantees life for both his children. "This doesn't have to play out like a Greek tragedy," I say.

"Fine," he growls. "As you wish. I only request Valentina gets to have one last Christmas at home."

"Fine, deliver her in January at Dante Micheli's wedding." And I almost laugh at how ironic it would be with two 'brides' in the same room. "But I don't want her to know about me, I'll tell her myself. You can tell her she will be wed in the new year."

It's getting late. We move towards the front of the room where the lighting is better. Only now do I notice the lines and dark circles around Luciano's eyes, and for a split second, I believe he might be telling the truth about the missing contraband.

But rule number one is, everyone lies. Until he's proven where the corruption is and who's accountable, I'm still taking him as a liar and following my rules.

I'm the victor tonight. Luciano is no longer the cocky, confident Sicilian. He will recover by morning, but this is one moment he'll never forget.

As I make my exit, I stare his guards in the eye, knowing they want to pounce but have no choice but to stand down.

Slipping upstairs, I find Savio in the main room. The music has stopped. It's our cue to leave before the intermission ends and the pomp and circumstance begins.

"What's up?" Savio inquires with wide eyes.

"We made a deal. I was the highest bidder, and Valentina is to be my bride. There's no way I would let that thug with the tattoos on his neck outbid me.

Valentina has until January to join me. In the meantime, Luciano can get his house in order. If not, it won't be pretty."

"Ouch," he says, flinching. "Still, he's a lucky man."

"Very," I concede without gloating. "Speaking of luck, where is Valentina? I'd like to get another look at my future bride before we leave. I want you to contact my attorney as the contracts need to be completed by midnight."

"I'm on it," he says, glancing around the room. "Valentina was just here."

I can't find my blonde-haired, blue-eyed vixen, but I find her friend flirting with some guy. I'm surprised she's not with Valentina. They've been inseparable all night. And why has Laura not noticed her friend missing?

"Hm." I'm perplexed. "The earlier commotion would create the perfect diversion for a lovely woman who is micromanaged," I murmur.

"Oh, no. You think she figured out what was going on here?" Savio asks, meeting my eyes. We're both thinking the same thing.

A bird in a cage sees an opportunity to escape. And she's in a city where no one would recognize her unless their motivations aren't honorable.

"Freedom for my little bird..."

"I'm so sorry. I should have watched her instead of the hallway," Savio says.

"No harm done. You cover this entrance," I say, exiting through French doors leading to the garden.

The brisk air greets me, like smelling salts to a man who's been knocked out. I'm alive, alert, and charged with adrenaline to find her before she regrets leaving the building.

The moonless night is not helping with visibility. The

short, small lawn lights lining the sidewalk's edge are more ornamental than useful.

Anticipating a game of cloak and daggers, I search for tall figures, moving or crouched. Valentina may be a target for those going after Luciano or Giovi. Killing her would make Luciano look dirty.

There are plenty of unscrupulous men underfoot tonight. Some could be contract killers from other mafias. Some could be from the De Luca family who are out to cover up the fact that they were stealing. The scenarios are endless.

Maybe, just maybe, Luciano was telling the truth, and he didn't cheat us. But if he didn't, who did?

What I find concerning is the fact none of the family guards are here, and even her overbearing mother didn't set off any alarms. In fact, where is her mother?

In the shadows, I see two men with ski masks slinking around the short trees and assume they are stalking her. Everyone appears to be on the same board game but Valentina.

Hiding behind a bush, I pick up a large rock and toss it to distract the men.

One of them takes the bait and doubles back, coming towards me. My heart races as I wait. From inside my umbrella, I slide out my samurai knife, the steel having been fired and folded ten times.

When he gets close enough, I slice his ankle with my blade. And before he can cry out, I pounce on him, wrapping my dominant arm tightly around his neck. I use my other arm to overlap it and pull as tight as possible, choking him out.

Seeing as how we all wore dress shoes, it left his ankle vulnerable. It's hard to walk with a severed Achilles tendon.

As an added measure, I stabbed his femoral artery to make sure he doesn't come after me or Valentina again.

One bad guy down, one more to go.

I stalk the next one with care, being careful I cast no shadow as I pass under the garden lights. I zig-zag until I see both my subjects six feet before me.

Valentina turns as if she senses something other than the winter breeze.

## 10

## VALENTINA

The drama caused by the man who said some important card was stolen gives me the opportunity to seize the day. I have no clue what card he's referring to, nor do I care.

I look for Laura and find her flirting with a handsome man. She's probably buzzed and oblivious to everything by now. She has zero interest in art and would rather be at a club with her friends, friends I've never met. I bet I know more about them than they know about me.

Mama is chatting with an old friend, and Papa and Giovi have been gone for some time. They're probably working the room, looking for another deal, or forging new contacts out of the public's eye.

Inching slowly towards the end of the room, I reach the French doors leading to the garden. I press the metal bar, assuming it's locked this time of night, and I'm surprised when it opens. As soon as my high heels touch the brick pavers, I jump for joy at my first taste of freedom in years.

I'm free. I don't have a guard on me, my parents—gone.

It's just me and the garden on this moonless night. I'm

quick to move away from the doors to avoid being discovered.

Taking a deep breath, the cool air enters my lungs. I take the first available pathway to who knows where. It's not easy to see in the dark. However, a glow in the sky from the city lights reflecting off the clouds afforded me limited visibility.

Damn, these stilettos. They are great for sex appeal but useless when walking on uneven pavers and pebbled stones. I must look like a newborn giraffe trying to stand for the first time. This is silly. I stop and gingerly slip one shoe off, then the other. Holding them tenuously by my fingers, they dangle by my side as I continue walking.

Shit. I left my purse and phone with Laura. No matter, I won't need it. I'll be back. It's not like I can run away. What I can do is revel in the fresh air and revel in the fact my father's guards didn't notice I slipped out. I chuckle, knowing others, including me, will catch shit later. Until then, I savor this rare moment.

I breathe in again with purpose before letting out a sigh. For once, I'm not thinking about my life. I have no idea where I'm going or how far I've walked, and it's sublime.

Shivers run up my spine when shadows appear out of nowhere, like someone is following me, and I turn to look, but nothing. I must be imagining it. Maybe being alone has made me paranoid.

I can tell I'm near the end of the gated garden when the sound of traffic breaks the serenity I'm experiencing. A car with a noisy muffler speeds by, causing annoyed drivers to blare their horns in return.

I can no longer ignore my gut instinct about being watched and turn to walk back to the museum. No one knows where I went, and the commotion inside must be over by now. I check my peripheral to make sure no one is following me.

Someone will look for me if I'm not back in five minutes. Won't they?

Laura only has eyes for Marco, and she's probably done flirting with her good-looking stranger. If she was brought on this trip to distract me, she's doing a poor job of it.

Something big is going on because Giovi looked more upset than usual today. He hates leaving Sicily for any reason, let alone a social gathering. God forbid he be social with anyone, especially strangers. He seriously needs a girl-friend if he's to ever procreate.

A twig snaps behind me. I whip around to find myself face-to-face with a masked man dressed in a black tuxedo. I quickly look down to check his hands for weapons and notice black gloves cover them, I scream.

Gloves, when it's not cold out, can mean only one thing. He wants to kill me and leave no fingerprints or DNA. Panic sets in as a light rain begins to fall.

Instinctively, I move backward. I can't breathe. I'm defenseless against him. He's tall, twice my size if he's a foot. I'm fucked.

"What do you want?" I bark, trying intimidation.

"You."

"Why?"

"No questions. Come quietly, and you won't get hurt." He's gaining on me as his long legs cover more distance than my backward retreat in this dress.

I don't trust him and take off running down the path I hope will circle back to the museum. I'm winded from sprinting as fast as I can. I haven't moved this fast since high school. My mind contemplates how far I can get before he nabs me.

Am I running fast enough? Looking back to find out will slow me down.

Fuck the path. It's long and winding. I make a quick pause to weigh both options in front of me before taking to the tree line. I find some bushes to hide behind. I squat as low as I can. If I close my eyes, maybe he won't see me. It worked when I was a child, and it was a masked killer in an American movie, but it gave me the illusion of being safe until I fell asleep.

Is it ridiculous in a real-life situation? Decidedly, my only chance to escape is not to be seen.

Someone grabs me from behind, and a hand covers my mouth before I can scream again. It's large, warm, and strong. It's a bare hand, not gloved.

"I'm here to help. Yell when I take my hand off your mouth to lure him here. Nod if you understand."

I nod. I have no alternative but to follow the stranger's demands. I'm at his mercy and hope he's here to help me. He's not one of Papa's men.

"After you scream, lay flat on your stomach behind these bushes, and don't look up."

His large hand falls away from my mouth, and I let out a blood-curdling scream before falling into the grass. I welcome the feel of the earth under me as I try to cradle its flatness in an attempt to become invisible. Instinctively, I put my arms over my head to protect myself from whatever is about to happen.

As soon as I'm on the ground, his long coat brushes across my back as he lunges toward the bad guy. The smell of damp earth infiltrates my nose, but a whiff of pineapple and musk is all my rescuer left behind. The notes of his cologne I'll never forget.

I don't look up, too afraid to witness my fate. Instead, I

pray to God as all good Catholics do in their hour of need. I close my eyes and hope for the best as grunts and groans ensue for the longest minute of my life. Then, a gurgling noise followed by silence.

I raise my head, peer into the darkness, and witness my rescuer stowing a blade in the handle of his umbrella. Ingenious.

I struggle to get up. The fabric of my dress is wet and heavy from the rain, making it hard to stand. The stranger extends a hand but as I reach up to grab his, he grabs my arm instead. He's stronger than he realizes, and I can tell a bruise is forming on my arm.

The fact he's not wearing gloves is my clue that the good guy won, and we will both live to fight another day. Well, he'll fight. I need self-defense lessons. Years ago, Papa did a hostage drill with me, but it's only suitable for the kidnapping-by-car scenario.

I can't see my hero's face in the dark, but I do notice a marking on his hand I assume is a tattoo. It's not what I consider to be normal. It's not filled in with color, nor can I make out the exact details, but it could be two lines in two different places and maybe a handle. Paying attention to details is something I learned in kidnapping drills. I was told to look for details to remember instead of panicking. In the real world, it's easy to say and much harder to do.

"No one will ever hurt you now that you are mine." His deep voice makes my heart flutter. His words imply he owns me.

Mine? What does he mean?

"Thank you for saving me," I murmur as I gather my dress in my shaking hands and lift the material to my ankles. My gown is stuck to my body, outlining every nook and cranny as I find it constricts my movement.

"Follow the rules so I don't have to rescue you again," he says.

I shiver and tell myself it's from the shock of the incident or the rain. However, I find the manner in which he is taking control of the situation calms me. As intimidating as he might be, I'm safe with him.

I look up, attempting to see his face, but the rain stings my eyes.

"Who are you?"

Without hesitation, he pulls me into his broad, solid chest. Before I can say another word, his hot, searing lips find mine with such force it makes me tremble. I'm intoxicated between the salt on his lips, the droplets of rain, and the rolling thunder behind us.

Our body chemistry merges, creating a combined warmth, and our kiss provides a refuge from the cold air and his cold demeanor. I can't open my eyes, so I shut them and tilt my head back. I fit perfectly into the crook of his arm. His deep kisses warm me in places I've forgotten. A moistness builds between my legs, and I can't help but kiss him back. My lips become eager for more.

I've never experienced any kiss with synergy like this. His hungry lips devour mine. He's demanding, pushing harder as if he's searching for something hidden as his tongue explores my mouth. He tugs at my bottom lip, sucking it into his, which I find wildly enticing. No man's ever been so forward or forceful with me.

I return his passion with my own, yearning to experience a man's passion. I press my lips to his with equal pressure. Our tongues mingle together, fighting each other for dominance before settling the give-and-take rhythm is established. This kiss rocks me to my core.

Warmth spreads through my arms and breasts like a

beacon of sunshine, and everything around me fades away. It's only me and the stranger who rescued me as the rain slowed. We're both wet, and my hair falls around my shoulders as my updo is destroyed.

His arm pulls me tighter to him, and my lungs scream for air as I've never been kissed so long. I need oxygen, and when I come up for air, someone yells my name.

He immediately pulls away, disappearing into the night.

I glance around my immediate surroundings to catch a last glimpse of him, but I know he won't be found unless he wants me to find him. With him gone, I experienced my first sight of a fresh, dead body. It's in the flesh and not on the TV. I want to scream but know I can't, so I cover my mouth with my hand as bile and champagne rise in my throat.

There's no escaping the sight of the dead man with his eyes open and his throat slit lying in a pool of his blood.

That could have been me.

Waves of nausea force me to crumple, but I force myself to stand and run toward the voice I recognize as Papas.

I run after I scan the garden one last time for the kiss thief, but he's not coming back.

Stealthy, like a ninja, he appeared and disappeared without a sound.

Papa's voice is full of panic as he calls my name again.

"I'm here," I shout, running faster. I want to put as much distance between me and the corpse as possible.

I didn't even thank the man who saved me.

My father runs to me, gathers me in his arms, and pulls me to him with such a forceful hug he squeezes the life out of me.

My lungs and legs struggle to fight off fatigue between the run and his arms.

"Are you okay?"

"I can't breathe," I gasp.

He releases me and takes my face in both hands, searching it for confirmation I'm not harmed. He backs, taking in all of me to make sure I'm intact. The light of the museum is spilling through the glass doors and windows. We stand on the pavers that I stepped upon and that lead me on this deadly journey.

"Thank God you're okay. We couldn't find you—I know how you love this garden."

"Yes, I do," my breath is uneven and catches in my throat.

Wet hair falls out of my updo, Papa tucks it behind my ear and kisses my forehead. He used to do this more when I was a child.

"Papa, what's going on? Why are you acting so strange? Why was a man after me?"

"Who was it?"

"I don't know, he wore a mask and gloves, and some man in a coat helped me"—my voice quivers—"he saved me. He killed the bad man. Papa, his body is covered in blood and back in the garden."

He turns, tucking me under his arm, "He'll make good fertilizer. We need to leave quietly. You're soaked, and your dress is muddy." He steps back, removes his dinner jacket, and drapes it over my shoulders to hide all evidence of the situation. "Look happy, but don't draw attention to yourself."

"Shouldn't we tell someone about the body back there?"

"We can't be associated." We swish through the doors as if nothing happened, my bare feet covered by my soggy dress.

We enter the main area of the event just as the music stops. Announcements begin to recognize the donors and sponsors who helped with the evening. We continue to walk past everyone, and it's beneficial their eyes are on the host and not us as Papa texts the others to join us immediately.

Mama, Laura, and Giovi are at the entrance as our limos roll up on cue.

"We're leaving like nothing happened," Papa commands.

Our guards open the doors of the two vehicles, and the drivers whisk us away. Mama and Giovi and a guard take the second car.

Now is the perfect time for Papa to yell at me for breaking the rules.

"You shouldn't have left the museum. How many times do I have to tell you?"

"Fine, I get it. I get it." My voice cracks from the strain of screaming earlier. I stifle sobs, remembering the sight of the dead man as trauma of the entire event unfolds as punishment for disobeying. "I'm sorry, I didn't know."

As the shock wears off, a wave of every emotion hits me. I wipe tears from my eyes with the back of my hand. Laura hands me tissues from her purse, and I blow my nose. Then she hands me my purse she's been carrying.

"I know," he murmurs. This is his first admission of how my life is stunted, and maybe he knew I was in danger all along.

The adrenaline from earlier is wearing off. I'm suddenly exhausted. I'm crashing hard. I just want to sleep. All I wanted to do was get away. I never expected it to end so badly. The man wasn't wearing gloves because he was cold. He was out to kill someone. He was out to kill me.

But the kiss—that was earth-shattering. I dare not tell Papa about that.

Who was my knight in shining armor? Will I see him again? Will I ever know who he was?

"Why is someone after me? What is going on? Did something happen?" I nag.

"Not now," he replies, and Laura squeezes my hand, signaling me to be quiet. "Besides, I'm handling it. Everything should be okay now."

"Where to, boss?" Our driver asks.

"The hotel. We'll leave at first light. Make the arrangements."

The car speeds up. I stare out the window. The streetlights become a blur.

Laura murmurs in my ear, "Put on a brave face. We'll talk later."

My toes, feeling the warmth of the heater in the car, remind me, "Daddy, my shoes, they are in the garden."

"Shit," he vents his frustration in Italian, then silence ensues.

Sensing something went down in the garden, Laura's hand tenses up in mine.

We all walk in at the hotel together, looking tired but not morose. It's important to look normal for the cameras, which will all malfunction before dawn.

Laura and I slink to our suite. I head to the bathroom and unzip the dress, struggling to get out of it. Laura comes in to help, and when we finally get it over my butt meant for twerking, it falls to the tiled floor in a wet heap.

Laura starts the shower and puts her index finger up to her lips to signal me to be silent. While I wait for the shower to warm, Laura leaves only to return with my dress on a hanger, and she hangs it on the bathroom door where it drips.

I've already stepped into the hot water and welcomed its warmth. Taking advantage of the background noise created by the shower, Laura undresses and steps in behind me. She closes the glass door before finally asking the important questions.

"What the fuck happened? I turned around after getting my flirt on with the hot dude, and you were gone. I thought you went to the bathroom. I checked, then your father and his guards appeared from the hallway. Something was going on tonight. There had to be some meeting. They looked all businesslike, and your father was *pissed*," she says.

"I know. I felt the tension in the air on the jet. I don't remember these things happening before."

"Well, now is not the time to fuck around with the guards or your father," she says, stating the obvious.

"I know, but it felt so great to make a decision and to get some air without sharing it with one of my rotating guards."

"Why wasn't Ridolfo here tonight?" she asks.

"Dad's crew, I guess. It's not a big deal. I messed up."

"What happened, exactly?"

"A man wearing gloves grabbed me and wanted me to go with him. But my gut instinct said if I did, I'd be dead. Then a man in a coat with a tattoo on the top of his hand saved me and disappeared faster than an apparition."

"No fucking way." Her eyes are wide with shock and horror.

"Yeah." I shiver even though the shower is warm. I make the water hotter, hoping it will erase the memory of the night.

"Laura, he killed the guy, like slit his throat and killed him. It was horrible."

"Fuck." She hugs me. It's just us sharing the sordid details of our lives when shit goes sideways, like when we were younger. Only then, issues didn't seem to be so life-threatening.

"I never imagined anyone would want to hurt me, let alone kill me," I sob into her shoulder.

"I know, we never do. But we're easier targets when we're outside Sicily."

I sob more; my freedom will never come back. It's over. I had a few minutes outside my cage, and it was disastrous. Realizing nothing will ever change makes me cry even more because there is no hope.

"Pull yourself together," Laura encourages me. "It will be okay. Your father is the Don, the Don of fucking Sicily. Powerful men create powerful enemies, but he will keep you safe."

"Sure." I agree to agree to avoid thinking about it. After tonight, I'm assuming anyone can get to me if they're motivated enough. Maybe the guards are to make us feel safer.

I'll have to find a way to live within his walls of safety and that someone out there means to harm me. Laura being here is helpful, and she turns off the water and grabs the thick towels for us to dry off.

We methodically go through our routine for bed. We remove our makeup and put our pajamas on silently, not knowing what to say or afraid the room is bugged. It's all the same tonight.

We have two queen beds, but when I get in mine and pull the covers back, Laura crawls in with me. Tonight, I need her close.

I sit with the covers over my legs as I pull the bobby pins out of my hair, letting it cascade around my shoulders. It will dry overnight.

"What do you think will happen with the dead man and my shoes? I left them in the garden."

She shrugs. "No idea. With luck, they will both disappear before the sun is up."

"Right." We are the mafia, and our slogan should be, *"We make problems disappear."*

"Shit! My phone." I get up, find it in my purse, and pull the charger out of my luggage to plug it into the outlet by the bed.

I wonder who my hero was, will I ever see him again? I touch my lips, which he kissed so fiercely, and they feel slightly swollen. What did he mean by *"you are mine?"*

"Did you take any pictures tonight?" I ask Laura, hoping she says yes, so I can look for the kiss thief.

"A few of the food mostly and the art, to show Daddy. Why?"

"I wonder if either of us have a picture of the man who saved me. There was that handsome man, remember he wore a coat."

"You really think a vigilante would be there tonight waiting to save you? Besides, there were a few people who kept their coats, just dropping in and not wanting to check them."

"Not that many," I disagree.

"True, okay, let's look." She swipes her phone from her bedside and crawls back in with me. We pull the covers over us like we did as kids, thinking it would keep us safe from the boogieman under our beds.

I usually don't photograph people, but we flip through my pictures just in case.

"Well, if he were someone important, he'd be savvy enough not to have his photo taken." I sigh and put my phone down.

"True. Let's get some sleep. Are you okay?"

"No, but I will be. If I act any differently, everyone will know what happened, and then we'll be in a shitstorm of all shitstorms. And Papa will look vulnerable. You can't mention this to anyone."

"Duh, I'm the one that helps you, not the other way around," Laura scoffs as she lays her head on the pillow next to me.

"Right." I pull the covers tightly around my shoulders even though I'm not cold.

I replay what I know about the man I want to thank. His smell, his voice, his tattoo, all clues. But he could be anyone.

And how did he know I was there?

And why would someone be after me?

"I bet it's the last time you get to go anywhere with me. I can't be sure if they wanted to kidnap or kill me. What do you know, Laura? Your dad doesn't keep you in the dark."

"I have no clue. Kidnappings are big. Maybe someone wanted money from your father. But he'll make sure they pay when he finds out who's behind this."

"I wonder if he'll ever find out," I murmur, staring at the wall and focusing on nothing at all.

"It's late. Go to sleep."

I can't sleep. I'm trying to remember the details. I don't remember much in the way of visuals but smells...

The stranger wore cologne because I got a whiff of it as he lurched over me. All colognes have bergamot and musk, but the sweetness of pineapple is more of a clue because it's unusual. It might be my only clue as to his identity. He must be in the mafia to have a weapon like that hidden in his umbrella. What a clever way to get his knife, or sword, past the metal detectors.

The way he said I'm his made me a believer.

**11**

---

# MASSIMO

I didn't exactly stick to my grandfather's instructions to take out Giovi tonight. In my defense, I did succeed in sending a warning to Luciano. The De Lucas are a powerful crime family with ties to New York and other major cities around the world. They've been in existence longer than ours, but we're gaining ground daily. And it's led to joint ventures to widen distribution channels.

We're more ruthless than the Italian mafia because we come from a country with a history of political turmoil and war. The resulting devastation takes a toll on everyone. For many women, the only solution is to offer themselves up as mail order brides. Their golden ticket out of poverty is to marry an American and move to the States.

Unfortunately, many of these women are tricked into human trafficking. Maybe it's why I felt compelled to help Valentina tonight. I don't care for that part of the business, but what my grandfather does for his own gain is on him.

Me, show mercy? Ha. Other than women and children, there is no such thing as mercy, and even at that, I don't go out of my way to be anyone's savior. Normally I don't interfere in situations like tonight's auction. For some reason, I couldn't let anyone else have Valentina. Sure, I made the man with the neck tattoo out to be the devil incarnate, but who knows? The fact I'm getting married is one for the books and Savio will throw it in my face until I wed my prize.

Luciano has something I want, and I enjoyed watching him squirm as I bid on his daughter.

Fuck him. He's lucky he got off so easily. If it were not for Valentina, Giovi would be dead.

I replay the night's events in my head. What can't be remedied with a knife stabbed in the main vein in a man's leg? He'll bleed out. I did it so I won't have to worry about crossing paths with him again.

Satisfied with my work, I take off at a dead run, knowing her attacker will be focused on her, which gives me the element of surprise.

Adrenaline courses through my veins knowing Valentina is in danger and could be killed if I don't get there first. Never have I been under such pressure to save someone. Usually, I'm the one hunting the prey, not the one saving it.

I find a second thug searching for her, and by sheer luck spot her hiding behind some low-lying bushes. Smart girl, I'm impressed. After my initial relief that he doesn't have her, I realize I must kill another man tonight, and none of this was in the original plan.

Sneaking up behind her, I clap my hand over her mouth before she can scream. Startled, she jolts from my touch and fends off my hand. But when I tell her I'm here to help, she immediately submits. Now to prepare for a fight. I unleash the saber-like knife from the handle of my umbrella and wait for an opportunity to strike.

Feeling her in my arms and seeing how her fitted dress

molds around her womanly shape is distracting. The wet dress clings to her curves, and my cock stirs. I need to be concentrating on killing someone, not fucking someone.

This has never happened before. I've never saved a damsel in distress, either. I've never even considered it, but there's something about Valentina, her presence raises my blood pressure and clouds my judgment. Having her as my wife might be more dangerous than anything I've ever done. I'm not one to bend for anyone except my grandfather, and even at that, I give his demands a lot of thought.

No one should threaten my woman and expect to live.

He fucking dies.

The moment is right, and I'm poised for action. I have the element of surprise on my side and strike first. He tries to punch me, but I swing my sword, and it connects with his neck, and he goes down.

As he lies there, lifeless. I notice a stun gun ring on his gloved finger, similar to brass knuckles. This tells me he's probably from Sicily because I've never seen guys here use these gadgets. The Sicilians love the theatrics.

Maybe they were sent by Luciano's thief in an attempt to kidnap or kill her. Sending men to carry out such a bold move is a huge risk, and the man behind this will pay with his life once Luciano finds him.

I turn back to Valentina, who realizes the danger has passed and is trying to get up. I don't want her to see my face and have her remember this terrifying event whenever she sees me at the dinner table.

Helping her up, nothing could have prepared me for the bolt of electricity running up my arm when I touched her. I've never been tased, but I imagine this is what it feels like. Plus, my heart is racing, and the desire to protect her is alarming. It overwhelms me.

Her hair is a mess, but it's quite sexy. The just-been-fucked look looks good on her. Her plump lips are slightly parted. I'm tempted to put my thumb over her inviting mouth, but instead, I kiss her.

That's right, I kiss her. Not just any kiss, a deep kiss, with my tongue inside her mouth and my cock pressed against her. I want to taste and explore every inch of her.

I can't wait to make her mine and fuck her long enough and hard enough to erase all other men from her memory.

She clings to me as our bodies melt together like heated butter and sugar, producing a sweetness I've never known. I'm lost in this moment as I run my tongue up her neck and nibble on her ear. I'm drowning in her deliciousness like a man without a raft.

Knowing I must leave, I kiss her again, deeper, pushing my tongue further into her mouth; she's sweeter than cotton candy. Her tongue meets mine, and they dance, first out of eagerness and sheer lust, then yielding and finding a rhythm, making me wish I could pull up her skirt and fuck her right here and now.

A voice is yelling, so there is no time for a goodbye. I abruptly pull away to disappear into the night.

As soon as Valentina leaves and I know she's with her father, I return to pick up the stilettos she dropped. The less evidence lying around, the better. Then I texted Savio to meet me at the Spanish Steps.

I'm still holding Valentina's shoes when Savio pulls up in a rented Mercedes.

"I don't think those will fit you, brother," he teases as we return to the hotel. "So, what happened?"

"Two men were after Valentina. I had to take them out."

"No fucking way. What the hell? That tells me Luciano's got problems in his house."

"Ha, you have no idea. He better keep my fiancée safe. The loss of these men will send a message to whoever sent them. She won't be coming to Florence until January. Her father requested she spend one last Christmas at home."

"You're going soft."

"Hm, I can see how you would think that, however I need time to get the house ready and she needs time to digest that she's getting married."

"I see," he says, not taking his eyes off the crazy traffic in Rome. It will stay this way until about two in the morning. Then the city sleeps for a few hours and starts up all over again, with rush hour lasting all day.

"She's not going to be happy, but she'll probably love the chance to be in Florence with the Uffizi. I saw her gazing at the pieces in the museum tonight, and she seems to genuinely like sculptures and paintings."

"She'll love your mansion then; not so sure she'll like the history of it."

"Awe, that's what makes it so unique." I smile for the second time tonight. The first was when I discovered Valentina.

We have an undeniable connection. She might fight it, but in the end, she will surrender herself to me. "Ah, home sweet home. I can't wait to shower and change." I'm relieved to see our hotel, the latest five-star monstrosity in Rome as the ancient city tries to meet the growing demand for accommodations.

Savio drops me off at the front before pulling away to find parking.

As soon as I get in the room, I drop her shoes into my luggage and remove my tux, putting it into the hotel's laundry bag to dump somewhere later. There is no need to take chances on how much blood is splattered on it. I shower and replay the kiss with Valentina.

I pop nicotine gum in my mouth and chew ravenously. I'm a bit jittery and tell myself it's from withdrawal.

This chemistry thing is new to me but exciting. I run my tongue over my bottom lip, remembering what it felt like to have them on her mouth, neck, and ear… I wonder what else I could've kissed before we were interrupted.

I long to see her again and shake my head as if it will break the spell she's cast on me.

After I've scrubbed myself from one end to the next to remove all traces of blood, hair, and thug DNA, I dry off. I slip into designer jeans, a polo, and black leather loafers.

I open the door leading to Savio's.

"You look refreshed." He smiles, noticing my wet hair and casual clothes.

"I can dress down or dress to impress," I reply, giving him a smirk. "We need a drink."

"For sure, we have to toast to your victories tonight, of which there were many."

"Indeed. I hope Grandfather sees it that way." He should, considering we have the Principessa as collateral if Luciano doesn't include us in his dealings with the oligarchy.

We make our way to the restaurant downstairs and find a leather booth tucked in a corner that cannot be seen from the lobby.

"What are you drinking?" Savio asks before heading to the bar.

"Whiskey, neat." I remove the gum and roll it into a paper napkin left on the table.

We never sit with our backs to any door. I tend to look for all the entrances and exits whenever I'm in a new space.

It's military training I received from Grandfather's top lieutenants, many who saw active duty and lived off the land most of their lives.

Savio returns with two whiskeys and eyes the room for trouble.

Satisfied we have no enemies in the restaurant, he holds up his glass. "To old times and new adventures."

"Saluti," I say, raising my glass, and we both take a swig. "Ah, that's nice."

"Top shelf, better be," he jokes.

"Thanks for coming. I still can't believe Italy fines people for sitting on the Spanish Steps, what the fuck is that?"

"Monuments," he grumbles. "Change, it's inevitable. Hell, next year you'll be married. Oh, that reminds me, our attorney is working on the contracts and making sure your specifications are in it."

"Great. Thanks for taking care of that for me. It will give me time to adjust to the thought of a permanent relationship. Plus, when she shows up in January, we can claim we met and fell in love at Dante's wedding."

I'm thinking about the repercussions of being involved with the Michelis and engaged to a Sicilian. Meanwhile, I'm a top man in my family's Albanian mafia. My life is becoming more complicated by the minute.

"How is that going by the way? The Michelis?"

"Interesting. No talk of striking at us but I'm not holding my breath. Sooner or later they will set boundaries with us."

"Sure, sure. I wonder what will they do?"

"No telling, but Argon is fucking up. He's supposed to stay behind the scenes, but he's throwing big parties with cocaine in the Michelis' bars. They have all the government officials who handle the liquor licenses in the palm of their hands so we can't compete with them."

"Not yet. It takes time."

"Sure," I agree and continue to sip my drink as I survey the room.

"Relax, few know who you are, and we're in Rome, nowhere near our territory."

"That's what puts me on edge." I lean back against the booth, suddenly tired. The adrenaline rush has left me exhausted yet invigorated at the same time. The night spent tap dancing with the devil has left me feeling the effects now that I've decompressed. Even though I'm only twenty-six, I feel like forty-six on nights like tonight.

"How did Luciano take being called out?"

"He deflected, denied it, but admitted something was going on. I think he might have a greedy bastard in his ranks. It may even be the reason Valentina was targeted tonight."

"They might have gone after whichever kid was easiest to get to," he suggests, moving his empty rock glass back and forth between his palms.

"True. We don't know their true intent with Valentina." And we never will with both men dead.

My intent is to get that little minx under me. The thought of her warms me more than the liquor.

We have another round and call it a night. It's late by the time I return to my room. Just then I get a text: Argon is dead, either from heart failure or murdered while on a ski vacation in the Alps.

Fuck! Not that I mind him coming to Italy, but Grandfather will probably come in to oversee this. Me being in the Micheli camp when Argon took his last breath poses a significant problem if they discover I'm an imposter and we're not on the same team. Before I left Florence, the government was watching a huge shipment, and one of my lieutenants gave them an empty Micheli warehouse they already suspected of belonging to someone in the family because of me.

It's sleight of hand stuff: get the polizia and officials where I want them to help my Albanian interests. The Michelis get a pass—just a minor inconvenience to them.

Is it more than a coincidence the government raid came shortly after Argon's death? Did the Michelis put a hit on him?

Was Argon even murdered?

"Savio," I call him on my phone as I take off my shoes. "Fucking Argon dropped dead on a ski trip."

"No shit. I guess someone took care of something we all wanted," he says out loud what I was already thinking. "The Michelis have been through so much with that crazy don, Conti, down here. I wouldn't be surprised if they didn't nip the encroachment in the bud."

"Time will tell. But either way, natural or not, Grandfather will probably show up since he was our banker. We'll need a replacement for Argon as well."

"Don't worry about it tonight," he says before we ring off to get some sleep. There's nothing I can do about the situation from here. The body will come back. Things will happen, and changes will have to be made because Argon laundered our money and hid things. I'll take it a day at a time. I can't leave the Michelis now, it would make me look guilty.

A conundrum for me to be sure. What the fuck have I gotten myself into? I'm on the inside of the family that we'd suspect if it was a hit, so maybe it's not so bad after all. The problem is I don't have access to what I need to know from the evidence files on Argon's death investigation.

I do know we don't want a turf war over this.

I'm glad my contract with Valentina was put to bed earlier tonight. I do love encrypted documents and e-signatures. I hope this mess with Argon is cleaned up before Valentina arrives.

Savio will fly back with me in the morning. I'll need to check in with both mafias. I owe Mama a visit too.

# 12

## VALENTINA

The day started with a German continental breakfast in the dining room, meaning there were meats and cheeses, not just pastries. I do like having choices of cold cuts, and the coffee is rich and robust.

However, no matter what Mama did or said, Papa snapped at her. It appears she can't do anything right today, and I find myself sympathizing with her as she tries to soothe Papa's foul mood.

Laura and I dodged them and kept quiet. I'm afraid to move out of sight due to Papa's mood. The guards look on edge as they sit around us in their street clothes.

By the time we arrive at the jet, it's noonish. I buckle my seatbelt and put on my earbuds to watch a movie on my phone as Laura reads through the Kindle app on her phone. Papa is talking on his phone, and the guards are vigilant, going so far as to look out the tiny window to ensure the tarmac is clear before taking off.

What are they expecting? A mafia invasion?

I get lost in my chick flick movie as the jet takes off, and an hour later, we are back on our home turf. Turf has never been such a welcomed word before the attempt on my life.

Papa's guards were with him when I disappeared, so there was no one else to blame but me, and possibly, he blamed himself. We walk to our waiting Mercedes limo van on the tarmac.

The flight home was unpleasantly quiet. I've never seen Papa so distraught.

"Giovi." I pull his hand to get his attention. "What went down in Rome? Where did Papa disappear to? What's going on? You need to help me."

"You've never been involved before. Why now? You love to put yourself first. Papa has shit going on, and you're not making it any easier. Obviously, we have enemies who sent a message." He lets out a huff as he dishes out his reprimand.

We used to be so close and now he's more distant than ever. Mama isn't in the mood to talk.

Laura tugs my arm. "Hey, relax. These men don't talk, nor do the locals. You know this, but you want everyone to break the rules for you. It's dangerous if they do."

"Yeah, but it's dangerous if they don't."

"It's the way it is." She shrugs. "Meanwhile, I'm sure my father will get wind of this from yours, and I hope we'll still be able to hang out. You became a dangerous woman overnight," she chides me as she bumps her shoulder into mine before we reach the van.

When we arrive home, Laura's father, Paulo Scalici, is at our house, and the men have a meeting before he comes out, says 'hi' to me, and then tells Laura it's time to go. He even carries her luggage and dresses for her as they leave with one of his men who opens their car doors and drives them. Laura's dad doesn't mess around. I know he has a gun on him, and his driver will have one as well.

It's not like ours don't. They don't walk around with them hanging out like a badge. Technology has made us international now, and I know from Papa's underboss, Gambino, that we're involved in places as far away as Belarus, Russia, and the United States. I surmised this from Christmas gifts, the ones that aren't envelopes filled with money that got passed around like cigarettes when I was a kid.

Then there is the Polish dark chocolate bar. They are two inches thick, the bitter kind, not the one that's watered down with milk because I got to eat the chocolate. I overheard someone joke about how their Russian vodka has the highest percentage of alcohol of all the vodka in the world.

I'm about to head upstairs when Papa calls my name. I wonder what he'll do to punish me. Reluctantly, I turn back towards the dining room as his office is just past it.

With trepidation, I walk into the room which has always been off-limits to us. I enter as he makes his way around a cherry wood desk and he waits for me to sit on the old brown worn leather sofa. He closes the door behind me.

The pictures hanging on the walls are of him with his friends in bars when he was younger. Some of these men aren't alive anymore. There is a picture of Uncle Federico Gambino and Papa from when I was little judging from the colors in the picture and a little girl in a tacky outfit, and it's not me. It must be Gambino's daughter.

Papa's has a family picture on his desk, along with their wedding picture. On the old bookcase beside is a 25th wedding anniversary picture frame; in it, they are in Greece. I remember how happy they were back then.

Papa sinks like a bag of bricks into his large leather chair behind his desk. In front of him is a wooden box, a gift from Russia. The box contains a pricey cognac.

Supposedly it's produced in Russia, but they import more due to the elite who demand it. I've heard it's a prized commodity for their elected officials, also known as the Bratva.

"Look, there's no way to make this easy so I'll just tell you what you want to know."

*Finally, some answers. Whew, this is good.*

"You know who attacked me in the garden?" I ask.

"No, that will take some time. But it concerns you."

"Oh?" I sit on the edge of the brown sofa cushion, bracing myself for something, but I have no clue what to expect.

He rubs his hand over his face. This isn't good. His hand remains on his head as his face is down. He finally looks up, takes a breath, and lets his hands slide away.

His eyebrows furrow, and his lips roll together as he pauses.

He pushes his chair back and stands, leans forward, and smacks both hands on his desk, scaring the shit out of me. He blurts out, "You're engaged to a man to be married next year. You'll have Christmas here, and then you'll travel to Florence to attend a wedding with me in January. At the wedding reception, you'll meet him and live with your intended until your wedding."

"What?" I stand, clenching my hands as my arms are stiff, glued to my sides. "You made an arrangement and told me nothing? I don't have a say in this?"

"Valentina, you always knew your husband would be picked for you."

"I should at least meet him and not be handed over like a hostage," I stomp my foot. I want to lunge at him.

His eyes bulge. I wonder if he's been held hostage. Did I hit my mark? Did I guess something he's been hiding? After all these years of guessing what's going on, did I finally hit the truth today?

"What are you not telling me, Papa? I thought I'd be married to a Sicilian."

"Me too. Honestly." He leans back in his chair, and our eyes meet.

So many secrets over the years, and it comes down to my arranged marriage.

"Who is he?" My fist ache from my squeezing them so tight as I wait anxiously.

"I can't tell you. He wants to do that himself." His gray eyes have a hint of blue now. This means he's no longer angry with me for my stunt at the gala.

I lower my eyes and put a hand to my forehead, thinking. Who could this man be?

"Okay, I'm promised to someone. Why does it matter if I know his name or not?"

"I don't know. All I know is there is a strict set of things which need to be carried out." He fidgets with a pen in his not-so-thin hands, but he's not focused like normal.

I want to protest more, throw a tantrum, and break shit, but when I see Papa sitting there, he looks tired. But I know it's more than that. His shoulders are slightly rounded, like a man who gave up. He's a man who lost something, and I think it's bigger than him losing me to this man with no name.

Fuck. I don't even get the last word on this to gain some satisfaction that he's a terrible father for letting me go so easily, without a fight. My understanding of psychology has come in handy, particularly today. I'm not able to gloat as pity rises in my gut. It's never happened before, I can't kick him when he's down and it looks like someone else kicked the shit out of him first.

No matter how much I hate being the daughter of a don with no free will, I can't fight him today.

He's lived a life of grandeur. He's a figure that's larger than life to everyone on the island. Today, I see the years of stress and they appeared overnight. Or, were they building up and I missed them?

"Does this have anything to do with you and Mama having words on the plane and the incident?"

"Yes, and no. I'm not sure what is related anymore."

He stands, throwing his chest out enough to square them, but it's shy of hitting the mark of the confident don I've always known him to be. It's as if I saw a stripped-down version of him a second ago. He's an Italian race car that was demolished in Rome, and overnight, he will emerge, rebuilt —all the blemishes—gone.

The breath I've been holding comes out in a long whew. I didn't realize I wasn't breathing. These revelations challenge me to put the puzzle pieces together.

## 13

# MASSIMO

"Hi Mama," I say, kissing her on both cheeks. She loves me, but she's not Italian and has never been as affectionate as I'd like. I must get that from my father's side of the family. Doesn't matter, I love her all the same.

She's busy making byrek, my favorite Albanian treat, which involves stuffing pastry dough with cheese and folding them into tiny triangles. She looks up to say, "Massimo, how are you? Work?"

"It's all fine, Mama." I sit at the kitchen table, and she brings me a glass of warm tea. It's a Sunday afternoon in early December. I try to take some time off, however, it rarely happens. How am I ever going to find time for Valentina?

The condo is larger than most, with three bedrooms and two bathrooms in a nice area of Florence. Not many can afford to live in the city anymore and most are moving out to the suburbs the upperclass once frowned upon.

Mama could have nicer things, but she won't take money from me. If she accepted my help, it would decimate Papa's ego. And she definitely won't ask for anything from Grandfather. Supposedly there was a big argument when I was little. I don't remember it, but I've heard bits and pieces about their strained relationship, and yet, nothing explains it.

They rarely talk. Mama still washes his money, I run the Albanian clan with a few top leaders, and life is good.

Today the condo feels damp from the winter chill. The hot oven will burn it off and the tea warms me from the inside. Last week, there was a shit storm of snow in the mountains, so ski season is in full swing. It usually is in December. Florence is cold and windy this time of year, hence the wool coat and scarf.

I can't stop thinking about Valentina and even jerked off last night fantasizing about her full breasts in my mouth and her tight pussy squeezing my cock. It makes me wish January was already here, but my word is my word. I trust letting her have time to wrap things up in Sicily will put her in a better mood. Besides, my house is being cleaned and prepped for a runaway bride.

I can't figure her out. Once she knows her family's life depends on her, I'm confident she'll be more accommodating. I'd rather have her with me of her own free will. But if push comes to shove, I'll lay down the law.

"So, you went to Rome with Savio?"

"Yes, business and pleasure," I say, stirring sugar into my warm tea. "Where's Papa?"

"He took your brother to get more books for school. He should've done the same for you. You could have been a doctor, you know."

"What's with always comparing me to Cosimo? School or no school, he'll never earn what I make."

"Not the point."

"Your point is?"

"Nothing."

"No, there is something. You look tired. Are you okay?" I have to coax her. She's stubborn, like me.

"Look," she pulls up a chair and sits close to me, "I have breast cancer and I want you to have this, in case I don't make it out of surgery or treatment." She fishes in her apron pocket and pulls out a folded piece of paper that she manages to slip into my hand. "This is our secret."

I try to read her tired face. The only thing I know for sure is that this explains why Grandfather hinted at spending more time with her. It's all clear to me now.

"Mama, cancer. You should have told me. I'll make sure you have the best doctors."

"I do already, that's taken care of. This cancer is not the only secret I've kept from you. Before I married Nico, I had a relationship with a married man. His name was Aldo Lorenzo Micheli. He is your real father... He was not going to leave his wife, so I married Nico when you were not even two. He adopted you, that's the paper." She taps the piece of paper in my hand. "Now put it away before Papa comes," she warns.

I slip it in the front pocket of my jeans.

"Why, why tell me now?"

"Because I have to come clean with my past and I didn't want you to hear it from anyone else. You deserve to know the truth but keep it to yourself. This makes you the heir to not only the Toska family empire but also the Micheli family empire. I should have known that your life was destined to be intertwined with them. Somehow, blood always finds a way back to its source."

I can tell this has been cathartic for her and I hope her

burden is lighter. What the fuck do I do with this information?

"Your grandfather loves you very much, but be careful. The minute you lose favor with him, things might go south. He never approved of me dating an Italian. Then, along comes an illegitimate love child. Well, that essentially ended my relationship with him, but he always wanted you. He's not the same with Cosimo. You're definitely his favorite."

After a long pause, I ask, "I'm the reason you and Grandfather aren't close?"

"Yes, however, I'm fine. I keep up my end of the family business, and we make good money here. I have Nico, you, and Cosimo. Nico raised you and loved you. However, neither of you were ever interested in the same things, not like he is with Cosimo."

"Humph." Does it matter?

Mama continues, "There were dark days for the Michelis back then, so I kept you safe. I never told Aldo about you. There was no point. He was never going to leave his wife or stop womanizing." She takes my hand and searches my face for something...empathy, maybe loss.

Nico and Cosimo come through the door, surprising us both, and she jerks her hands away to avoid their questions.

"Hi Papa, Cosimo, how are you?" I ask, pretending everything is normal. I'm shaken by the news of Mama's illness and my new family tree, so I put on my best poker face. And I'm annoyed we didn't have a chance to discuss her doctors or treatments before we were interrupted.

"Fine, fine," Cosimo answers in Italian.

We visit briefly, then I get a phone call, and I'm out the door.

My mind is all over the place. For some reason, I remember Marchello is passionate about expensive watches and sneakers. We bonded immediately over our shared interest in vintage Nikes. How do I know that's not genetic? Maybe this is why I never felt at home in Nico's house. I was too young to understand, and yet I was probably picking up on some unspoken undercurrent of energy. Negative energy.

I wish I got to know Aldo before he died. I wonder what we would have thought of each other. Oh well, as Mama explained, he loved his wife, and with three boys and a mafia war to fight, I'm sure he had his hands full.

I hug and kiss my mama and make sure she calls me if she needs anything. Nico is a good man and will take good care of her. I had no way of knowing then that I wouldn't have time to help her much as my life was about to change drastically.

# 14

## VALENTINA

It's strange living at home knowing I'll be moving out soon. I knew this day would come, and for whatever reason, I thought I'd have more time to prepare and maybe even have a choice in the matter. How could I have been so naïve? I should have known better.

"Laura, how are things going?" I sit on my bed, talking on the phone. I'm wearing a tracksuit because it's comfortable and I need that right now.

"Have you talked to your mother?"

"Some, she wants me to learn how to cook all of a sudden. And she wants to help me start looking at wedding dresses. She's been acting nervous. I think my papa is in some serious shit."

"Hmm. Yeah. I mean, our families do some fucked up shit."

"Tell me about it. I still haven't heard from my fiancé. It's been weeks and no call, nothing. I don't get it."

"You'll hear from him at some point, I'm sure."

"How is Marco?" I switch the topic to avoid talking about

a man who can't be bothered to call or court me. He's treating me like I'm invisible, making me feel powerless.

"Marco loved the pictures of me in that dress and was terribly jealous, which made for incredible sex."

"Really? Jealousy drives a man crazy, huh? I guess a healthy dose of it is okay."

"Yeah, you don't want the crazies. Do you think this guy you're marrying will be faithful?"

"No clue. I think it's better not to have any expectations. I hope he's faithful, but you know Italian men. They all meet up on Saturday nights while their wives sit at home watching nighttime soap operas and eating chocolate. I don't want that to be me in twenty years."

"Me either." Laura pauses

"Did you tell your father what happened?" I ask.

"All I know is your father did something, and as a result, the guys are a bit jumpy. The consensus is that your family is the target. Don't you know anything?"

"Right, in a world where we call men 'uncle' who are not blood relatives, and none of the kids at school come over to play. If they did, it's short-lived, and we are tight-lipped. I have no idea what really happens under my nose. Uncle Federico hasn't been around so much since his daughter, Ignazio, is out of town again. God, I despise her."

"Yeah, she's a bitch on wheels for sure. I wonder if she was locked in a sanitarium all those years. No one asks any questions, and she just popped up out of thin air after two decades of visits twice a year."

"Well, that family gives me the creeps," I add. "I wonder what the story is behind that."

There's a knock on my bedroom door.

"Yeah?"

Ridolfo comes in and hands me two small boxes. "It's for you."

"From whom?"

"No clue, you're supposed to get it so now you have it."

Ridolfo leaves, closing the door behind him.

"What's happening?" Laura asks.

"I got presents, I think. Let me hang up and check it out." We make a kiss, smacking our lips together, and ring off.

It's Christmas Eve. We'll go to Mass tonight as a family. We don't go overboard with gifts like in America. We prefer to give food, bread, jams, wine, and small items, especially now that we're grown up.

Giovi has an apartment, but after the event in Rome, he's been living here again. Papa forbade him and his crew from hanging out at any restaurant or bar, so he has gone nowhere besides work, for the past month.

Sometimes I feel like a criminal under house arrest, minus the ankle bracelet. I'm not in the Christmas mood and resorted to shopping online for family gifts. The only part I enjoy is wrapping them and making sure each gift is pretty.

Curiosity gets the best of me as I pick up the box wrapped in thick, shiny red paper. I experience a rush of excitement like when I was younger and used to look forward to St. Nick every year.

I run my fingertips over the box. It's almost too pretty to rip open. I carefully remove the white bow and beautifully tied ribbon before tearing off the paper.

Wow! It's a new phone. I can't wait to use all the new features and try out the camera. I look for a note, but there isn't a card.

I know from advertisements that this is the latest release.

I turn on the phone, and after it boots up, a notification pops up saying there is a message waiting.

This phone is different from mine. However, I managed to find the messaging box.

*"My little bluebird, I can't wait to see you again."*

My pussy throbs with anticipation, and my heart is beating out of my chest. It must be from my fiancé, and he wants to see me. But who is he?

He must have seen me, but where? It had to be in Rome because I don't get out much. There were so many people in the museum I'd never be able to single out just one man. I hope it's not that creepy dude with the neck tattoo. Surely, Papa wouldn't have anything to do with him.

Or has he sunk that low?

In my excitement, I rip open the second box. Mama gets jewelry in boxes shaped like this.

I peek inside the felt-lined box and find a jeweled necklace with blue gems, must-be sapphires, and more diamonds than I can count.

I lift the necklace. It's heavier than expected. Draping it over my hand, I look closer at the sparkling diamonds circling each sapphire in a unique design. I've never seen anything so exquisite and wonder if he designed it himself, just for me. If so, it could be the only piece in existence. Like the relics we walk around daily.

Now I'm being ridiculous. A man who hides from his future wife is not a romantic. If anything, he's looking for a piece of arm candy he can pose, dress, and decorate with expensive jewels to impress his friends and family.

He's egotistical and a showoff.

And yet, what I'm thinking doesn't stop me from placing the necklace around my neck. It's gorgeous. I'm all thumbs as I fiddle with the lock that prevents the clasp from coming undone. This type of closure does not go on a necklace made with fake stones.

Leaping out of bed, I run to the dresser to check my reflection in the mirror. The necklace is stunning, and the sapphires bring out the blue in my eyes. What did he call me?

Bluebird. He must know my eyes are blue and wanted the necklace to compliment their color.

I squeal and run downstairs to Mama.

"Mother of God, that is beautiful," she gasps.

"You know who sent it, don't you?"

"Your father can't tell anyone. A few men wanted to marry you, but they didn't seem to be the type to keep their mouths shut. That's all I know," she adds hastily, knowing I'll have a million questions.

Without taking her eyes off the necklace, she says, "You'll make a stunning bride. I have collections of pearls your father gave me. He lacks the imagination to pick something so colorful and expensive."

"Right," I forgot about how much this must have cost. "It's safe to assume the man in question has money."

"That I'm sure of." She raises her hand to stop me from asking her to guess its value, and I don't need her to guess. I'll look it up later.

Why would my fiancé send me something so expensive before the wedding? He doesn't know me or my taste. He hasn't bothered to contact me for weeks, and then he sends me extravagant items.

I wonder if he's passive-aggressive.

I have no way of sending him a thank you. I don't know his name.

Suddenly it hits me. I can text him, maybe even call him because he texted my phone. *OMG, I have his number!*

"I gotta go," I say, dashing upstairs to my ivory tower as Laura calls it.

*"Who is this?"* I text back.

*"Did you like your gift? Merry Christmas."*

*"Thank you. I would like to know where to send a thank you card."*

*"Nice try, little bluebird. We'll meet soon."*

*"Who are you?"*

Three dots appear, and then nothing. He's gone.

Sneaky like a fox I'd say.

I guess this is like a bat phone from the movies: call when needed, and maybe I'll get back to you.

*Damn!*

Meanwhile, I can't forget the man in the garden and his deep voice. I've thought a lot about the tattoo on his hand. I'm beginning to think it was a sword with a knife threaded through it, going in one side and out the other. I wonder what it means.

His cologne throws me off. I've never come across it before and I may never find the man who wore it that night.

I get up from bed and lock my bedroom door, slip my clothes off and crawl under my bed sheets, feeling my firm, rounded breasts while I use my fingers to enter myself and I'm instantly wet thinking of him.

I rub my nub, then push them deeper to massage the spot inside me that makes my back arch. I want more, and as my nipples harden, I take the opportunity to tweak my hard nipple and stroke my nub, making my lips and clit engorge. I continue to play until I'm ready to burst. I hold back coming right away as the second pass is always more intense. I come thinking of the man in black who saved me.

I moan as I come a second time, surprising myself. I

didn't know that was possible, but I stored it away for future use just the same.

No more texts show up on my new phone, and I'm not giving him the satisfaction that I give a shit. If he wants to ignore me, two can play that game.

It's time to go to Florence. I'm anxious as I prepare to leave. I still have nightmares about the last time we left Sicily and I don't know if those will ever go away. Laura is the only one I can share my night terrors with. There are nights I wake up in a sweat, remembering the dead man and his throat gushing blood. My parents would never understand.

I packed a large suitcase to take to the hotel where I'm to meet my fiancé. I'm still in the dark as to his identity. Mama is holding back tears, which surprises me. I thought she'd be happy I'm finally leaving home.

Giovi wishes me well and is abnormally nice to me as we hug and kiss each other's cheeks goodbye. The fact that he's still living at home tells me the family is in danger, and I worry about us all.

Laura is here to see me off, and I give her a long hug and promise to keep in touch as we suspect I won't be coming home any time soon. We both are misty-eyed as our fathers shake hands before we return to the car to head to the airport.

Papa tells me not to worry and pats my hand to reassure me. Even with the driver and four men with us, he seems preoccupied by business, and our men are on high alert.

On the private jet, I open a beer for Papa and pour

champagne for myself. It's just past noon, and I need it to take the edge off.

"Any change on the front?" I ask him, speaking in code for the mafia situation.

"Not much, but you've helped me out more than you'll ever know. I'm sorry you don't get to pick the man you marry. I have a lot on my mind and appreciate you not fighting me on it." He sips his drink.

"True. Thank you for saying that."

He nods.

"What are we doing in Florence anyway?"

"We're going to a wedding."

"It's someone in a connected family, isn't it? The ones getting married?"

"Yes."

"Would we normally not go?" He's great at not revealing much and keeping me on a need-to-know basis.

"We don't know the family. It might be an attempt to reach out for new business. Let's keep positive thoughts, eh?"

"Sure," I put my earbuds in and watch a newly released movie. It's in English, so I have to concentrate. Having so many shows on TV dubbed in Italian with English subtitles has helped to keep me current with American phrases and slang.

The years at school in Switzerland are a distant memory as I embark on my next role in life, that of a wife.

I'm glad I went to college, and even with a degree, there's no way I could make it on my own. Surviving on the salary of a child psychology degree is impossible. Instead, I live at home and use Papa's money to buy expensive things to fill a hole inside of me, one that's void of a career, love, and affection.

As a result, I have so many clothes and shoes I couldn't possibly wear everything even if I lived a hundred years. All of this has been my backhanded way of getting even with Papa. Now, I'm going to have a new man to provide for me, and he better love me instead of trying to buy me. Sometimes, I don't know if the men in my world know the difference.

Maybe there isn't a man who will love me. Maybe it's just a fairy tale, and I'm not sure I'm a believer.

**15**

---

# MASSIMO

Before Christmas, the news of Argon's death reached me through Besnik, one of my loyal bosses. I'm not surprised. I'm a bit miffed. We must find someone to replace Argon. With his incredible aptitude for numbers and moving money around, he was the one who kept our cryptocurrency. He's the only one who knew the passwords and changed them numerous times a day. If the money is lost, our heads are on the chopping block. We're in a bind to find the information only he knew.

Argon was to blend in, not make himself so prominent. Only his best friend Besnik knew what he really did for us. But once he left home, where he played the doting father to Prende, he lived a larger-than-life role amongst his peers. He became a liability, and he was disrespecting the Micheli family. I wouldn't doubt they didn't off him, but there is the issue of that damn code that is hidden somewhere, and we need it.

On the heels of his death, one of my lieutenants inadvertently showed up at the wrong time, posing as officials to raid one of the Michelis' warehouses. Again, nice plan, but not approved by me. I wonder how long I have before the Michelis begin to look at recent hires. My name is on that shortlist.

Did the Michelis murder Argon for retaliation? Is Prende in on it or just a pawn in a larger picture? I've seen Marchello with her, as I've had my men watching her and others in the family.

What a shitshow. I have my hands full trying to control men who act on their own will, for their own gain, and never think of how it affects the rest of us. This is all piled on top of the fact that I still haven't processed my mother's illness and the truth about my biological father.

The news about Cosimo being my half-brother makes sense. It accounts for my wider face and a few other things that never made added up. Things like why Cosimo has baby pictures, and there are very few of me. Mama said she didn't have money to develop photos back then and reminded me it was before cell phone cameras. I know Mama, and she has them hidden somewhere. She'd never throw a picture of me out. I'm her firstborn, for heaven's sake.

Now, it adds up. All the excuses and little lies over the years to cover up my real identity. Mama might think she's better than grandfather, but they both told lies that led to more lies and brought me to this moment of truth.

Who am I? What family do I belong to? Will I fit in with either family once everyone finds out my true background? Or will both sides want to kill me? Neither side will know where my loyalties lie, and I could be eliminated simply because I'm of mixed blood.

Albanians and Italians intermarry but never have I heard of one having mafia royalty on both sides. Clearly, Mama loved Aldo and turned her back on her family until she needed Grandfather for our safety. In hindsight, it's a good thing she did. Since Aldo died so young, Mama would have given up too much to stay with him. No one could have known he'd go so young.

So, I'm a lovechild. Nico must've hated keeping the secret and knew he could never take the place of my real father. He's on the lower echelon because of Mama, as he's Italian on both sides of his family. My mother sure gets swept off her feet by Italian men, that's for sure.

It's crazy how a person can be attracted to a particular type when it comes to looks and fall so deeply in love that one has to have them at any cost. But that's what Aldo was to Mama. In my eyes, it was her weakness that led her astray.

Then she found Nico, someone she could live with for the rest of her life, and she didn't have to hide him from anyone. He loves her, and they have Cosimo.

Nico tried over the years to get close to me. Now I understand these looks are from frustration. I'm sure he's miffed at his failure to keep me away from the street life and out of Grandfather's clutches. It's why he kept Cosimo in sports, something I never cared about, and why he was so hard on me when I stayed out past curfew.

In his defense, he did his best to keep me safe and on the path to a different life. He just wanted more for me and his son. I can't be angry with him over good intentions.

For me to be legally adopted, papers giving up Aldo's rights must have been forged. I guess Mama was still in love with Aldo and put him down as my legal father, which pissed off my grandfather, who wanted to erase all ties with the man. No one was to know the truth about my lineage.

What am I supposed to do with this information? For now, it's best to keep it a secret. It never hurts to know more than my enemies. In this racket, I never know when I might need to use it.

Grandfather knew the Michelis were my blood, yet he let me infiltrate them and thought it was brilliant. The darker side of Grandfather is coming to light. He'd never hurt me unless it was an unforgivable deed. I'm not stupid enough to give him a reason to have to kill one of his own.

Mama's warning to be careful around him is not to be taken lightly. I must cover the bases. He took the news of Valentina better than I anticipated. I'm sure he enjoys having the upper hand, and nothing is better than a captive audience who knows they need to please you, and for now, I'm pleasing him in his eyes. But I'm my own man, and I know I'm appeasing him.

I've been assured Valentina is watched closely as Luciano knows the lives of his family depend upon her being delivered to me. I'm sure a part of Grandfather hopes something will go wrong, but that won't get him the oligarchy seat he wants. Using Luciano for information that enables access to the 12 is his endgame. And Luciano needs to be alive for that. Grandfather can't just step in, especially if foul play is suspected.

Grandfather doesn't need to know everything when it transpires. Details are best if doled out on a need-to-know basis. This strategy has always kept me one step ahead of others around me.

First, I have to get past the holiday mass with my family. Then, it will be New Years where Savio will be getting drunk and picking up woman to spend the long and lonely night with. That will take my mind off of Valentina. She's pissed that I haven't responded to her text messages.

She gave up on getting information out of me. I'm

enjoying the amenity, yet I can't forget her eyes. They haunt me.

I spend Christmas with my family, and New Year's with Savio is a bust as I'm not interested in the friends we've amassed, and even though he invited women for me, I act like an ass and get drunk. Before midnight, I fall into my bed, thinking of those perfect eyes I long to see again.

BEFORE THE WEDDING, Besnik helped facilitate the return of the black book with the passwords we needed. I orchestrated that, but no one needs to know except Bresnik. Grandfather had to use it to show off and act like the don of all dons, as I can't give up my identity yet. I'm the mole in the Micheli organization.

I gave Micro, my guard, the job of the botched snatch and grab of Prende's purse that he farmed out to a new soldier. My mistake is not specifying someone with a proven track record and isn't learning on the job. Two drugs were found in Argon's body. Either could have killed him. I suspect Digitalis did the job.

Two anonymous identities wanted him dead. I suspect the Michelis. That's obvious. I've picked up enough to know that Dante likes making little waves and enjoys being under the radar. His legit businesses are something I'm envious of and something he should be proud of as he hobnobs with Florentines.

He's building luxury condos in a prized location in Florence, and his construction business has the contract for the new city hall. He's able to finesse his way through the political jungle to get things I'm making inroads with, but it isn't easy because we are not Italians.

Life is complicated. Dante is my brother, and I want to be part of his family and success, but at the same time, I feel like I'm betraying the Albanian side of my mother. Now I know why my grandfather kept me close all these years, knowing my true identity. He knew I was born into this life double-fold; he has a dedicated mafia 'son' at his side, and now I know why I fell so effortlessly into my mother's clan.

Grandfather must be pleased with himself that I'm working for him and against the Michelis. He even planted the seeds that I infiltrate them. In time, he will want more information on them so he can ruin them. I see where he's going with this.

In the end, Grandfather blows into town to retrieve the book from Dante and Marchello, who are now tied to us as Prende is Argon's only child. In the deal, we allowed her to marry Marchello, and we no longer launder money through her flower shop, but I see it as a small price to pay to keep the peace. I'm sure she didn't want to marry the man that was chosen for her. I can't blame her for that. She's far too innocent and sensitive for the life she's had with him and I suspect Marchello is the lateral move. As long as secrets are kept, it's easier to appease her. If she loses her shop, we'll buy it and run it ourselves. In the meantime, we've avoided making an enemy.

I remind Grandfather and my lieutenants that the book was the objective, not trying to control Prende. She was never really connected to the mafia and turned out to be oblivious to her father's dealings. Besnik always claimed this to us, and I believe him.

With that wrapped up, Grandfather still wants to know who killed Argon, and I know it's because he's anxious for a justification to retaliate against the Michelis. The family must have been a thorn in his side all these years as he bided his time for retribution over one of them sullying his daughter's reputation. That can't be forgiven.

Aldo might be dead, but Grandfather would have no qualms about using Dante to gain more legitimate business with the government and laugh at the irony of it. Knowing what I do now, I have one up on Grandfather. I don't want a war between our families unless one is warranted, so I need to get to the bottom of who killed Argon as quickly as possible.

I'm DRIVING to the wedding reception in my sports car, dressed in a suit that will raise some eyebrows because of the limited funds I make working for the Michelis, but I don't care. I will make a good impression on Valentina and let her get to know me before the news breaks that I'm the one she'll wed.

I hand over my keys to the valet at the hotel before meeting up with Tommaso.

"You look great."

"Thank you, so do you," I say, ignoring the fact that his suit doesn't fit him as well as it should. It's loud with Italian flags on it and red suspenders. His wife is wearing a low-cut dress, more appropriate at a disco than a wedding reception.

Orchestra music provides a fitting backdrop for meeting an untold number of dons and bosses that must be here. The *Godfather* theme song would be more appropriate. Tommaso doesn't know I'm biding my time as I look towards the door numerous times, waiting for my fiancée to show up.

I sense a ruckus and turn to see Valentina. She's in a black taffeta dress that's fitted at her tiny waist before flowing out in pleats. The deep-cut neckline shows off her porcelain skin, a perfect canvas for the necklace with its dark blue sapphires. The precious stones are eye-catching, but nothing is more beautiful than her.

Heads turn as she breezes into the room on her father's arm. Her walking in her four-inch heels. . . flawless. Perhaps I'm biased. I cough in mid-sentence to cover up my surprise. I can't give myself away. If Tommaso catches me looking at her, he'll know something is up, as I'm sure I'm gawking.

She's mine. I'm not ready to share her with anyone. However, she must have learned a few things while she was at the best college in the world. She's spent her earlier years living around some of the wealthiest kids from around the world while in Switzerland.

Her eyes scan the room, no doubt playing hide and seek with mine. I have nowhere I'd rather be than beside her. She approaches, and I take in the blue eyes that have haunted me. Someone distracts her, and she turns, bumping into me.

"Scusi," she murmurs with a tweak of cuteness. There's no need for an apology. Any man worth his salt would be thankful for the physical contact.

As she turns back, our eyes lock.

"Ah, no problem. Massimo," I introduce myself, extending a hand.

"Valentina." She slips her small, delicate hand in mine, and I raise it to my lips, giving it a quick brush before relinquishing it. "Do I know you?"

Blood pounds in my ears. My thoughts are scrambled like eggs.

"Possibly. Are you with the bride or groom?" I know she'll remember meeting me soon unless the night's trauma jarred her recollection.

"Groom's side." I manage a small smile. Is she always so inquisitive?

"You?" I'm a bastard for asking because I already know the answer. In fact, I know everything about her except what she looks like naked. I can't wait to find out but deter more primal thoughts as my cock hardens against the lined pants.

"Hmm. Business, just a guest," she answers.

I shrug it off, snagging two champagnes from a passing tray and handing her one.

"To the bride and groom," I toast, clinking our glasses together.

"Good fortune to them both." Her sweet voice floats to my sensitive ears and I revel in the moment. These life events are few and far between for me.

We both take a sip as I raise my glass.

"May they be so lucky to have a life of happiness."

"I'm sure they will. Dante's quite the catch. It's in all the newspapers." I take in my half-brother as he is all smiles and networks around the room like the gracious host he is.

"I wish I believed in love." She sighs.

"Really, you don't? I thought every woman wanted their man to save them from the evils of the world."

"One would think so, but then again, not all men are such great catches." She pouts, but I find it enchanting. I want to hear more from her sweet lips.

"Ah, Valentina, I'm going to the bar," Luciano says in her ear as he drops a chaste kiss on her cheek and throws me a glance before moving on.

I gave him a wink. The package was delivered.

"Who is that?" I ask.

"My father. He made me come to this wedding," she volunteers, then changes the subject. "I love Florence and the Uffizi. I hope I get to see it soon. Do you like art?"

"Yes, yes, I do." I smile. This is falling into place perfectly. "I have quite the house, actually. You'd love it."

"Really, is it haunted?"

"No, just the opposite. It's filled with incredible art pieces."

"Oh, you must tell me about it one day. What do you do for business?"

"Business," I say, spreading my arms, "with men that do business. What about you?"

"I'd love to work as a therapist. I have credentials from an esteemed institution, but I haven't been able to secure a job. Papa won't allow me to work for the government. He says they are evil, but it's the only way to ever get experience and set up my own office."

"I see his point."

Just as we're getting to know each other, there is a blood-curdling scream, and people move away from the bar. The commotion is cause for alarm, and I protectively put one arm around Valentina.

"What's going on?" she asks.

"I don't know, but I don't like it."

I motion with my head for Tommaso to check out the situation. Then, more women scream. I look for Dante and see his brothers and his guards form a protective circle around him.

The area between me and the bar is now clear. Luciano is on the floor. My instincts tell me he's dead.

**16**

———

## VALENTINA

The flight was quick and painless. We checked into a suite at the same hotel as the wedding reception. Even though we can see the Arno and the Uffizi from the window, I doubt I'll have time to visit the museum or walk the bank.

It's cooler here this time of year and I'm wearing a long-sleeved dress, and the plunging neckline is perfect for showing off my necklace. The material is heavier than normal as this is supposed to be the most prestigious event I've ever been to.

The necklace is the most expensive piece of jewelry I own and the only piece not given to me by my parents. There were diamond earrings for my 16th birthday and strands of pearls for graduation because it was their way of saying 'well done' without a hug. Goodness no, Papa holds me at arm's length. We don't have the relationship he has with Giovi. I assume it's because Giovi has to learn Papa's business.

My time with Papa is coming to an end. I'll be with my fiancé after this trip. He must have something very big riding on my marriage because he's not given me one detail about my future husband, and I've given up asking. I knew he wouldn't cave. I'm not a child anymore who can pout until I get what I want.

When I was younger, he'd love to tease me and give me ridiculous clues about my gifts the night before Christmas.

Papa tells me to dress with care and mind my manners, leading me to wonder if my fiancé will be at the party. Because I'm wearing four-inch-high heels, Papa insists we take the elevator down. Ridolfo goes with us because he has been around my entire life and knows me best.

Music spills into the hallway as soon as the doors to the meeting room are opened. The fresh flower arrangements and dolphin ice sculpture are breathtaking. I've been to my share of mafia weddings, and trust me, this is the most elaborate.

As we circle the room, my stomach is full of butterflies. Everyone looks important, and for the first time in my life, Papa is one of many powerful men in the room. It's easy to pick them out by their posture and the custom cut of their suits. I spot the groom right away. He's tall, dark, and handsome. The bride has a sexy devil in her bed.

I can't stop my instincts from identifying the undercover guards. It's a game Laura and I played since we were kids. I've gotten better at reading people since I went away to college. Laura knows more about the inside workings of the mafia as she listens in on her father's work calls and keeps track of the businesses he visits when he runs errands with her. She's never shied away from the darker side of our world.

I accidentally bump into a handsome man and we introduce ourselves. His name is Massimo. I feel guilty about flirting with him, knowing I'm engaged, but I'm spellbound and can't pull myself away from his eyes. I wonder what he feels behind his dark eyes. Something is familiar about him, but I can't place it. He's like a magnet, and I'm a steel pole. I'm drawn to him by a force I can't control, not that I want to control it.

Needing a drink, Papa heads to the bar, leaving me to chat with Massimo as we drink champagne. I'm loosening up as the alcohol hits my empty stomach.

A curly brown lock drops onto his forehead, and I push it away from his eyes without a thought of how intimate the gesture is. He smiles, his smoldering dark eyes meet mine. I catch my breath, unable to look away. God, he's gorgeous. His nose and strong jawline belong to a Renaissance sculpture of a Roman god. His full lips are red, perfect, and slightly parted as if he's about to kiss me. My chest constricts in anticipation as my heart thumps in my chest like a racehorse. There is a familiarity about him, but I brush it aside, surely I'm imagining it. I'd never forget meeting a man like him.

Then…

People are screaming and running towards us. I look for Papa, but Massimo grabs me and covers me with his body as if to shield me from bullets.

The area in front of the bar clears, and Ridolfo is kneeling next to my father, pumping his chest. Papa's face is gray, a pale gray I've never seen before. Frightened for my father, I cry out, but Massimo's strong arms hold me back.

I fight against his strong arms. I can't break free.

"Please, it's my father." I look up and plead with my eyes.

"I can't let you go. It's not safe. Your guard is with him. The medics will be here soon. We have no idea what happened. You need to stay with me."

Massimo knows Ridolfo? I don't remember them meeting, but nothing makes sense now. My brain is in shock after seeing my father lying on the floor, and my body is fuzzy with hormones that kicked in with Massimo holding me.

"You can't help him, but I know he'd want you to be safe."

"Am I safe with you?" passes her lips as a whisper.

"I'm your best bet of getting out of here unharmed."

"I didn't hear a gun. There's no blood." I look at Papa lying so still it makes me shiver.

Massimo loosens his grip to take his suit jacket off, then drapes it over my shoulders. Oddly, I don't take the opportunity to escape.

I can't leave Papa. I hear the siren of the ambulance outside, and then medics rush into the room. I look at the exit where guests are making a fuss and see the polizia blocking the door and sealing the room off with tape.

"What's going on? This isn't right. Why are the police here?"

"I don't know, but stay with me. We might be questioned by the authorities."

"For what? Papa must have had a stroke or a heart attack," I murmur in disbelief as I watch Ridolfo stand as the medics work on my father. I see them place Papa on a gurney.

"I should go with him," I cry out as Papa as I watch him being wheeled away.

"It's not safe. Whoever got to him could get to you, and that would be the worst-case scenario," he says.

"Let's ask Ridolfo," I suggest as a compromise.

"Fine," he replies. I see that my guard is heading to meet us.

Massimo's arm is still around my shoulders as we approach my guard, and Massimo asks him what happened.

"I don't know. He seemed to have a difficult time breathing, grabbed his chest, and fell over. It was so fast."

"You're in shock, Valentina," Massimo says. "You need to sit."

"Yes, you don't look so well," Ridolfo agrees.

"I don't feel so well." My voice fades as I drift into a sleep I cannot fight. Closing my eyes, I slump into Massimo's arms.

## 17

———

# MASSIMO

My bluebird is in my arms, but this is not my idea of a good time. I'd rather have her leaving scratch marks on my back with her nails and calling out my name as she comes.

But I am happy she's here at last. This past month has been the longest in my life, and now that I'm with her, it's as it was always intended to be. She passes out from what I believe to be shock. The police took our information and allowed Ridolfo and me to leave with her. The fresh air should bring her around.

My plan is to head to the hospital if she's not up in a few seconds. Ridolfo and I exchange a worried look, hoping Valentina wasn't targeted as well.

I find it hard to believe someone would take them both out at the most public event of the year, but I have to consider all the options. Valentina being harmed isn't an acceptable outcome.

She's mine, and I'll kill any man who harms a hair on her head.

By the time we get to my car, she's coming around. She must've just fainted.

"Are you okay?"

"Yes," she replies.

"I'll take her somewhere safe," I tell Ridolfo. He shakes my hand. I thank him for taking care of Luciano, and I carry Valentina to my car.

"Where is Ridolfo? He'll take care of me. I have to go see Papa." Her voice is frail and vulnerable. She's in no shape to go anywhere but home. "I can walk," she protests.

Ah, my bluebird is feisty once again.

"Your Papa is at the hospital. Ridolfo will check on him. You need to remain hidden until we figure out what the fuck happened," I grumble.

"Oh." It seems to have sunk in that she might be in danger.

I strap her in my sports car, and we leave the cityscape behind as we drive the hills to Fiesole and my mansion.

"You can't mention where I live, I'm in the middle of some personal stuff right now," I caution her. "Besides, it's best not to advertise where we live as a rule."

She nods, looking out the car window as the sun sets and darkness falls.

A tear slips from her eye, and she sniffles.

My phone dings. I look to see a text from Tommaso. Luciano is dead.

What a fucking nightmare. During the commotion, I saw my grandfather at the bar and wondered what he was doing here. He never mentioned he was going to be here. Did he kill Luciano with a drug? Everything was under control. He has no reason to eliminate Luciano, and I hope to God Giovi is okay in Sicily.

"Valentina." I wipe the tear from her cheek. "You need to

call your brother and tell him what happened. He might not be safe."

"Oh, my God, you think a hit has been put out on my family?"

"We can't rule it out, can we?" I glance at her to check her coloring, she seems fine.

I like asking her questions. It gives her an opportunity to come up with her own answers without being micromanaged. I trust we'll arrive at the same conclusion. That strategy produces a pliable woman, one who's not resentful or angry.

Valentina opens the small purse she's had with her all night and takes out her phone.

"Giovi, Papa is in the hospital, he collapsed at the party. I think you may be in danger. Be very careful, promise me."

I can make out Giovi's voice. He's rattling off in a Sicilian dialect that I can't follow very well, but I can imagine with great certainty that he's worried over his father. He has to batten down his fortress and select his best men to protect him, men he can trust.

Valentina fires back at him before she kisses the phone and hangs up.

"He's going to hole up in the compound and send others out to investigate."

"Good." I hope no one else dies tonight.

It's going to be a long night. I park my car in front of my castle, for lack of a better word.

"You live here?"

It appears my future bride doesn't think I'm capable of greatness. That hurts.

"Did you assume I'm a pauper?"

"Oh, no. I didn't mean. . ."

"Actually, you'll love the house, but there will be no tour

tonight." I get out of my car to help Valentina when I see Savio walking towards me.

He asks, "Brother, what happened?"

"In a minute." I nod to Valentina in the car.

"Oh."

"Right. Valentina, this is my best friend, Savio."

"Hi," she says, putting her hand in mine so I can help her get out of my car. It sits very low to the ground.

She needs help walking on the gravel in her heels, so I scoop her into my arms, and she falls against my sturdy chest, and it fills my heart that I can comfort her.

Savio heard about Luciano and came to my house, knowing I'd come here, my fortress, in a crisis.

"Call more men to guard the house," I instruct him.

"On it." He pulls his phone out and walks behind us as I carry Valentina into our home for the first time.

This isn't what I had planned, but hell and brimstone, what will befall us next? Maybe I don't want to know the answer to that.

The house is lit, and Samira greets us at the door, wearing a house dress and comfortable shoes. I arranged for her to be at the house this evening in case I needed anything when I brought Valentina home.

"Are you okay, Massimo?"

"Yes."

"Can I make tea?"

"That would be great. This is Valentina—Valentina, Samira, my housekeeper. I let Valentina down.

"That's an odd name," Valentina mumbles, and I shoot Samira an apologetic look.

"Why don't we sit in the living room?" I steer Valentina to a room with the warm glow of the wood burning in the fireplace. The long room has Italian-colored yellow walls and huge wood rafters for the ceiling, making a large room feel homey.

Valentina's heels tap as they come into contact with the wood floors, and she sits on a large sofa with overstuffed cushions and lays her purse beside her.

"Let me get your shoes off." I undo the tiny clasps around her ankles and resist the impulse to caress her feet.

I'm a monster to even have such thoughts at a time like this.

Samira comes in with hot tea on a tray for everyone. I grab a throw with Sherpa lining and wrap it around Valentina as she curls her feet under her and sinks into the couch.

Samira hands her a cup of tea. Savio sits opposite Valentina, and I sit beside her.

"Valentina, I have news of your father."

"Oh, tell me he's fine," she pleads, holding onto hope in what we both know is a hopeless situation.

"Your father is dead. There will be an investigation." She doesn't need to hear the word autopsy right now.

"What?" Her lips quiver as she processes the information, and tears stream down her face.

Savio and I exchange looks. We know we didn't do it, so what the fuck is going on?

"Call Giovi again and let her know you are with me."

Valentina breaks down and cries. Samira shows up with tissues, and after Valentina regains her composure, she calls her brother again.

It appears her mother just got the call from Ridolfo, who waited at the hospital, and Giovi has more men at the house for protection.

Her voice ripples with sadness as she hangs up with her brother.

"I can't believe Papa is gone," she murmurs, sipping her tea and trying to process everything. Then the fog lifts and she turns to me. "What am I doing here with you? Who are you? I know I know you. Rome?"

Oh, boy. Here we go.

"I'm Massimo. I had to get you out of there."

"Who do you work for?"

"Complicated answer."

"Uncomplicate it. How do I know you are the good guy? And not holding me for ransom?" She sits taller on the sofa but is poised to make an escape.

"Hmm, your guard let you leave with me. Surely that means something?"

"Ridolfo has been with me forever."

"Exactly, he's trusted by your father and you."

"Which means I'm a hostage?"

"Not exactly. I'm your fiancé."

## 18

# VALENTINA

Dazed over the loss of Papa and the fact that him walking me so proudly into the reception this afternoon was the last time I'll ever feel his presence is tragic. I never got to say "I love you Papa," one last time. I can't remember the last time I said those words. In hindsight, I was selfish and behaved like a spoiled brat.

His marriage was for the good of the family business, and it's one that gave me private schools, jets, and luxuries most people never experience.

Now I find myself in the home of a stranger who Ridolfo is fine, and it dawns on me...

"How did you know Ridolfo's name?"

"We've met."

"You're leaving out details," I say as my mind struggles to put the details together.

"Not important." Massimo smiles at me and takes my hand into his own. "You're safe. We're not the bad guys."

My eyes connect with him and suck me in. I'm falling for him, like a bowl of my favorite gelato. I can't get enough.

"Wait. The reception of a couple I don't know, Papa is murdered, and you're there to save the day? I don't think so."

"Timing, that's all."

His hands warm mine, and the heat travels up my arm. I can't deny the tingles that go with it. His hands are surprisingly soft, not a paper pusher, but not manual labor. He has no calluses.

Uncomfortable with his hands on mine, I immediately pull mine free. I cover my mouth to keep from shrieking and leap to my feet. My teacup flies across the room, landing on an oriental rug that must be irreplaceable if the pattern is authentic. Judging from the ornate items in the room and the lighted works of art adorning the walls, everything in the room must be collectible antiques.

I sprint to the end of the room, looking for a way out as anxiety wells in my chest.

"You won't get far, Valentina." His calm voice stops me in my tracks. He's not a man to mess around with, but more than that.—his voice.

I know that voice now that I'm not looking at him, and the pineapple smell jogs my memory. The hair on the nape of my neck stands up like a cat cornered by a dog.

I turn, facing the one man I've been longing to meet, the man with the sword tattoo. The tattoo on Massimo's hand looks like the one on the man who rescued me in the garden from the few details I observed before he fled.

I lift my eyes slowly. This is the man I owe a debt to. This is the man who slit someone's throat to save me. This is the man who kissed my lips and left me thinking about him for months.

"You." I can barely say a word as I look at his dark eyes. I remember them. They reflected the same loneliness I see in mine.

He saved me again tonight. His hands are a contradiction in motion, capable of saving a life or taking one. All mafia men can kill, but this one strikes me as exceptionally competent.

"How did you know? That night in the garden?" My voice quivers as I get closer to answers.

"After meeting your father and Giovi, I noticed you were missing. I figured you went out for some air, and thank God I did, or you wouldn't be here," he says, almost bragging.

"Do you know who was sent to kill me?"

"No, but the two men there that night are dead, so they aren't a threat anymore."

"There was more than one?" I ask. "It's incredulous that two men were out to harm me."

"Two." He puts up his fingers as if I need a visual aid.

"I helped him get away without being noticed," Savio pipes up, definitely bragging.

I turn my gaze, observing him for the first time. He's clean cut, has dark hair, darker eyes, and is as tall as Massimo as he stands to stretch his long legs.

I move quickly back to my purse to pull out my phone. I have the number of the man who sent me the necklace. I fidget with the phone.

"Don't bother calling the police." Massimo reaches to take my phone.

I pull it back.

"I'm not. You think I'm an idiot?" I press the number on the phone. Massimo's pants buzz. His phone must be on vibrate.

"You, you are the man who sent me the necklace." My hand goes to my neck, and my fingertips caress the precious stones.

"Yes." He bows his head slightly to confirm my guess.

Facts, yes, this is good.

"You are my fiancé?"

"Yes. I never dreamed we'd meet under such circumstances." He spreads his arms out apologetically.

"So, Ridolfo knew the wedding was the place for you to accept delivery of me?"

"Yes, don't blame him, he did his job. As did your father."

"Why? You could have anyone you want. Why me?"

"Why not you?"

*Why not?* I was going to go to someone. I should have been married off already. So why did Papa wait?

Massimo is a fine specimen of a man to be shackled to, and I'm safe with him. I'm not blind to the fact he's a trained killer. He took out not just one but two men that night! I'm impressed.

He might be a hired assassin. I take a quick visual inventory of the room. It's not a modern house, but it's been nicely restored. I check the view out the window from where I stand and see the glow of city lights in the distance. It's safe to assume that's Florence.

"Did you really want to go with the scary man with the neck tattoo?" he chides me.

"What do you know about him?"

"Nothing, but I didn't trust him for one thing," he puts a hand on his hip, "he was bidding on you, too. I wasn't about to let him win."

I'm turned on by his assertive nature and how he lets me speak my mind, but he can use an attitude adjustment.

"Wait a minute. Bid?" I'm stunned again.

*What the fuck is bidding done for?*

"Yes, it was quite shocking to me, but we got a tip." He

glances at Savio, then back to me. "And I had to see what was going on."

"Yes, I swiped neck-tattoo-mans card so Massimo could go downstairs to check out the situation."

"Of course, I had to find out what the private meeting was about," Massimo exclaims like he's won a court argument. It's as if it excuses his behavior of stealing and interfering with other people's lives. "And that's when I was appalled by the fact that men auction off their daughters."

"No." My jaw drops. "Papa wouldn't do that. Arranged marriages, sure, but bidding on us like we're cattle? That can't be true."

How could Papa turn me over to a stranger in exchange for money?

"Think what you want," Savio says. "I was there, nicked that man's card to get in the room. Some time passed, but when he noticed it was missing and caused a commotion, you must have used that as your opportunity to escape."

The timing flows. I'll give them that.

"So let me get this right. You felt sorry for me and bid on me?" I throw a hip out and put my hand on it, standing my ground. I'm not something you buy at an auction, like unclaimed luggage. I'm the don's daughter.

"Yes, why else? I don't need a wife. My life is busy and complicated. I had business to discuss with your father. You were more valuable to me than anyone else in the room."

"What do you mean by that? Was he in trouble?"

"He owes me money, lots of it. As for his dealings with others, I know nothing. But with me, he was in trouble."

Massimo heads to a free-standing bar at the end of the room, takes the top off a decanter, and pours the contents into two snifter glasses. Judging from the amber color of the liquor, it must be cognac. It's a status drink in certain circles. The more expensive, the better.

"So, who killed my father?"

"Don't know; trust me, we want to know as much as you do. Your father is no good to us dead. We need to ask ourselves, who has the most to gain by his death?"

He stares at me over his glass as if daring me to provide him with a list of names. Is he baiting me, or is he on the level? I can't figure him out.

*Damn.*

"I suppose the next in line, who would technically be my brother, but Giovi wouldn't do that. He's not ready. He likes not being the one to make the difficult decisions."

"Let's not get into details tonight. It's getting late. Samira has a room for you I think you'll like. We'll talk in the morning. The house is guarded, and we're all safe. That's a win. Right?"

"I guess so." I could have been dead on the floor like Papa twice over by now. And both times this man is present. He's either my knight in shining armor or the dark cloud over my family.

"Good, we understand each other." He unbuttons his jacket and tosses it in a nearby chair. "Samira," he calls.

A woman appears. She reminds me of my grandmother, only younger.

"Please take Valentina to her room and get her settled. I'll send a man to your hotel room to get your things as soon as the police release it. Right now, it's part of the investigation."

"When will we know the cause of death?" I straighten my shoulders, forgetting how this makes my boobs look bigger. Here I am, trying to assert myself but only succeeding at showing off my breasts. But his eyes remain on mine, which tells me he's not a total douche.

"Days, maybe. I'll let you know."

And just like that, he dismisses me to join Savio over a chess set on the coffee table.

Samira is elderly but assertive, putting her hand on my back to move me along.

I follow her as I'm exhausted. My feet seem to be walking themselves, exposed to the cold marble floors, and we pass a room roped off like a museum. Maybe it is one. This appears to be an old house with some rooms updated and some rooms are still under renovation. I gather this is a large mansion and the work to keep up with it must be constant.

"This way." Samira leads the way down a hall and opens a door. The room has a small fireplace, and the wood beams overhead have been painted and pair well with the color of the walls. The thick cream drapes over the windows should block the morning light. The bed is huge and elevated with an inviting comforter and plush pillows. I even have my own bathroom with a claw foot tub and a bidet.

"Do you need anything?" Samira asks while she stands ready to close the bedroom door.

Plush towels in a pretty rack in the bathroom, and I realize I'd love nothing more than a hot bath and sleep. I didn't eat dinner, but I'm not hungry.

"No, I'm fine, thank you."

"I'll see you in the morning then." She leaves, closing the door behind her.

I text Giovi to make sure he's okay.

He's okay, but I can tell he's worried.

I peel off the dress I never want to wear again and leave it on the floor. I run water in the tub until it's hot enough to boil lobster. It feels good to soak, and when it cools down, I slide under the water and scream so no one will hear me. I come up for air, and my cry is more of a wail. Papa is gone. A killer is on the loose, and I'm in a stranger's mansion, but he's to be my husband.

To top it off, I don't want that dark-eyed devil downstairs to feel obligated to 'save' me from myself or anyone else ever again. I don't need his help. I don't want him to be with me out of some obligation he's stuck with by a contract with my father.

I'm not a chess piece. I'm an intelligent woman who wants to be swept off her feet with love. Until that happens, I'll never be happy.

I cry and moan in grief and shock. Then, I pull myself together. This is the last time I cry for anyone.

The hot bath was amazing, but the bedgasm from the most comfortable mattress, crisp sheets, and fluffy comforter greet me an hour later. It puts me into a sleep so deep and dreamless I'm reluctant to wake up. Dreamland is uncomplicated.

**19**

———

## MASSIMO

I carry the chessboard from the coffee table, and we head towards what used to be a sitting room, but it's more of a den now. It's the one room in the house that looks and feels manly with a black leather couch with stud trim and two high leatherback chairs that are more reminiscent of Capone's era than mine.

"What's your next move?" Savio asks.

I try to pretend he's referring to the game sitting between and tell him he can start, but he doesn't move.

"God only knows, man. You saw some of those men. They looked like they would use her to get favors from her father or use her, and not in a good way."

"Like you're not." He sips his drink and looks comfortable in his favorite chair. He's like a dog with a juicy steak bone when he's got me on the hook. It doesn't happen often, so I can't say that I blame him.

"What?" I swirl the cognac under my nose and inhale deeply, appreciating the caramel and vanilla notes.

I tip my head, sizing him up.

"He owed us. If it wasn't for the debt combined with his

involvement with the oligarchy, he wouldn't have shown up on our radar at all. Grandfather had a good idea. I just saw an opportunity to sweeten my pot and get the same result. Maybe a better one," I say.

"Ha, I know you. You're claustrophobic on a long dinner date, and she's a flight risk. She has some spunk for a principessa." He grins at me, knowing there's more to this story.

"Does she? Seems to me she's got a target on her back, and her father is dead."

Savio straightens in his chair. "Fine. To be continued. I go first." He slides the first pawn.

I RISE EARLY, call Grandfather, and tell him I saw him at the wedding.

"I stayed in Florence after I got Argon's book to have fun and see some friends. I wanted to meet Luciano, seeing as how I'd like to get to know him better. He runs tough streets."

"Hm, I thought you hated Italy."

"Truth be told, I wanted to see my daughter."

That I can understand. Mom had breast surgery to remove the cancer and is resting at home. I need to see her, but there never seems to be enough time. Plus, I'm still not over the secret she kept. Ironically, I would have figured it out myself if I were able to spend more time with the Michelis.

"So, would you like to come over?"

"Valentina is there, right?"

"Yes, thankfully. I was able to get out of that hotel when she fainted." I pop nicotine gum in my mouth to get my fix.

"That was a surprise. With Luciano dead we have to worry over who will lead the Cosa Nostra. The authorities questioned me. I'm surprised they didn't tell me to stay in the country."

"They don't have to. Albania just updated its treaty with the U.S., United Kingdom, and Italy a few weeks ago. They are uniting to 'better confront crime', they say. Extradition is easy now."

Grandfather coughs, and I wish he would give up those damn stogies. I'm glad I stopped smoking. With Mama having breast cancer I'm now concerned about a Grandfather who prefers the older, non-traditional methods for ailments. I mean, horse cream for ligaments can work on bursitis, which he has in his left arm, but it won't cure lung cancer.

"Fuck, I hate the way these countries are going. We built Albania out of war and chaos. This is our thanks," he grumbles. "Tell me what you find out about Argon. I have people working on the inside."

Great, more officials on the payroll.

"I'm working on it," I reply.

"You'll be even busier with a woman in the house. I didn't mean you had to get a wife right away, Massimo. I just didn't want you to be alone forever. It's not good, you lose the will to live when you have nothing to look forward to."

"Are you okay?"

"Of course, I'm too miserable to die. I'll go when I want to go. By the way, I saw Dante frisked at the wedding, and they arrested him."

"What? You're withholding the most important news of the day!"

"I thought you might be busy mounting that filly all night." He laughs at his joke.

This is fucked up and disrespectful to talk about my future wife that way.

"A marriage is still a marriage no matter how it begins." I make my point and he gets the message.

"Sorry, she's a gorgeous girl. I'm sure you'll be happy. Let me know when you set a date."

"Fine, I'd better go see what I can find out about Dante."

Fuck, he's my brother, and now I'm the one keeping secrets from a dangerous man.

"Do your sources have more intel?" I ask.

"He'll be bonded out. The cops found a vial of something in his pocket. Maybe it was used to kill Luciano. But that's too easy, it had to be planted."

"There's a conspiracy going on, first Argon, now Luciano. And it's two totally different syndicates. What is the connection?"

"You think there is one?"

"Wars are typically tit for tat and between the same families, like when the Contis and Michelis went at it. Bad blood or one crazy asshole. But this doesn't sit right. It's not the normal progression of heightened tension, followed by retaliation, and then a sit-down or another retaliation."

There has to be a connection between the two murders. I feel it in my gut. As a man who has killed plenty, I'm usually right.

"You might have a point. I need you to make sure the shipments from De Luca's family are on time. I need to line up details with our friend in Belarus. The Russians don't like to be kept waiting. Ironic considering they don't give a fuck about their own people."

"I'll do that, too."

My to-do list is growing longer. My other phone rings. Tommaso.

"Gotta go."

Grandfather hangs up.

Do I trust him? I'm on the fence with that one. He might want that seat at the table sooner rather than later, but to show up in person is too obvious. Or is it the perfect cover?

"Tommaso, what's up?"

"It was good seeing you last night, but I need you to come in. The family is worked up over Dante being arrested over an obvious setup. I mean, it's like an amateur hour with the detectives."

"I wasn't aware."

Valentina picks this moment to come downstairs wearing the dress shirt I left at the end of her bed. I hope it will hold her until Samira gets her new clothing, as her luggage is stuck at the hotel as part of the investigation.

No doubt she'll be called in for questioning, and so will I.

"I'll be there as soon as possible." I hang up. I turn to face my fiancée. "Good morning. I left the espresso machine on for you in the kitchen. Samira will be here soon with some clothes for you."

She's at the bottom of the staircase. Her hair is tousled, not messy. Sexy as hell. If I weren't distracted with work, I'd fuck her on the steps.

"Thank you. I need an espresso." She runs a hand through her long bangs, tucking her thick blonde hair behind an ear. "The kitchen? And I'm starving. You know, we never ate dinner last night."

"There's some food in the fridge. Make yourself at home. I have guards everywhere, and the house is secluded, so don't get any ideas." I show her into the old farmhouse-style kitchen with the long family table in the middle, covered with a checkered tablecloth, chairs, and two benches.

I love how her tits and ass move under the fabric of my shirt. It's one of my favorite dress shirts with pale gray vertical lines so I'm glad she didn't burn it in effigy after our last conversation.

"Skillets are there." I point to them hanging on hooks above the island.

This is my favorite room in the house because the kitchen is the heart of the home. It's always warm with the light coming in through the windows and large doors and the view of the hillside is relaxing.

"You hungry?"

"I am, but I have to run. It's a busy day. The police will probably set up a time for you to be interviewed at the station. I'll get us an attorney just to be safe. You don't know anyone who would want to harm your father, do you?"

"No." She turns on the espresso machine, and the hum of the machine interrupts us.

"Are you sure? It's very important that you're honest with me. No matter what our arrangement is, it's my job to protect you. I have a lot of shit to get done today. You know how to reach me, so keep in touch. If I call, make sure you answer it."

"Or what?"

She turns to face me with her cup in one hand. I swear she's trying to make me horny as hell knowing I have to leave. Is she really teasing me?

"You want a good spanking? Keep it up. I know plenty of ways to make you obey. Follow the rules I have for you, and we can work on some of the things you want. It goes both ways. Remember that. And don't tell anyone but your friend Laura, Giovi and your mother where you are and who you're with. It will be dangerous otherwise. Speaking to them is dangerous enough."

"My father's enemies?"

"His and mine." I can't let the Michelis know she's here. That would make me look guilty.

I turn and walk to the front door just as Savio shows up.

"Can you keep your eye on her? I have a long day."

"Sure. I just saw Dante on the news. Crazy, no?"

"That's one word for it. I'm fact-finding today, so do what you can to keep her occupied. She can't be seen here."

"Gottcha, but the estate is off the beaten path, I doubt anyone will happen upon her here." He walks into my house to spend the day with my woman. He's my best friend, and I trust him with my life, but I'm miffed I'm not the one home with Valentina.

I have plenty of money, but there's no escaping the life I lead. Even those of us who get out of prison often end up back in the slammer because we can't stay out of trouble. As Ma said, it's in our blood.

Now that I know who my true relatives are, I'd say I wouldn't make it long on the straight side of the law.

I arrive at the warehouse. Tommaso is in a tizzy.

"Dante's been bailed out, but we suspect he's being framed. How do two important made men in two different families end up dead? We knew Argon was in our territory, but it wasn't us."

"Who was it?" I sit across from him as he has another cup of coffee, sitting at a rickety table in a rickety room he calls an office.

"We're trying to figure it out. Someone is after Dante." He slurps his coffee as I sit patiently in an indirect way.

"That was quite the spectacle yesterday."

"Sorry, I gave you a hard time on not having a date. Who was that woman you were talking to?"

"Someone new." I shrug.

"Might want to tap that. If only I was younger...."

I smile. Even young, Tommaso wasn't the player he makes himself to be. Now, in his late forties, or early fifties, with his kids grown, he can relax more since they are out on their own.

"What can I do to help?" I ask, trying to speed this along. He's not one to spill the beans without a trip down memory lane.

"There was a raid on our warehouse, have you heard anything?"

"No. Did they find anything?" I ask, knowing the answer.

"Thankfully, no."

He shrugs his shoulders and looks in his coffee cup. The Michelis have already looked at me as a possible leak.

"So, what's the plan? How do we prove Dante isn't responsible?"

"What man would do that at his own wedding? In *The Godfather*, he took out his enemies while at his kid's christening, but it wasn't like the red wedding in *Game of Thrones* where everyone is a sitting duck. And how did the police arrive so quickly? That never happens. Someone is playing with us."

Now he's making sense. But who? Losing De Luca messed us up as well. I'll have to keep tabs on Giovi and make sure he's safe in Sicily. That might mean a trip south sooner than I anticipated.

"The drug they found on Dante was Digitalis."

Now Tommaso has my full attention.

*Fuck.*

Digitalis. That's what killed Argon. Do they know that? It has to be the same killer, but why target the Albanians and now the Sicilians?

Someone is framing Dante for these murders. Men at his

level don't do their own hits unless it's very, very personal. He would never risk it. His business can't afford to lose him. Each brother has an operation. Dante oversees it all.

"Let me know if you need any help. I have to visit my mother."

"Sure, sure." He waves me off.

Fuck, I'm so busy my head is spinning, and I want to be home in time for dinner. I hope Samira makes something good.

I run my fingers through my curly hair, pushing it back. My life was great. I had a routine that worked and now. I'm going to be strung out to help the Michelis track a killer, while keeping Valentina hidden so as to not look guilty of the murder—and deal with police interviews, all while not blowing my cover.

I'm fucked.

Keeping Giovi safe isn't really my bag. But I will marry Valentina and keep Grandfather happy now that his plan to become involved in the oligarchy has become compromised. If Giovi is taken out, it will ruin Grandfather's plan.

But first, I have to figure out how to untangle myself from the Michelis and remain in one piece because I can't afford to get caught.

Make no mistake, Valentina will marry me. I just have to live long enough to make it to the wedding, but it doesn't mean I'm waiting until then to sample her delectable body.

I can hardly breathe thinking of her. She occupies my mind like no other, she has from the night at the museum. I tasted her lips then, but it was nothing compared to what I have in store for her. I imagine kissing her entire body and drinking her sweet nectar. I'm so hard my throbbing cock hurts.

On the way to see my mother, I dispatch Ridolfo to the

house to fill in for me as it's too risky to show up at the police station together. I had a feeling he'd come in handy. I have to have trusted men everywhere to get out of the fix I'm in, and for now, Valentina's former guard can help out.

As I mull over the new information I received, I wonder what Dante's next move will be. Being set up is never fun. It takes time and many manipulations to pull these events off. Someone knows more about our syndicates than they should.

It seems to me that this is the work of a dedicated person on a mission, and they can't be working alone.

**20**

———

## VALENTINA

I wake up to the howl of wind and the squawking of birds. It reminds me of a Hitchcock movie. I didn't mind sleeping in the nude last night. Between the comfortable mattress and the clean, fresh sheets with their high thread count, my traumatic day ended peacefully and I'm still alive.

I call Laura. I missed her calls yesterday and need to contact her before my battery dies. Otherwise, I have to use Massimo's bat phone.

"Hey, I was worried about you." Her voice is scratchy from crying. "How are you?"

"As you would expect, traumatized, worried. I don't know what killed Papa, and you would not believe who my fiancé is."

"What do you mean?"

"The man that saved me in the garden is my guy. And get this, that museum was used to auction girls off to the highest bidder."

"What? I never heard of such a thing."

"Me either. He saved me from being purchased by the

creepy dude with the neck tattoos. So now I am forced to marry a man who took pity on me."

"I don't think that's the truth of it. I mean, he saved you in the garden and you were with him at the reception?"

"Yes."

"Sounds to me like he has a crush on you."

"I don't think he has enough room next to his ego for anyone."

"Don't underestimate yourself. You're a catch."

"Maybe when Papa was alive, but now. . ."

"It will be okay." She tries to reassure me, but I can't wrap my head around anything positive at the moment.

"I have to go before my phone dies. I'll text when I can."

"But you're okay? Do you have a place to stay? Is the guy nice?"

"Oh, yeah, Massimo is his name, and he lives in a mansion of some kind."

"Sounds exciting. Stay in touch. I'm sorry about your father."

"Thanks, I'll be in touch."

We hang up, and when I get to the end of the bed, I notice a man's dress shirt. Oh my, there's no way we did anything. Is there?

He was totally captivating last night, with his cognac in his hand, and so smug when he told me what really went down at the museum gala. I believe Papa had to be desperate to do what he did, and I hope to find answers to my questions, knowing it might not happen as quickly as I want.

I pull the shirt on and roll up the sleeves. I need an espresso and head down a marble staircase that never ends.

I find Massimo, and he shows me the kitchen and the espresso machine. Before heading out, he tells me Samira will be here shortly with new clothes, toiletries, and a phone charger.

He breezes out, and the scent of warm pineapple greets my nose. His cologne. Oh, God. It is him. The man from the garden, it's not a dream.

I wonder what his story is. He seems a bit sketchy, but as I watch him leave, I can't stop myself from checking out his ass as he walks away in his fitted suit. His Italian loafers make no sound on the floor as he walks to the door.

I stand in the doorway with the cup of espresso in my hands while the lips between my thighs become slick with desire.

Who am I kidding? There is no way a man like him would want to be with a Principessa. Besides kissing me in the garden and some flirting, he's avoided me at every turn.

Massimo opens the door, and Savio rushes in.

"Buongiorno," I greet him. At least he smiles when he returns a greeting. I assume he's my new babysitter.

"Ah, espresso, I can use another." He helps himself to the kitchen.

"Let me guess, Massimo asked you to sit with me while he's gone."

"We help each other out. I can think of things that are worse." I notice he doesn't keep his back to me for long.

"Don't worry, I didn't take any knives." I roll my eyes and finish my drink. "Any food around here? We never ate last night, I'm starving."

"I'm sure there's food here that isn't stamped with an expiration date from two years ago."

"So, what exactly do you and Massimo do?"

"That depends. We do what we need to. You know our world, we know yours. We are just a different nationality. That's all."

"You both look pretty Italian-ish to me." He's wearing fitted jeans and Italian loafers. He takes off his coat, putting it on the back of a chair before pushing up the sleeves of his black sweater.

He chuckles, drinks his espresso in one gulp, and opens the fridge.

"Albanian. Well, we're half Italian, but Albanian mafia."

"So, you were at the gala. Any idea who wanted to kill me that night?"

"None." He turns around with eggs in his hand and asks how I like them.

"Scrambled, please."

He pulls a skillet off the overhead hooks that hold several pots and pans before he begins to crack eggs.

Samira lets herself in, carrying numerous bags, and I look at the digital clock on the wall. Shit, it's noon. I really did sleep.

"Where did Massimo go?"

"He has tons to do today. I'm arranging for an attorney to go to the police station with you." He cooks the eggs in under three minutes and serves them to me on a plate. "Sit."

I take the plate and sit at the long wooden table.

He sits across from me. "It's important that you don't mention anything that's gone on, the museum, the men, none of it. You know how it goes."

"Yeah, I know." I'm ravenous and inhale the eggs like a hungry wolf. Isn't that a Duran Duran song?

"There are things going on, and until we know more, we need to be careful."

"Like someone might be out for me?"

"Maybe. We hope to find out more soon. Capisci?"

"*Si.*"

He turns to Samira, greets her, and tells her to take care of me before he leaves.

"Samira." I nod.

"Good afternoon. You slept well?"

"Yes, thank you."

She puts her bags on the table. "Massimo wanted you to have these. There are phone chargers and clothes, and your dress shoes from the museum are in your closet," she informs me.

"Thank you."

Then it hits me, does he have my shoes? That was thoughtful. However, if he's a serial killer he knows not to leave any clues at the scene of a murder. So, there was no evidence I was in the garden that fateful night. I'm touched that he returned after I left to retrieve my shoes.

Samira nods and sets off to clean the kitchen.

Meanwhile, I'm excited to see what is in the bags, the first one contains jeans, dress pants, long-sleeved shirts, undies that make me blush, and matching bras that look like they are the right size but made to wear on a runway. He even thought to get socks, and there are boots in large boxes and another bag with numerous sneakers, all designer names.

I enter the kitchen. "How did someone buy all this in under two hours?" I know the shops don't open earlier than ten.

"We had a few people working on it," she says, and her eyes soften. "I'm sorry about your father."

"Thank you."

She nods.

Conversation over. I take the bags, head to my room, and open the closet, and there are my shoes, and they've been cleaned. There are hangers for my clothing so I make two trips up the staircase with my hand and arms full of bags and boxes to find a home for it all.

This mansion is larger than I imagined, and I'm anxious to look closer at the artwork and see what other treasures this home holds.

After putting away my clothing, I charge my phone before putting together a matching outfit. This mansion needs to be explored, but before I leave the room my phone rings.

Mama. I pick up the call.

She's crying. Sure, she and Papa have been married for over thirty years. I can imagine the shock of it. I don't sympathize with my family for what they did to me—tossing me to the wolves to save their cushy asses.

In a way, it improves my opinion of Massimo.

Mama is rambling on.

"Mama, did you know Papa was selling me to a stranger?"

"What? No, he said he arranged something," she sniffles. I'm not sure I believe her.

"Well, I'm with my future husband. Everything is fine for now. But tell Giovi not to trust Papa's men. I think Papa was murdered."

She bursts into tears again, and I make an excuse to hang up. I can't deny I'm glad to be away from home now. Giovi can handle it.

I try on my new wardrobe. The clothes fit, like really fit, and are comfy. I think someone has better taste than me as I put the phone on speaker, lay it on the bed, and tug on the socks and sneakers. This will help with the cold marble floors.

Once downstairs, I asked Samira to show me around. The fog has lifted, revealing empty olive trees on the hill behind the property. I see some men walking around outer buildings and know they aren't gardeners.

Samira heads to the kitchen. I continue to walk around the house, taking in the paintings on the wall. These aren't cheap, they are exquisite. Then I stumbled upon the roped-off room that I caught a glimpse of last night.

I peek inside and find a beautiful mural on the ceiling. I recognize the artist, and it dawns on me that Massimo isn't just wealthy, he's insanely rich. This artist has work in the Uffizi. I sit down, lean back in an old, red velvet-covered chair, and stare at the mural. I feel lucky to be one of the few people who enjoy the colors and imagination. And to think things like this exist in a private residence.

I have more questions than answers when my bat phone goes off. I should learn how to change the ringtone, and I chuckle.

Massimo is in a good mood, it appears; he's sending Ridolfo to go with me to the police station with an attorney for the interview.

"That's fine. Why is Ridolfo still here?"

"I wanted him to stay in case we needed assistance."

"Oh." Hmm. He's a man that plans ahead.

"Don't get any ideas. He knows what's going on and that you are mine. But he'll keep you safe."

"You can't go with me?" I try to hear where he's calling from, but it sounds like a car's Bluetooth speaker.

"No, don't mention my name or where you are staying. Say you are planning to head home to Sicily today. Don't screw this up; it could jeopardize your family," his voice turns serious, almost threatening, and I sit up straighter in my chair.

Why do I feel like I have to please him? Why does my heart flutter and make me feel weak when he gets domineering? I cross my legs as my pussy pulsates with the inflection of his voice. It's deep and rich. It's powerful and demanding.

"Fine," I reply sternly after a pause to make him wait.

I subconsciously wait for the special phone to ring even though I deny it to myself. I've spent the past few months waiting for a call from him, running my fingers over its shiny exterior, and now he's....my reality.

*Damn him.*

No boyfriend ever made me toe the line like him, yet I find myself compelled to do what he wants.

"Glad we can agree." He hangs up.

He's all work. But surely he must play as well.

I find Samira in the kitchen prepping a roast for tonight.

"Does Massimo have a girlfriend?"

"Ha, they are not good women like you."

"What do you mean?"

"They fall for him, and he'll have none of that. They get angry. The last one tried to ruin the mural." She shrugs.

This seems like a Greek tragedy playing over and over again.

"Are they wealthy?"

"Some are, some are not worthy of him, but he sees through all their games."

Interesting.

The door opens, and Ridolfo walks in with one of Massimo's men. I run and give him a big hug. Savio left earlier, so I'm relieved to see a familiar face.

To my surprise, he hugs me back. "You, okay? He's treating you well?"

"Yes." My arms slip from his neck as he says we need to go.

It appears the guard is driving us. Ridolfo preps me for

the questioning as we ride in the luxury SUV. I'm to say I stayed with Ridolfo last night. I don't understand Massimo's need for secrecy, and I hate telling lies, but my family's lives depend on it. I know Massimo's more than capable of killing anyone.

Massimo, being Albanian, must've pissed Papa off. So proud of his Sicilian heritage, I'm sure a mixed-blooded baby from us would have killed him. Massimo has something on him for sure.

"Ridolfo, do you know of any contract between Papa and Massimo?"

"Very little."

I keep my voice low so the driver won't hear.

"If Papa made a contract, can't it be dissolved now that he's deceased?"

"That's a question for an attorney, but don't ask this one, it's his," he warns.

"Isn't there a way out of this? Can't I go back to Sicily?"

"Let's go one step at a time. You might need Massimo. Your brother might not be able to protect himself, let alone you."

I love my brother and am beginning to feel more and more like him every day, making decisions based on what the family needs instead of my own. I understand what his days must be like now that he's in charge during what could be the most dangerous time for our family's survival. I worry about him and hope loyal men surround him but how can he be sure?

He's my best bet to get out of this contract. Whatever went wrong, maybe he can fix it and buy me back.

## 21

## MASSIMO

"Mama." I greet her with a hug and kiss on both cheeks out of respect rather than the forgiveness she wants. "How are you?"

"I'm fine but sore. These pain meds make me loopy." She struggles to sit up in bed and I help her, adjusting her bed pillows.

I try my best to be pleasant as we visit. I listen to Nico as he cooks and tells me how well Cosimo is doing in school.

"That's great, Papa.

"Mama, I met a girl. I like this one," I say.

This news is the best medicine. She perks up, wanting to know more.

"I'm getting to know her. When you're feeling better, we'll get together."

She grabs my hand as I sit by her bed and lean in to hear her.

"That would be great, be good to her." She smiles.

"You get some rest. I'll see you soon."

I can tell Mama's exhausted, but having a woman in my

life will give her hope for grandchildren and a reason to live. With the amount of time I spend working and my track record with women, she had probably given up on grandkids.

Nico and I nod as I make my way to the door. I'm no longer angry with him. He had the impossible task of trying to fill another man's shoes and loved me in his own way. That's more than I can expect for a man who raised another man's love child as his own.

Once in my car, I call Grandfather to make sure he's on his way out of town. He wants me to solidify our relationship with Giovi and is more than happy I have Valentina to facilitate a likely regime change. He believes Giovi will be more motivated to stay in power with his sister's well-being riding on it. He may be right, but I'd never let anything happen to her.

Giovi's situation is as unpredictable as it is unproductive. He has to keep men loyal to him when the men might not be confident in his abilities since his dad was whacked. He also has to keep the syndicate's products moving, or he'll have issues with cash flow and soured contacts he needs to keep afloat. Any failure to meet terms with us will void our stay of execution.

Like I always say, everyone lies. At some point, greed involving money or power fucks up everything. I don't relish the thought of war, but I sure as hell will fight for what's mine and take out any person who deserves it.

"Giovi will have to be in control to protect his family. We have to make sure of that. Congrats on the girl, she's very pretty. You're a lucky bastard," he says, and the implication strikes me as inappropriate. I'm his grandson. Would he really muscle in on my woman?

"Maybe," I reply before hanging up. He's overstepping. I don't appreciate the connotations.

Is Grandfather fucking with me? The words of my mother can't be ignored. But would he have a reason to knock me off, or set me up? I can't fathom it. He spent the past two decades mentoring me and teaching me survival in the wild. He has no children. He treats me like his son. It's partly why I'm so wealthy.

I toss my second set of gum before I arrive at the police station to give my statement before Valentina's appointment. I can't be distracted from my duties, and just like the police, I need to figure out who killed Argon and Luciano.

In our line of work, men at the top know the status of relationships between our friends and foes. The Michelis lie low and, like me, they don't instigate if they can negotiate. So, I don't think they are involved in these hits. I suspect there is a larger play going on. A conspiracy. But to what end?

It was a quick in and out at the station. The police and detectives are overworked, and I don't expect the wedding guests to provide any useful information. The Michelis must be as confused as the police.

Dante and Marchello were not supposed to see Luciano at the party. He was not invited, but I bribed the wedding planner, Gabriella, so Luciano could get into the affair and bring Valentina. Gabriella promised they'd be in another room, and the transfer would go off without a hitch. So, how did everyone end up together?

If Dante and his family had no way of knowing Luciano would be at the party, there is no way they had time to plan his murder.

Whoever whacked De Luca knew he was attending the wedding in Florence. That finger points south to Sicily.

Which means we're not going there for the funeral later this week. It's too dangerous.

There's no telling when someone is going to move against Giovi, but it's inevitable. Even my black heart hurts for him. The Sicilians are known for guerrilla warfare and planting explosives. I'm not into shooting people in the streets, but I can blow some shit up.

As for Grandfather, Dante and Marchello met him when he returned Argon's black book of passwords. Even though that situation resolved itself on good terms, they weren't best friends, and his presence at the party would have set off red flags.

Not many would recognize Grandfather. He doesn't travel much, and he stays out of the news. But lately, he's had his nose in everything. First the reception and now my personal life, which is concerning. I don't know why he's interested in my operation in Italy.

One of the things on my to-do list is to swing by our legitimate business office, the one under the real estate sign. We use it to buy up property and pocket cash for rent, another way to launder money. We also have a trucking and moving company that doubles as a front.

Besnik text, he'll meet me there. It's been months since I've seen him, and his timing is good. He was there when Argon was killed. I have more questions.

I'm on a tight schedule but still find time to daydream about Valentina, remembering her long legs and lovely figure dressed in my shirt this morning. When she reached for a cup, the shirt went up, and I saw her curvy butt cheeks. Savio probably got to enjoy the same view, but it couldn't be helped. She needs clothes, and until we get her belongings from the hotel, I have to improvise.

As soon as I get to the office, I pull out my phone and text her.

*Hope you are having an excellent first day at the mansion. I'll be home for dinner.*

She texted back, *I can't leave so I'll be here. Some kind of roast, I think it's veal. Smells great.*

I smile—finally, a woman who loves to eat. And the dish Samira is making is more of an Albanian dish than Italian. I hope Valentina is open-minded to trying new things.

I have a new world to show her in the bedroom. Sure, she's no virgin, but it's likely been years without a boyfriend, so my hard cock will fit nicely in her tight pussy. She'll never think of another man after I fuck her.

Besnik enters, interrupting my wicked thoughts. He's aged since Argon died. It took a heavy toll as the two went back years and were very close. His burly gray beard and overgrown hair tell me he's still not himself. He lumbers into my office with no concern for his own safety. It's just the two of us anyway, and it's the middle of the afternoon, so nothing is likely to happen, but one never knows.

We shake hands and exchange pleasantries as he sits.

"Have any new facts surfaced about Argon's murder? I don't think it was the Michelis who killed him. In fact, I'm confident someone set up Dante to take the fall for De Luca's death. It's too much of a coincidence. Did you see anyone out of place, unusual, or suspicious the night Argon died?"

"It seems like it was forever ago as I go over it in my mind. I keep thinking if we didn't go, maybe it wouldn't have happened. I should have never let my guard down. We were drinking at the bar, and Prende came in and had a drink with us. We only had a few men with us, but they are trusted, they live here and are not suspects."

I lean back in my office chair thinking.

"Do you have any pictures from the trip?"

"Some, maybe, I never thought to look at them for clues. We're men, not so much into pictures," he explains.

"If you find any with people in the background, please text them to me."

When I stand, he knows we're finished.

"Sure thing, Massimo." We shake hands, and he walks out with me.

I've never been so anxious to get home before. I am curious as to how Valentina's day went in her new home. I regret the timing wasn't better for us to get to know each other. I wish I could have taken some time off to get her acclimated. I can't wait to see how the new clothes fit. She'll need to get out and shop. I'd enjoy seeing her trying on clothing and having her model it for me.

That would be quite the turn-on. I'm getting hard thinking about it and remembering the garden kiss that is seared in my memory like a cattle brand. I can't shake the heat that warms me from the anticipation of seeing her again.

How can I keep my distance and fuck her at the same time? Is it possible? She's different from the other women I've bedded, and yet I can't figure out why she has this effect on me.

Ridolfo should have her home from the police station by now. Micro drove them, and some of my other men are protecting the house. One can never be too safe, and the recent chain of events will put everyone on guard. Who knows what the killer's next move is?

What if someone is out to destroy Dante? He was obviously framed for the murder. The news reported he was arrested after something was found on him that could have been used to kill Luciano. Investigators would be stupid to release all the details. I can read between the lines.

I hope Besnik comes up with a clue. I hate feeling helpless. I need to be able to protect myself and my beautiful fiancée.

**22**

---

# VALENTINA

Massimo returns home in time for dinner at eight. I greet him at the door, wanting news about Papa but also because I'm bored.

Massimo does not sugarcoat it. "He was poisoned with Digitalis, a common drug for the heart. His body will be sent to your family soon."

"He was killed. Who would want to do that?"

"That's the question of the day, trust me. I've heard nothing from my men." He hands his coat to Samira and walks away without a word.

I follow Massimo into the kitchen where he pours us both a glass of wine, handing one to me. Our fingers touch, and his warm flesh brings back the memory of that night in the garden when he reached out to help me stand.

"Giovi and Mama have to plan a funeral. I want to go home for it."

"Absolutely not," he declares, his voice rising. "It's not safe." He softens his tone when he looks at me. "Let's eat."

Samira appears and announces dinner is ready.

He slides his hand to the small of my back, and the

warmth of his touch radiates through my sweater. I fight off the impulse to turn around and kiss him, to feel alive and wanted. The scent of him makes me want him more. I'm excited and feel a slickness between my legs. Thankfully, we reach the dining room before I slip on my juices because I want him.

The table is set to perfection with fine china and cloth napkins. The candles have been lit, and it feels like a romantic dinner in a mansion with a mysterious man I'm inexplicably drawn to. He's dark and brooding, a man of few words and more secrets than a confessional at St. Peter's.

"I don't use this room much, preferring to eat in the kitchen because it's convenient, and I usually eat alone," he explains while pulling my chair out for me.

"How did you end up at the museum in Rome?" I ask, fishing for details, anything that might give me a clue to Papa's life and death. But mostly to avoid silence and distract me from my wanton impulses.

"It's not relevant." He cuts into his veal with the same energy I reserve for tiramisu.

"What is your last name?"

"Rizzo," he swallows, "I know, I'm Albanian and Italian."

"Interesting. What business did you have with my father?"

"We're not playing this game, Valentina. I'll tell you things you need to know when I decide you need to know them. Don't ruin dinner."

"I'm not. I'm asking adult questions, and I want your opinion on my brother. My family is dropping like flies, and you tell me it's none of my business," I huff.

I'm pissed at trading one cage for another, worried about my family left unprotected in Sicily, and I'm fucking sexually frustrated. So much so I wish he'd just fuck me on the table. The tension between us is so unbearable I can't keep from wiggling in my chair with anticipation.

He chews another bite as if he's ignoring me on purpose. The thought that he might be hungry doesn't cross my mind.

"I've lived through a war with the other mafia family on the island and it was terrible. Is someone going to challenge my brother to take over as Don?"

He shrugs, lets out a sigh, and then says, "I can see you're going to be relentless, so I'll tell you the truth. I'll never lie to you," he says, ending his sermon with a gaze that shakes me to my core.

I'm vulnerable. It's new to me. I've never felt it before. My hands are shaking. I keep them in my lap so he doesn't notice my nervousness.

"No one ever knows, even going into a war you think you've won. Your father ruled with an iron fist. The odds are good Giovi will be okay. We have to wait." He sips more wine and asks, "How is Ridolfo?"

"Good. Why did you keep him here?"

"I thought he'd be a comforting face for you." His voice is soft, and it's filled with concern, it's almost like he cares for me. "Besides, he needed to be here for the interview, and you never know when his service might be needed. The interview at the police station? How did that go?"

"Fine. They didn't seem to be too invested in the case if you ask me."

"I got the same impression, but to them he's just another dead member of organized crime. And, for all we know, the detectives have been threatened not to pursue the case."

"You're joking."

"I don't joke."

"Obviously," I say, adding emphasis to make it clear I

speak my mind. I'm still adjusting to life without Papa, but I have a loyalty to my family and want to be there for them.

"How can we help Giovi?"

"I hope he can help himself."

"How can you say that? And what of the contract with my father? He's gone. The contract shouldn't be good. Did he die before it was executed?"

"No, it was executed the night of the gala, but I like your enthusiasm to find a way out of marrying me. I don't know if I should be impressed or insulted," he says with a cocky smirk.

I'd love to say *insulted* but he's obviously someone important and I'm afraid to be disrespectful. He can make my life uncomfortable.

"So, how long do I stay here? What is in the contract? Do you have a list of obligations for me? If you ask me, the contract expired with Papa's death."

"One, it's a contract, not a will. Two, no obligations are mentioned other than the fact you do need to be my wife and have my children." He glares at me. "And the rest will unfold according to your behavior."

"Oh, so a good girl gets rewarded with shopping. Do you think you can buy me?" I sit taller in my chair as I spit out the words.

"I already bought you, sweetheart," he says, and I'd love to knock that smirk off his face.

"You went about it behind my back. It's not the same as earning it."

"And what would you know about earning anything?"

"I wanted to work. Papa wouldn't allow it. I wanted to use my counseling degree, but he said it was too risky."

"He's right, but maybe I can come up with an alternative that would appease you." He finishes the food on his plate and wipes his mouth before laying the napkin on the table.

"Are you going to eat or talk all night?"

I take a bite. I'm nowhere near done.

"Have you heard from Giovi?" I ask.

"Yes, he seems fine, competent."

I wish I was home for his sake, but I know I'd be one more person he'd have to worry about.

"How was your day?" I ask, deciding I can't beat him at a game where he holds all the cards.

"It was like all others." His vague answer is not lost on me—the mafia life.

"Men and your secrecy," I scoff, taking my last bite of veal and risotto.

"It keeps our families safe," he reminds me.

"I know, so you say," I reply as I blot my mouth with the napkin.

"Shall we retire to the living room?" He stands and waits for me.

I walk behind him, eye-fucking his toned buttocks, which calms me down.

"I love your art collection," I mention in passing as I blatantly stare at his backside.

"Ah, yes, I noticed at the museum, you were one of the few guests who enjoyed the viewing."

"You do, too."

"Yes, I don't know why. I like fashion and pretty things. Well," he motions for me to sit on the sofa, the same one I sat on my first night here. "I'm partial to having nice things.

"That's obvious."

I sit, and he helps himself to a cognac at the bar.

"I suppose so. What is it you desire, Valentina?"

"To be of use in some way. I want to help others." I'm not

going to confess I've never been in love and that I want him to fuck me till I can't walk.

He nods as he approaches me. "Let's watch some TV. I need to relax."

I comply and follow him to the living room, where we both sit on the sofa.

Sitting beside me, he picks up a remote on the coffee table and at the press of a button, a TV comes up from inside the cabinet that holds books and a vase of flowers.

"Neat trick," I chuckle. No wonder I couldn't find the damn TV in here.

"I liked the wine at dinner." I start a new conversation.

"I'm happy it meets your approval," he replies. His eyes pass over my breasts, and I don't have to be experienced to know that I am distracting him.

He's a man looking to dip his cock in me, only he owns me, and I doubt he'll make it special. We're not a love match. No doubt he'll approach sex like work. I see him on autopilot, going through the motions with no attachment. Killers can't possibly feel emotions like love. Real lovers have a mind and body connection as well as a physical one, in my opinion.

"What do you have planned for me? I can't mill around the house with nothing to do all day," I say;

"It's just for now."

"I miss my friend, and I'm stir-crazy. Can you find a way for me to find a job?" I reply.

"Ah, I have your background report. I know you're educated."

"So, you know everything about me now?"

"I would say I know enough to understand your wish to be more productive in society, and that's honorable. Maybe you can be a therapist for men in the mafia," he jokes.

"Very funny." My sarcastic tone makes it clear I'm not amused.

"All kidding aside Valentina," he says, setting his glass down and leaning into me. "I have plans for you, us."

Sex appeal drips off him like rain, like the night we met. The adrenaline and excitement that night weren't just from the events in the garden. I realize now that it's him. I want him. But I want him to want me, not pity me.

How can I protect myself from being heartbroken by a man that clearly has no time for a wife? He's never had a long-term relationship, according to Samira.

I can act like he doesn't have an affect on me. But who am I kidding? My panties turn into a sponge when he walks into a room. I felt it the instant I bumped into him at the wedding, without knowing it was him. Our lives are entwined, and if we have kids, I'm forever bound.

I long to be kissed like that again but Massimo seems preoccupied. I try to keep my mind busy as anticipation spreads like fire down my torso, my abs, and coming to a rest nestling inside my pussy, where it pools into a warm, moist triangle.

Damn him for having the looks and sex appeal of a hot Italian movie star. He has a power over me that makes me forget my limitations. His is full of possibilities and excitement, and I find I'm jealous that we're in two different worlds under one roof.

"Do you kiss every woman you rescue? Or was it just me?"

His face is inches from my own as he slides a hand around my neck, his fingers gripping my throat.

"I never rescue anyone," he whispers. His mouth tastes of vanilla from the cognac, and the pungent aroma of the liquor swirls around us as his lips claim mine harshly.

I'd pull away, afraid this would turn rough, but he slid his hand up my sweater, loosening my bra and freeing my breasts. He pulls the sweater over my head, and my blonde hair tumbles around my bare shoulders.

He nuzzles my neck, and his essence washes over me, a virile man looking to mate. He runs his tongue down my neck, nibbling as he goes, sending shivers up my spine. I close my eyes and feel his hot breath on my skin, the skin between my voluptuous breasts. I arch slightly, willing him to take me. The anticipation of his next move is driving me insane. I'm tempted to open my eyes and watch him but find it more exciting not knowing where he'll go next.

"Ah," I moan in surprised when his lush lips devour my nipple. His fingers play with the other nipple, gentle at first, then give it a tweak. I gasp and arch back, but he still holds my head and limits my movement.

The chemistry between us creates an eruption like Mt. Etna with hot lava flowing between my thighs, but I want it to be his cum as he claims me as his.

I'm immobile. Subject to his control and desires, I can't deny my rapid heartbeat, and my arms are around his neck as I feverishly return his kisses.

My body melts into him from the heat of our spontaneous foreplay. I tip my face towards him because he is the nectar of the gods, created for women to swoon at his feet and birth warriors for him.

I'm lost between the rush of adrenaline and blood pounding through my veins. He pulls me to his broad chest, a chest I can't get to with all these damn buttons in my way. Why does he always wear impossible clothing?

Fuck that. I can't prolong the inevitable. I grab his dress shirt and rip it open. Buttons fly across the room. Before they can hit the floor, I'm sucking on his neck and feeling his abs under my fingertips. Months of pinning away for him make it impossible for me to refuse him.

I'm putty, powerless against him. I can't hold back and tug at his chest hair, then run my fingers through it, reaching his nipples, rolling them between my first finger and thumb, harder and harder until he releases a moan.

I let up, rubbing my palms gently over his nipples before I move them up to his shoulders. Raking my nails gently down his back digging into him, and then gently over the same area as my fingertips caress the craters as they move up to his neck again. I can't miss the goosebumps under my fingertips that cover his skin.

I run my hands across the top of his back, urgently exploring it until I hit resistance. Scars. I move slower, tracing the lines of the raised skin as I peer into his eyes. Yes, he's lost men he's loved like brothers. As young as he is, he's had more experience in life than most his age in his line of work.

He's an expert at everything he does, a perfectionist. Someone who always wants more. Will I be enough for him?

Perspiration builds on the nape of my neck as we hold each other, locked together like a puzzle and needing the other to complete the final spot that is empty, like our hearts. His eyes mirror my own, exposing a vulnerable soul. It's as if he's known me forever. We're both still, no words can explain what passes between us.

"I'm afraid," I whisper against his neck.

"Of what?" His voice is raspy and uneven.

"Of losing myself in you and never finding me." My breath catches in my throat.

"I won't let you lose your way," he promises.

I blink my eyes, holding back the mist, but one tear

escapes. He kisses it away like he's done it a million times, but I know better. He's a loner, a killer, a man without attachments.

He gingerly drops kisses over my face, then my neck. Running one hand down my arm, he takes my manicured hand and sucks on my first finger, then the next, circling his tongue around each one as if it is my clit.

Massimo pulls away, and the brief fear he'll leave me is dispelled as he stands to shuck his shoes, pants, socks, and boxers.

His heart, soul, and body are naked as he stands before me.

For months he had no contact with me. I thought the rejection would make me hate him, but it made me want him more. Did he do that on purpose? I built him up in my mind, the hero complex alive and well.

I tell myself not to want him. There is no way I'm going to risk my heart on this man, one who uses a blade and his hands to kill for me. I don't know who he is or what he does. His life—still a mystery.

Naked in front of me, he pulls me to him, undressing me as my jeans and panties join his on the floor. He swoops me up in his arms and carries me up the long staircase to his room. It's as if the beast has claimed his princess at last.

**23**

———

# MASSIMO

I carry Valentina to my room upstairs. My arms hold her like she's as precious as a valuable gem, and although she's light, she's not frail. Her hair tumbles onto the pillow as I lay her on my bed.

"Don't move." I light a candle on my nightstand for an ambient glow.

I sense her checking me out before I turn back to her.

"You're beautiful," I murmur as I position myself between her legs and lean over her.

"No," she shakes her head.

"Yes, you are. I'm going to spend the night showing you."

I spread her tanned legs. She doesn't resist.

"It's been so long," she confesses.

"You're mine." With her admission, I can understand some of the buzz about her at the auction. Most would think she was a virgin.

I run my tongue up one leg and then the other as she shifts under me. I can't get enough of her sweetness, but I remind myself to take it slow.

She tastes like vanilla gelato on a summer day, but I'm taking my time instead of eating it quickly before it melts. I lick around the outside, teasing her, flicking my tongue to drive her stark, raving mad as she clutches the blankets on the bed. She moans and squirms as if it's painful, but I know it feels good, and she'll beg for more if I stop.

Using my fingers to enter her, I continue to lick her inner lips, making sure she can watch as I do so.

"I want to introduce you to enhanced pleasure. It will be new to you but you'll be safe. Do you trust me? "

"Yes," she half moans.

I reach above her, pulling straps from the bed's corners, and slip the Velcro cuffs around her wrists and ankles, securing them in place.

I massage her feet. With an "Oh," she squeals and twists away from me.

"Keep your eyes closed." I retrieve a feather teaser from the drawer in my nightstand and gently touch her stomach with it, making her quiver.

She complies like I knew she would. She didn't expect me to make love to her, but she's reveling in her desires and seeing me in a new light. I can't help but drop my guard when I've waited so long.

I don't think she minds not being in control right now. She's out of her childhood bedroom and becoming a woman. My woman.

I run the tickler over her breasts, breasts that are begging to be touched, the nipples hard and erect. And yet I restrain myself. Using the feathers to excite her more, I drag the tickler to her trimmed mound and run it between her legs and the inside of her thighs.

Her breathing is rapid. She pulls against the wrist

restraints. I toss the tickler and drop kisses on her side, her abs, and come back to her full breasts where I grab them with the strength in my hands, causing her eyes to open wide with surprise.

"Ouch," she moans.

"Sorry."

"It felt kind of good," she grins. "I can take it," she adds, but I can tell she's exhausted from the intense foreplay. She's at the end of her patience as I rub her clit. My fingers are soaked with her.

I lick them. She's as sweet as I expected and then some.

"What do you want?" I demand.

"You."

"I don't know if you've had enough yet," I tease.

"Fuck me, now," she demands through gritted teeth. Her body quivers in anticipation as I kiss her between her thighs, licking her nub and sucking her nectar.

I know what she wants as I lean over her, our eyes meeting as I reach up and unclasp the restraints around her wrists. She immediately clutches my large cock as perspiration beads on my neck. I'm prepared to make her mine at last.

I circle my engorged cock around her opening, rubbing her juices around her vaginal lips as she moans and squirms as if it hurts, but I know she's ripe with desire.

I lean back and unclasp her ankles.

"Now," she weakly protests my delay and tugs at my chest hair, bringing our lips together for a succulent kiss; like a plant that needs water, she needs me to fill her up.

"You are mine, Valentina."

I enter her, dipping the fat head of my cock into her opening, one last tease. When she struggles against the restraints, I know she's ready. I plunge into her hard, giving her all of me at once, and there's a lot of me.

She gasps, catching her breath, and I see a tear in her eye. Fuck me, she's touched. this excited me even more. I move to slow down, she lifts her buttocks off the covers and grinds against me, greedy for more. She meets me thrust for thrust increasing the tempo. Her moves are natural and fluid.

Her arms are tight around my neck, holding onto me as if her life depends on it. I pump her hard, my cum filled balls slapping against her ass cheeks. Her nails are like talons clawing at my back, partly from pleasure and the other anchored on the headboard to keep herself from crashing into it.

Using one hand to support myself, I make sure I'm stroking her swollen clit, and only when I feel her pussy tighten around me, do I let her come. I explode into her. She cries out in ecstasy while I muffle my low moan, not wanting her to know how much I'm enjoying this.

She has blown away all my expectations. She's the only woman I've ever been this excited to fuck, and if all goes well, we'll both be happy with my arrangement. The agreement was she take birth control, so I don't have to deal with messy condoms, but I filled her up nonetheless.

I roll off onto my back. "I'd like you to move into my room. There's no need for two beds. We'll set a wedding date soon."

"Wait. Wedding date soon?"

"There's no reason to wait. It's an arrangement."

"I guess you have a point," she confesses. "But I don't even know what you do."

"I'm connected, as you know, and that's all you need to know until this body count stops."

I leave the bed long enough to clean up in my bathroom. By the time I return, she's fallen asleep. I lift the blankets and slide her under them.

She opens one eye to ask, "Who else died?"

"A boss of mine. But I'm involved in many different families at the moment, so never speak business with anyone. Do you understand?"

"Yes." She pulls the covers up and closes her eyes. I pull her into my arms knowing full well the engagement ring I picked out months ago is in my nightstand.

I'll have to find the perfect moment.

Valentina got her belongings back from the hotel, and now we need to shop for clothes she'll need for upcoming events.

Instead of shopping online today, she gets to touch and feel everything as we scurry from store to store in the streets of Florence. She's ravenous for the freedom to be like others our age.

Savio and my guard Micro are with us today for protection. Micro is a trusted and seasoned soldier in his forties. He's in great shape and adept with his hands, knives, and guns.

I could've used Ridolfo, but after the police interviews, he was dispatched back to Sicily. I only hope that Giovi has his best allies around him. It's hard to tell who to trust in times like this.

All day, I've been on the lookout for any Michelis or members of their ever-expanding family. With the brothers settling down and getting married, before long they'll have enough kids to support a soccer team.

Valentina walks out of the dressing room wearing a cocktail dress that shows off her young body without revealing too much. She looks happy as she takes a picture of us. She's slowly defrosting my grim outlook on women.

"Don't share or post pictures of me to anyone," I warn.

"I'm just sending it to my best friend Laura," she assures me.

"Mm." I watch her walk away, taking in the sway of her hips and the click of high heels. I don't care what she wants to buy or what it costs, as long as she has me in mind when she wears it.

I should ask more questions about Laura, but I trust Valentina's judgment. She knows to be careful. Besides, women need other women to talk to. Who else will she call after our first argument when she wants to complain about me?

I take her distraction as an opportunity to pull Savio aside and ask him for a favor.

"Savio, can you call one of our friends at the hospital? See if we can take advantage of Valentina's degree and get her a job working with kids. It's the best way for her to use her skills and help others."

"That sounds like a great idea. Sure, we have enough pull."

"Great, keep me posted." I give Valentina my attention as she walks out of the dressing room with a sales associate who has a difficult time holding all her items.

While the cashier uses my black card to pay for everything, I tell the guys to bring the car around and make sure we're not being followed.

A few minutes later, we're in the SUV. Valentina thanks me for shopping and tells me how much she loves Florence.

Of course she loves Florence, the art capital. She has taste. I'm hungry from all the shopping and direct Micro to a café for food.

I text my mother from the car to see how she's doing. She's fine, improving daily, and, of course, wants to see me. I'm busy but convince her I'll drop by soon.

"Are you working?" Valentina asks.

"Yes, in a way." I turn to meet her eyes. "You don't have to worry about another woman."

She purses her lips in thought. "I'll trust you until you give me a reason not to."

I love it, she's not in a position to dictate anything, but she tries all the same. I respect a woman with enough spunk to make the best of a situation and do what's best for her family. Family is her weakness, as it is mine. This is another reason I travel light, and now I find myself in a compromising position.

We're in the middle of a light lunch when I receive a call from Tommaso. Dante wants to see me. I give Savio a look and shrug to indicate I have no clue what this is about.

The meeting is at his office downtown, not that far away. Part of me is nervous because a sit-down is rarely a good sign. I'm nervous someone ratted me out. My lieutenants would never do such a thing.

But when you get whacked, most never see it coming.

All my actions and decisions since Valentina carry more weight. She depends on me, the same way my men depend on me to employ them and pay them so they can provide for their families.

Their wives are more street-smart than Valentina. Valentina has never been taught to survive on her own. Hell, I don't even know if she likes kids, I assume she does as she has a degree to work with them. Besides, hospitals have good security systems in place to keep her out of harm's way. I have contacts there, so it should be easy for them to find a fitting job for her.

We wrap up lunch quickly and head out. Valentina asks if everything is okay and I tell her I have a stop to make, and that she's to remain in the vehicle with Micro.

She furrows her eyebrows with worry. I squeeze her knee to reassure her as we pull up to the doors of Micheli Enterprises.

THE SECRETARY GREETS me and takes me to Dante. I haven't seen him since the reception. I'm nervous, and my stomach is in knots from the tenuous situation I find myself in. I'm in a dangerous position and can't get myself out quickly enough.

I worry that he will find out about Valentina. How can I be with the daughter of a murdered don and not be a suspect? Or what if he has found out about my Albanian lineage, considered by some to be royalty? He would have to ask why the hell am I working for him.

Dante stands to greet me, walks around his large desk to shake hands, and motions for me to sit.

"Massimo, thanks for dropping by."

"Sure thing. What can I help you with?"

I sit in a leather chair, knowing he wouldn't whack me here, but keeping my guard up just the same. Until I can clear things up, I need to be vigilant.

"It's more pleasure than business. Juliet and I are having a private ceremony in Greve at her parents' restaurant to make sure nothing goes wrong this time."

"I understand that."

"We can talk more at the wedding when we're all together. The police still have me on their radar, and all the bad publicity has stalled some of my larger building projects."

Dante is pensive for a moment. I force myself to relax. He has the presence of a don— a don who rules based on respect and purposeful decisions. He doesn't impress me as being an asshole like most men in his position. I love my grandfather, but he can be a pompous ass.

"You've been doing good work and, depending on your skill sets, you may be able to help me. This wedding planner, Gabriella, is not who she says she is, and until we find her, I'm not comfortable. We need some camera footage from the police evidence locker, but it's impossible to penetrate. Can you use your contacts and see if we can obtain her real identity?"

"I'll look into it."

"Please do. Let me know if you get any leads. I don't think my family is safe with her on the loose." He stands, and I can't mistake our tiny mannerisms, and I crack a knowing smile. "She was suspiciously absent after De Luca went down, and she spoke many languages and isn't the type to not show off. My guess is she can only stay hidden for so long."

"It would seem that way. I'll see what I can find out."

The meeting is over.

"We're not sure what's going on. However, my fingerprints were not on the vial found on me. Even the police know it's too obvious."

"I'm concerned as well." I stand. "I knew Argon was overstepping his boundaries."

"Yes, but the Albanians are pushing their way into everything. They have a pipeline to Eastern Europe I don't have. I'm fine with keeping everything in Italy and knowing my men."

"Nothing wrong with that," I respond.

"Hey, bring a guest to the wedding. Also, don't share the information with anyone." We shake hands.

"I'll see you Sunday, a real romantic Valentine's Day wedding," I add.

"Silver lining, I guess. Juliet is happy. That's all that matters."

There's a pep in my step as I leave. I just had my first one-on-one with my half-brother. I'm stressing less after the meeting, and watching him and his interactions with others gives me an understanding of the family dynamics. I've been the outsider in my own family my entire life and never knew why. Now everything is coming together.

I hope Dante's on the level and the Michelis do not find something in the evidence locker that will jeopardize our relationship and put me in a precarious position. I'm not even sure it's possible to breach the evidence locker.

Even if my brothers were to find out about me, I don't want to order a hit on them, particularly when they didn't steal the cryptocurrency and were kind enough to return Argon's black book.

Dante was smart not to steal the Bitcoin. He's demonstrated he has principles. If you work for a Don with no principles, like that fuck Conti, you never know when he'll go crazy and shoot the person next to him because he didn't like the way the guy was breathing.

I'm glad Conti's gone. According to the news, his sons disappeared and were later found dead. Some woman runs that outfit now with an underboss. She keeps a low profile.

It's not like we keep a family tree on all the mafias. Even

if we did, it would never be complete with all the illegitimate kids. Some of the men have a way of remaining under the radar. We only learn of some men with inflated egos who flaunt themselves, but by then, they have been caught by the law or killed by an enemy.

**24**

---

# VALENTINA

Massimo is gone for what seems like hours, but looking at my new watch, it's only been fifteen minutes. As promised, he returns from his meeting, entering the vehicle and sitting beside me.

Micro begins to drive.

"I've been invited to Dante's wedding," he announces. "It will be a small affair in Juliet's hometown, so you'll see more of Tuscany, and we'll have a nice weekend."

He sits quietly, but the smug smile tells me something else went on in that meeting.

Everyone has secrets, and Massimo is no different. It's as if his entire life is smoke and mirrors. He runs here and there, and after a week with him, I still have no idea what he does when he leaves the house.

Could it be plausible deniability to protect me? It could be a mistress, but I don't think he'd have enough energy after going twice in one night with me. He's ruined me. There is no way another man could meet or exceed the sex we share or the heights we ascend.

Afterward, before I drift off in the darkness of night, I

often wonder if he would have picked me if it wasn't for the tattooed creep at the auction. The contract I once resented is now my saving grace as I don't want to lose him. He has to marry me, but my pride would prefer he marry me for love, not obligation.

I hate when the girls in the shop check him out, and I know they wish he were with them. Who wouldn't? I used to be that way watching Laura with Marco, not that Marco is as hot as Massimo, not even close. It's just that she had someone to love her and see her for who she really is, to share things with, and I didn't. I'm tempted to call Laura and share my sexual awakening, but I'm afraid it will break the spell if I share it with anyone.

I can't imagine my life without him. Yes, he's killed people, but he's also complex, and like me, he's beginning to enjoy life. I catch him smiling when he's not looking at me, and sometimes when he is, we'll share a laugh, a quip, a commonality that tells me we're not all that different.

I love it when Massimo chases me through the house and up the steps, laughing hysterically. It's fun playing games that young lovers do. On other evenings, he teaches me how to play chess, or we'll watch a show together.

He brings me flowers, and there are so many Samira and I put them in vases throughout the house. I'm beginning to get attached to fresh flowers, not just because they're pretty but because he put thought into them and picks them up himself.

He comes home every night even if he has to run back out. When he comes home late, he doesn't reek of alcohol. We're in our bubble, the place where magic happens and life is good. But after every high, comes a humbling low, and I can tell we're both thinking about it without discussing it.

Papa's funeral was private, only family and low key. I

urged Giovi to hold off on the service, but he said it would show he was weak and unprepared to step into Papa's shoes.

He's still living with Mama, and I don't see that changing even if he gets married. He said the bosses and appropriate command staff have all paid their homage and allegiance, but something in his voice concerns me.

I'm not sure Giovi is telling me the truth or what he thinks I want to hear. Surely, he understands I'm not as naïve as I used to be.

It's Valentine's Day and time for Dante and Juliet's wedding. The ceremony is on a Saturday so we're spending the weekend, booking an Airbnb in Tuscany.

We're on the way, Massimo at the wheel of his blue Italian sports car. Savio and Micro follow in the SUV.

"I hope Juliet's wedding goes off without a hitch this time."

"Me too." Massimo turns the radio station to one with only Italian music.

He seems nervous, which is out of character. Something is up.

"Dimmi?" I ask.

"Tell you what?"

"Why are you so flustered today? I haven't known you long, but you're not yourself today."

"Mm, well. I need your absolute trust."

"Okay,"

"No, it's not that simple, Valentina. Our lives and the lives of others depend on this."

"I'm good. I can do this. I mean, we're going to be married, so bring it."

I love American movies, and not all their phrases can be translated.

"Bring it. Bring what?" He chuckles, having never heard it used before.

"Tell me. I can handle it," I plead.

He shifts into a lower gear as we're driving fast, and the road has a sharp bend. One mishap, and we're over the side of a rocky mountain.

"You ask who I am, who I work for. I work for my grandfather. He's in charge of all organized crime in Albania."

"Ah, that explains the house you live in."

"Yes, he doesn't have kids. Something else you should know, I decided to infiltrate the Micheli family a few months ago. One of our important men was breaking rules inside their territory."

He glances at me to make sure I'm keeping up.

"Got it." I can't stop looking at him.

I never want to wake up with anyone other than him. When he looks into my eyes and caresses my body like he adores me, I forgive him for avoiding me in the beginning.

Now that I'm on the verge of getting answers and learning who he is, I'm all ears.

"So, our guy, Argon, was murdered on a ski vacation shortly after I left you in Rome. When Argon died, I suspected the Michelis. They had a motive, but now I know it can't be them because the same drug was planted on Dante and was used on your father. Plus, why would Dante, who obviously loves Juliet, ruin his own wedding?"

I gasp. "So, this is a bigger issue than just my father..."

"Yes, I think so. But who? Both victims are from two different families. I don't understand it. It's like a machine with many moving parts."

"Sounds to me like someone didn't want the wedding to take place. And you had arranged for me to be there?"

"Yes, I thought it would be a special event, and you would be my date—so to speak. Your dad wasn't supposed to attend the actual reception. He was just supposed to deliver you to me, so that means the killer had to know he planned to attend."

"Yes," I agree, hanging on to the door handle as we skid around a corner. "So, who knew my dad would be there other than you and, I assume, Savio?"

"The wedding planner, the pilot of the jet, and anyone he may have confided in," he suggests.

"Papa had a rat in his family? Impossible. I mean, he had cameras and listening devices everywhere." It's like he could read everyone's mind, so he probably had everyone bugged. "That explains how he knew when Laura and I were planning to sneak out on our sleepovers as kids. Papa knew things for sure."

We make the bend, and the map in the car shows we are close to our destination.

"So, how did you get invited to this wedding a second time?"

He smiles. "Double jeopardy."

I giggle as he pulls up in front of a small house, an Airbnb.

"This looks very nice, Massimo."

"Say it again."

"What?" I give him a questioning look but smile.

"My name."

"Why?"

"I like to hear it from you," he says, leaning toward me as we unlock our seatbelts.

"Massimo," I whisper, not sure why I'm taunting him by trying to sound sexy.

"Um…" His lips cover mine, and I can't help but yield to him. My eyes close, my tummy gurgles, and a knock on my window makes me jump.

"What the fuck?" I burst out, frightened that a bird or something worse hit the car.

Massimo chuckles, and it's the only reason I don't get worked up about it. Then I see Savio looking at us through the window and making a goofy face.

"Let me guess, he's single."

"You're catching on, my little bluebird."

I like the way he says it. He makes it sound endearing. Is he capable of love, or am I dreaming? How could he love me? I can't dress worth a shit. He had a stylist work with me, but I'm still challenged. I can walk in heels. That's a given for every Italian woman. But no matter how I try, I'll never be Sophia Loren.

Savio and Micro park beside us and grab our overnight bags. Massimo surprised me with a set of luggage to match his, which is thoughtful. I'm told it's an expensive brand.

We check in under his name Rizzo, and it's funny because his name on the mail says Romano. I understand why he told me the truth about himself. I'm involved in both lives indirectly, but today, the two worlds collide.

"How are you introducing me at the wedding if we're the opposing mafia?"

"I'll say you're my fiancée whom I met and fell in love with at his ill-fated wedding, the one you weren't invited to." He shrugs and laughs. "I have no clue."

"We aren't crashing this wedding, are we?"

"No, in fact, I expect there will be business going on, and that might be why I was invited."

"Business?" I ask, drawing my finger across my neck.

"Oh, stop, it's not that dramatic. As I said, that would then make it two weddings with dead bodies. I think we're safe."

I'd be more relaxed if I knew for sure his life wasn't in danger. No doubt I'm aging myself with all this worry about his gorgeous ass.

"I need a drink, let's have something. Champagne, can we do that?"

He turns to me as we enter our master bedroom, his eyes taking in every thought and emotion, and he nods. He understands I need it for my anxiety.

"Sure." With no room service to call, he asked Micro to get us some items at the local store and grab some snacks.

It's sweet that he thinks to put something on my tummy before alcohol, as I'm such a lightweight.

"I guess we should get dressed," I suggest, putting my luggage on the bench at the end of the bed and opening it.

"Yes, we have just over an hour."

## 25

## MASSIMO

Valentina's eyes are wide with anticipation at the turn of every corner on the curvy road to get here. I enjoy the fact she's not cooped up at the mansion. She actually has me singing the latest Italian pop tune in the car with her. I'm glad none of my men are around. She's lighthearted, and it's contagious.

She reminds me of my younger, more carefree days, and maybe life's responsibilities have weighed me down to where I'm not as much fun as I used to be. Being with her reminds me that growing older doesn't mean I have to live in solitude or loneliness like Grandfather. Perhaps the wisdom he's gained over the years will help me from making mistakes he's regretting in his old age.

We arrive at the rented house an hour or so after we leave home. I let the men check the place before letting her follow behind them. She immediately checks out our bedroom suite. The house is quaint. We have everything we need for a secluded getaway except groceries, and our privacy is lacking due to the continued presence of security, who are in the house next to ours.

I pull out the bag with all our fancy clothes, and Valentina begins to dress. I sneak looks at her as she changes her skimpy panties and uses a beige bra instead of the black one she wore here under her dark sweater.

I methodically pull up my dress pants and don an undershirt, but I can't stop staring at her as she steps into the vintage cocktail dress. It's a rare dress. I hired a saleswoman to track it down for her. She saw it in a magazine and loved it so much I thought it would make her happy.

I have her engagement ring hidden in my luggage, hoping that I'll have an opportunity to give it to her this weekend. We take Valentine's Day seriously as we started the celebration born out of love for our country, and now it's an international day to celebrate love.

I hope we'll be able to travel more and eventually have a kid to carry on the family name. The issue is, what name will he carry?

My adoptive dad has a son of his own. The Michelis, well, I'm not sure it's safe to come out of that closet yet, and if I did, I'd then be a fourth son, but not a full-blooded son. I'd never be looked at as one of the original three as I'm dirty born. The love child that lived in exile with my mother's clan. A child they don't know about, or so I presume.

"Oh, Valentina, I forgot to tell you. I made some inquiries regarding a job for you."

"Doing what?" She sits on the bedroom bench, strapping her shoes around her dainty feet. She finishes before she cocks her head up to look at me, her blue eyes showing excitement through her long eyelashes.

"And what would that be?" She sits up and watches me puttering around the room.

"Working as a counselor with children at the hospital in

Florence. It'd be like play therapy, and you'd be able to help them without sitting in an office unless it's needed."

I add cuff links to my shirt's holes, use the cologne, and reach for my jacket.

"Really?" Her face is bright, and there's a twinkle in her eye. A twinkle I wished was for me.

"Yes, they have good security, and I think you'd like it. You said you wanted to work. You can meet with them when we get back."

"Oh my, this is incredible." She stands and takes a tiny jump of glee. "I never dreamed I'd be able to have a normal life." She crosses the room, throws her arms around my neck, and kisses me.

I don't care how badly she crushes my dress shirt. It was a wrinkle-free shirt a second ago. It would have pissed me off with other women and led to an argument whereby the woman would tell me how arrogant I was.

"Hum," I mumble, taking her sweet, sweeter kisses because she offered them to me on her own accord. I'm not going to spoil the moment and tell her I'm donating money to cover her salary and new equipment to the children's ward. The donation is something no one but my accountant needs to know about. I don't do charity for charity's sake. There has to be something for me.

That's how the mafia makes a profit. No one gets something for nothing. But if this gives Valentina her dream of independence and a job she's always wanted and helps kids in the process, so be it.

I return her kiss. My cock hardens thinking about last night's hot sex as I slide my arms around her now, our kiss deepening. So this is what it's like giving a woman something she wants. I guess I get affection in return. Interesting. What's more perplexing is that I like it.

I lean into her, intending for her warmth and attention to lead to more, but she gently presses my chest an inch off her breasts. "Oh, I guess we'd better get going," she says, as she knows we don't have time for a quickie.

I turn to adjust myself in my pants as Savio snickers. Micro checks the directions and heads out to grab the SUV so we can ride together.

The irony of normal is lost on Valentina. We're the mafia's normal. As if anything about our expensive spa days, our unique home, and the luxuries we partake in like shopping and dining is normal. We pretend we're normal, but when people ask what we do, it's a lie. I try to keep things simple, as most big men do. There is always a price to be paid in the life we lead. Seldom are the solutions desirable or straightforward.

Valentina's never been on the streets. She doesn't grasp our world like other wives married to those under me. There is a hierarchy and pay scale differences. Valentina might have her friend Laura whom she can confide in. I remember the girl at the gala that must be her. They seemed inseparable. I wonder how Valentina could have been out of everyone's sight long enough to get to the garden without being missed that night.

I put an envelope inside my suit pocket for Dante. Valentina hands me the infamous necklace to put around her neck. I'm all thumbs. It's not because I can't do the task. It's that being so close to her does weird things to me. Her skin is softer than cashmere, and her body gives off a sweet smell, creating an elixir I'm addicted to.

I extend my arm so she can slip hers through mine and I escort her to the vehicle waiting outside. Her dark blue cocktail dress goes well with her icy blue eyes, and only I know how they hide the passionate woman behind them.

We arrive at the small restaurant in the village owned by Juliet's family. Savio and I exchange a look behind Valentina's back when we see the meat market sign next to it, the look that only a wise guy could appreciate.

Everyone's men are milling about, trying to be inconspicuous, as I was told Juliet's parents are in the dark about what Dante's family does, but the tabloids have strained their relationship with Dante since De Luca's murder.

We enter the rustic restaurant with wood beams overhead and all the tables have been arranged with fresh flowers on every table. A banner that says *Mr. and Mrs. Micheli* hangs over what I assume will be the reception area, as there is a cake table under it.

Soft music floats around us as well as what will be a flavorful prime rib that's cooking. It wafts into the room from the kitchen.

Tables set for eating are on one side of the room, leaving space for dancing later on the other side. It's far from what was planned last month, but it's homey. I like it.

A tiered dessert plate is filled with heart-shaped cookies dipped in red, white, and green striped frosting. It's homage paid to St. Valentine which started in ancient Roman times.

The cake is three tiers of chocolate covered in red frosting with swirls of frosting threaded like a ribbon around the individual handmade roses that adorn it.

A woman approaches us, she's shorter than Juliet and has a beautiful face without the need for the makeup she wears. Her brown hair is in a trendy blunt cut and she wears an elegant dark green dress. She must be in her late fifties, if I had to guess.

"You must be Massimo, I'm Mrs. Accordi." She takes my hand in hers and shakes it.

"Hello, so nice to meet you. This is Valentina."

Valentina smiles as the two exchange the proper Italian greeting of kissing cheeks.

"Welcome, have a drink at the bar. I hope you're hungry. Juliet's father is a chef and is cooking enough to feed the entire town." She smiles and excuses herself.

"She's nice," Valentina notes as we grab one of the many glasses of champagne. They all have a heart with Dante and Juliet's names inscribed on them.

"Cute glasses. This is a nice restaurant and I'm sure he does well here," she remarks.

"I heard he is a fourth-generation butcher, so be prepared for the best beef of your life," I whisper in her ear before giving it a nibble.

She giggles. "We're in public," she complains.

I know she wants more. I'll wait until later as my cock stirs in my pants. I slide behind my bride-to-be so she can feel my cock against her.

"You are so frisky all the time. You are a sex addict," she teases.

"Hm, and you aren't?"

"I didn't say that. Maybe I should be happy that I got you and not that goon at the gala."

"Now you're seeing things my way," I reply as I move so I can plant a meaningful kiss on her lips.

It seems like we're getting along as if we're a couple who isn't forced to marry. But my trust in women is limited, more so since Mother's confession, and I still have to remind myself that as much as I make concessions for Valentina, she might still be a flight risk.

Family ties run deep and none more so than Sicilians. For all I know, her brother could be working on a way to steal her back if he didn't have his hands full right now.

"I arranged for your interview when we return home,

but no more talking of work this weekend, it's Valentine's Day, and we're celebrating."

"Fine." She makes it sound like a protest, but she enjoys our nights of passion as much as I do, judging from her moans and numerous screaming orgasms as she comes over my cock.

"We must not disappoint St. Valentine, and we need to make sure this wedding works out for these two. They deserve it," she says before taking a sip of champagne I obtained from the bartender. The room fills up, and there are chairs in another section of the building for us to sit for the ceremony. Chairs that have red bows tied to their back.

Dante and his brother enter from a back door, all dressed in tuxes. An older woman is with them and I'm assume it is the reclusive Mrs. Micheli. Her hair is a shiny platinum color, which is the newest trend. Her hair is wavy, coming to the top of her shoulders. She's about five-five in height, with dark brown hair and a curvy figure. She's talking to her sons, and they are bantering back and forth as they enter the building. It sounds like they get along like a big, happy family, which might not have happened had they known about me years ago.

I marvel at how one event can alter a person's life. One lie, one affair, one child. Secrets that may last forever or come out at the most inopportune time. I'm torn. Since my mother told me of my father, I've been wanting to meet them, and now that the moment has arrived, I'm looking into a different world. It's not better or worse than my own, just different, and I'm torn on whether I should keep the secret forever or find a way to bring out the truth without destroying both of our families.

Did my mother's guilt get to her, or in her sickness, was she reminiscing about Aldo and wondering if things might have been different? I can't ask her personal questions like that.

"Are you okay?" Valentina puts her hand on my arm and draws me back to the present.

"Sure, just taking in the members of the families."

The Michelis notice us and make their way to introduce themselves.

"You must be Massimo." Mrs. Micheli extends her hand.

"Nice to meet you; this is Valentina," I reply, and they exchange a hello.

"This is Sal, and this is Dante." Marchello continues to announce each family member until we are all shaking hands.

"So nice to meet you. I thought Tommaso would be here."

"He and his wife had a touch of the flu and weren't able to make it. Trust me, Tommaso would never skip an event with free liquor or beer," Sal chuckles.

"Congratulations, Dante." I nod to him.

"Thank you. Glad you could make it."

"Wouldn't miss it. This is Valentina." The men give her a quick kiss of greeting.

A woman who moves with the stealth of a predatory cat slips behind Sal and wraps her arms around him. She gracefully clasps her hands around his neck and holds herself against him.

She's easy on the eyes with a muscular body judging from her developed shoulders and strong looking back. I catch a glimpse of it as she turns to grab a glass of champagne off a tray passing by. She wears her dress as a functional accessory with a slit up one side; it's red and has a deep V cut in the front, adding to her femininity as her breasts are perfectly aligned in it. Without her impeccable updo of her ashy-blonde hair, she would otherwise be mistaken for an MMA fighter. I heard she boxes.

I'm dying to know her story and how she and Sal met. Sal owns the bar Argon pissed around in, and I'm sure it's a front to launder money. I heard from Tommaso she is the beautiful Francesca, and she flexes her fingers possessively on Sal's arm. I peg her to be in her late twenties, lithe on her feet, and she's surveying the room as if she's a professional. But of what?

She has tear-drop diamond earrings and a gold necklace filled with princess-cut diamonds. Her look confuses me, as her beauty and practicality are combined. Could she be their bodyguard? Is she casing the joint? Her lovely smile threw me off guard as I anticipated she'd be cold and blunt.

"I'm Francesca. So nice to meet you both." She smiles and greets us as she continues to caress Sal's hand. I'm sure they're in love, but she doesn't bear his ring.

She is like a cobra behind her piercing green eyes, ready to strike anyone who would hurt her or Sal. All her moves appear to be deliberate, even professional, as she came to round us up. The wedding is about to commence, and there are a few others in the room whom I don't know and assume they are bosses that are important to Dante or other family members. Some may belong to Juliet's side.

I'm confused by Francesca's behavior. Sal grabs her, making a joke about her always working and that we're all safe due to the secret location and last-minute timing of the affair.

Marchello moves closer to me. "So, I see we have the same dress shoes."

I look down, sure enough, we do. What are the odds?

"Okay, if we have the same watch, I'm leaving," I joke.

"I'm using an older one, vintage. . . classical. It seemed

fitting for a simply elegant day, timeless." We chuckle at the pun seeing as how it is a wedding on St. Valentine's Day, the most romantic day of the year.

"That is so true." Prende joins Sal. "We were married before the holiday in December, and I did all the flowers for both events."

"You are incredible. I'll have to make sure to use you for my wedding and special affairs," Valentina says.

"Oh, you're engaged?"

"We don't want to take away from the bride and groom, so let's not talk about it now. Today is Juliet's day," I add, and we excuse ourselves only to run into Juliet's mother again.

It's a small affair with few people to talk to, or in our case, move away from so we don't disclose any unintentional information that could land us in hot water.

Mrs. Accordi mentions the nice day and hopes we aren't bored in her small town.

"Oh, no," Valentina reassures her. "It's a nice town, and the drive was incredible. How is the bride? Nervous?"

"After the last affair, yes. Now she's fretting over every little hair on her head. We should be on time as long as her father leaves the rest of the cooking to the staff." She excuses herself again. I presume to get everyone rounded up for the ceremony.

"I love this town, it's so relaxing," I say.

"Yes, but I bet Juliet has become accustomed to life in Florence. She likes working for Dante's company," Prende adds.

"I'm sure, and don't forget she has Dante, the most eligible bachelor in Tuscany." Francesca smiles.

"Funny, I thought you were." Valentina smiles at me, and it's times like this my heart beats faster and I feel invincible.

Is she happy to be out of the mansion, or is she happy to be with me?

She's grown on me over the past weeks. Not that I didn't have months of wet dreams and masturbating while thinking of her. Not all men would do that. Some would hit the massage parlors or find a one-night stand, but I haven't thought of another woman since I saw her outside the museum.

It was my lucky day to be at the right place at the right time to see her, then to find out she was the daughter of the man who owed us money made it even more fortuitous. A deal had to be made.

I'm counting my lucky stars as they say that I went back for one last look at her and saved her in the garden. I hope this weekend will be lucky for me again. I want her to wear my ring so everyone in the world will know she's mine.

We've moved to where we're standing with other guests waiting, and a handsome gentleman is beside me, gray hair, built, definitely ex-military, I saw him near Dante at the botched wedding.

"Massimo." I offer my hand.

"Riccardo."

Okay, not that big on social skills. "You're with the Micheli family?"

"Yes, always, I knew their father as well." He has the stance of a soldier and is in terrific shape for a man who is in his mid-forties.

"Oh, really. I heard he was a good man."

"He was. Did you know him?"

"Sadly, no." It hit me that he would be here today if he was still alive, and because he's not, there is a sadness in my heart. I would love to have met him. In fact, I might have learned of him earlier if anything were different, maybe if he wasn't married or if he was divorced. My life might have been different if Mama had told him about me.

The music changes, and a cute American girl, her maid of honor, holds a small bouquet of red carnations and red roses as she walks down an aisle flanked on both sides by dozens of rose petals.

Next is Juliet, who slips her arm through her father's. She's wearing a wedding gown rumored to be made by a fashion designer for her ill-fated wedding in January. The long train is covered with hand-sewn beading that matches those on the bodice. It has the vibe of the 1940s, with the A-line shape, fitted but not tight around the waist, made of white taffeta. Tje sheen sets off her olive complexion, dark black hair, and eyes. Her hair is braided in an intricate updo as she walks proudly into the room.

Her mother has tears in her eyes, watching her walk towards the altar, where she joins her maid of honor and her future husband at the mini altar.

The photographer is snapping pictures like crazy, and there is a second person taking pictures, many women have their cellphones out for the same reason.

The priest performs the short ceremony, as it's not a formal Mass, but enough to satisfy the court of law and the Catholic Church, even without a church steeple over us.

After the formality and late into the night, the men meet at a table for cognac and cigars. I'm invited.

"I hear you're doing good work, Massimo." Dante kicks off the information meeting.

"Thank you."

"We wanted to see if you knew anything about De Luca, seeing as how you are with his daughter tonight."

"I can understand your concern." I pull up a chair and take a freshly poured drink. "I assure you it's coincidental."

"I'm sure. Otherwise, you'd have a hit on you," Sal chuckles.

"What is that story and how she and her father ended up at our reception last month?"

"Luciano was delivering her to me there, it was just an exchange as we met in Rome at a gala, an arranged marriage, so to speak. I spoke to the wedding planner, and she said it's no problem getting them in for that."

Dante ponders this for a moment. "That fucking wedding planner keeps coming up. She was in the wind before all hell broke loose."

"I wanted to protect Valentina as that was her father, and I had no clue what was going on and if her life was in jeopardy." This isn't a lie. I was concerned.

"And what was Fitore doing there?" Dante looks down his long nose at me as his head is tilted over his right shoulder, trying to connect the dots.

Here's where Grandfather fucked me. He met with them over that fucking black book, and now they know who he is, and everyone saw him there. He also managed not to be locked in the room with the rest of us.

"That is one I don't have an answer for. I don't know why he was there. It might look bad on me now, but he's my grandfather. He told me afterward he was getting to know his business associate."

The men fall silent. Minds are thinking. I don't know if this will help me as the minutes turn into hours, and my guards lie low outside. I can't panic.

"And what business do they have?" Sal asks.

"Ironically, it's family business."

"Your family business. What would an Albanian grandson of a don be doing working for me?" Dante asks.

"I did it to keep an eye on Argon; he was fucking up with

your bars, and I wanted to protect him. Then he ended up dead on vacation, but I don't think you guys did it. Since he died of the same drug as De Luca, I'm trying to figure out who killed them both. It has to be the same killer, right?"

"Yes." Francesca joins the table and stands behind Sal. "We want to know who framed Dante."

"I haven't learned much of De Luca's operation; they owed us money, and I have a feeling someone inside his house is stealing from him. That's why I paid him a visit in Rome. We made things right, and it bought him the time he needed to find out who was making him look bad. Then he died."

"His underboss would have the most to gain, Gambino." Dante sips his drink.

"No, De Luca has a son he's primed to take over. Giovi."

"Wait, Gambino was in the same hotel with Argon," Sal says. "What are the odds he's at both events? The murder of Argon sets Dante up to look guilty, as does the murder at your wedding."

"Who was near you that could have planted that vial on you?" Francesca asks Dante.

"It's not like we haven't been over this a million times in the past month, guys, it was my wedding day, I had a few drinks, and the wedding planner looks guilty as hell. We just need to know who the fuck she really is."

"What do you mean?" I ask.

"Her ID says she's Gabriella Loren, but that's not her name, and we need to find out her real name," Marchello explains.

"And, while we're on the topic of who's who tonight," Dante stomps out his cigar, "why should we not take your life for infiltrating our business? It makes sense, as it just so happens we wanted Argon dead to send a message to your pompous grandfather. He's such an ass. We have to protect our own, but you in our ranks is inexcusable."

The way Dante delivers his words is that of a killer: calm, no fuss, emotionless.

"True. However, I've done nothing wrong. I was looking to find information on Argon, and then De Luca died. I was looking for an out after I met Valentina. It was dangerous to do what I did, even a bit impetuous. But I want to get to the bottom of both murders as I'm engaged to De Luca's daughter, and her brother should be the next in line with the Cosa Nostras, not Gambino."

"What are you not telling us?" Francesca asks.

Hm, one killer to another knows tells, and she read something on my face.

"Like what?" I play it off, hoping I'm wrong.

"You look like Marchello, the two of you in the room together—it's like watching fucking twins. You have the same mannerisms. How old are you?"

"Twenty-six."

"I'm twenty-six," Marchello exclaims and coughs on his cigar smoke.

"Holy fuck," Dante mumbles. "You're our half-brother, aren't you?"

**26**

———

# VALENTINA

I notice Massimo has been with the guys at their table making guy-talk. It's not like I haven't seen it before.

The girls are all taking pictures and talking as we finished eating an hour ago and the dancing is subsiding. Mostly only immediate family is left. I'm lonely and step out front to call my brother. I see Savio and Micro hanging around in the cold night, so I'm safe.

"How are you?"

"There's been some Molotov cocktails going off in the streets. It's not safe down here. Mama stays home and we have everything delivered."

"Oh shit. Giovi, you need us."

"I want you safe, you can't do anything. I have to try to keep Papa's legacy. You know how it is."

What he's saying is this is a game that isn't over until he or his opponent is dead.

"What is your plan?"

"To stay alive."

"Don't joke." But, in the face of death that's so close, I can understand him being glib as strange as it sounds.

"I think Papa knew who was stealing from him, that's why he was murdered. He made him look bad and then he died, unable to exonerate himself. It's a brilliant plan, I just don't know who is behind this yet. I'll find out who was skimming from us."

"That's unbelievable." And now I know why Papa sold me the way he did. Of course, Massimo would have plenty of money to walk away with anyone that night.

"Tell me about it," Giovi says. "I have a loyal army around me and we just have to find the man behind the thugs running through the streets."

"Oh, Giovi, I'm so sorry."

"Don't be sis, I love you. I'll be fine."

"I love you too. I think Massimo can help you. He's incredibly wealthy."

"And what if his grandfather, the Don of the Albanian mafia, is in on this plan?"

"I don't think that's true, but, I don't know. I'm not privy to all of Massimo's dealings but, his grandfather has been on his nerves recently. He only mentions it when I ask what's wrong when we play chess."

"You, chess?"

"I know, right? I love Florence. I'm getting a life."

"You sound happy," my brother says.

"I think I am." I smile into the cool night. Massimo makes my newfound life more meaningful, and the job shows he's listening to me and wants me happy.

"Good, enjoy. Don't worry about me. You know how hard-headed Sicilian men are."

"Don't I?" I tease. "I love you, Giovi. I better get back to the wedding we're attending."

"Go, talk soon."

I wave to Savio and Micro, who nods in return as they

rub their hands after pulling their jackets closer to themselves.

As I enter the restaurant, I'm immediately aware that something has changed. The air is charged, and the men have been joined by Francesca and Prende. Curiosity gets the best of me.

I walk cautiously and listen to see if anything is being said before I officially arrive.

"Hey, is everything okay?"

"I'm just taking in the fact that we have a brother we never knew," Marchello says.

"I have proof—the adoption papers," Massimo states.

"That's not necessary. In fact, I think we've all known for some time that our father could have had a kid out there with as many women as he had over the years. He hid it from Mama. Maybe she pretended not to know."

"So where does this leave us?" Sal asks.

"We'll have to break the news to Mama; I'll do that, but not tonight." Dante drains his drink.

"Fuck, what is it with weddings?" Dante asks.

"The night's not over yet, maybe you shouldn't test fate," Marchello says.

"They figured out who I am." Massimo looks up at me. "What you didn't know was that I've been working under-cover so to speak in their syndicate to keep tabs on one of my bosses who was in charge of moving our money around, Argon, who was murdered in the Alps."

"Oh." I must look like I'm going to faint as Massimo stands and helps me to the chair.

Juliet comes to the table. "Hey, everyone is leaving and," she takes in our faces, "what happened?"

"I'll tell you later," Dante promises.

"Let's call it a night. What are you doing tomorrow, Massimo?" he asks us.

"Resigning."

The men chuckle.

"Let's meet in the morning for brunch when we're sober, and we can go over things together. I'm sure we can find this Gabriella Loren," Francesca suggests.

"Who's that?" I ask.

"We think she's behind the murders of Argon and your father. We just don't know why," Massimo says.

"I don't know much about the men murdered, we're so far south. I see the news, but I don't know Argon except he worked for Massimo."

"He was also Prende's dad," Massimo states.

"Oh, I'm sorry, Prende, you're married to Marchello?"

"Crazy, but true. Long story." She smiles as she cuddles up to her husband sitting at the round table.

"We need to know who would want to sabotage Dante's wedding. I mean, maybe Argon's murder was an outlier. A crime of opportunity? Or just to make Dante look guilty before the bigger kill? She might be using Argon's murder to cover up the real reason for the second murder," Francesca thinks out loud.

"Who would want you to not be married?" I ask.

All eyes at the table focus on me.

"No idea. My father's dead, and my mother was unknown, presumed dead. I was adopted," Juliet states, "but my adoptive parents don't know I know."

"Seems to be a trend of that, I only found out myself that my dad adopted me," Massimo chuckles.

"Yeah, we need more alcohol or sleep," Sal states. "My head is swimming."

"It's a good question," Dante speaks at last as he runs his

hand over his chin in thought. "We never locked down where Juliet's mother is buried, but that was what we were led to believe. Besides, why would she hide all these years and surface now?"

"Because she can, maybe the reason she hid has been removed."

"I'll ponder that. It's a new perspective." Dante stands. "Until morning then." He hugs Massimo.

This is huge coming from him. Massimo is accepted.

We all say our good nights and we head back to our little house for the night.

By the time we get to bed, I ask Massimo what all transpired at the table.

Now that all the secrets are out, we might be able to work together to find out who killed my papa.

Massimo's phone dings.

"Ugh. I don't want to work."

"It might be important at this hour."

He picks up his phone. "Just pictures from one of my bosses from when Argon was murdered."

"Open them."

"You're a bit pushy," he teases.

"Well, if it holds a clue to my father's death, I want to know."

"Fine." He shares his phone with me, scrolling through the pictures.

"Hey, I know that one." I point to a man in the background of a picture.

"Who is it?"

"That's Gambino, Papa's underboss who would be in control at his death if not for Giovi."

"Fuck. Have you talked to your brother recently?"

"Tonight, he said he has loyal men around him and

there are Molotov cocktails going off in streets near Papa's businesses. Nothing major has happened. They're being as safe as possible."

"Shit, no telling who's on Gambino's side, and he must have been stealing from your father too; your father was in debt to us, and if he stole from your father, he's got money to finance a war. He must have been planning this for some time."

"Impossible. How could he pull that off? Papa knew everyone. Sicilians don't talk. No one would raise a hand against Papa."

"How close is he to your father?"

"He's like a brother, I call him Uncle."

"That makes it all the more plausible. He would have known where your father was and weaknesses in his deals to steal from him. He used your father's trust against you all."

"I have to call my brother."

"Text, they might have his calls bugged."

"Fuck, I never thought of that. Shit. A month off the island, and my brain goes to mush."

"No, I think it's hormones."

I pretend to punch him in his arm.

He laughs. It's nice after the stressful night he's had and knowing he could have been dead tonight if things didn't play out perfectly.

I text Giovi the information that Gambino is the culprit, and he says he's on it.

"Okay, that's done, but my brother will need help. We don't know who else is involved in this."

"We'll figure it out in the morning. Go to sleep, little bluebird." He turns out the light and pulls me to him. I take comfort in his arms and realize how much I love being in them and that he protects me. Even before he knew me, he protected me.

I drift off wondering if Gambino sent someone after me at the museum. Surely he would have known Papa would have been there as Mama and I worked on the invitations for a month.

My head hurts from thinking. I fall asleep, but it's short-lived as I worry about Giovi.

"ARE THOSE BIRDS CHIRPING?" Massimo murmurs as he pulls the pillow over his head.

"You mixed alcohols," I scoff.

"It's a guy thing, besides, it might have turned out to be my last supper if Mama didn't tell me they were my relatives."

"Yeah, that was insane. I mean, it's cool you were a love child."

I get up and bring him painkillers from my makeup bag, give them to him, and he downs them without water.

He pulls me to him, rolling me over. My back is on the mattress.

"I thought you had a headache," I tease, feeling his hard cock on my thigh.

"Hm. You're the cure." He nuzzles my neck. I squeal as his chin is scruffy without a shave, and it tickles, but I'm excited at the same time.

Light is coming in the window as he slips my silky nightie off my right shoulder, kissing it as he does so, then he slips the left side down and nibbles my neck and my shoulder and I reach for his cock, grabbing it, and rubbing my hand up and down his shaft.

"Mm." He continues to undress me and once my nightie is off, his finger traces my jawline and ends on my mouth, where his finger slips in, and I suck it.

I flip over and kneel over him as I take his hard cock in my mouth and suck on it as he moans in pleasure. I circle my tongue around the head of this shaft and take him in my mouth, all the way, his cock touches the back of my throat.

His buttocks rise off the bed. He pulls me up so that my breasts are on his chest. His lips find mine and I meet his urgency with my own. I'm hot. I have to have him.

I slide my right hand down his torso, feeling his muscles, and grab his ass hard, digging my nails in.

His hand now holds my chin as he focuses on my eyes for a second before he flips me again. He grabs my wrists and holds them over my head as he licks one nipple, sucks on it, and grabs my breasts so hard it hurts, but the hurt gives way to pleasure.

"Ah." I writhe beneath him. I want his throbbing cock to fuck me now but he pauses instead.

"Not yet, bluebird."

He buries his mouth between my breasts and then moves over to suck my underarms which ramps up the anticipation. It's as if a cord on my orgasm has been opened and is dying to be released. The man is a sexual genius.

He sucks my other underarm and with one hand on my wrists and the other on my buttock, he grabs it, and as I moan, he finally enters me, slowly.

He's driving me insane with passion. I want all of him. I want him now, but he makes me wait.

I'm helpless under him; he's in control.

I want to scream for him to fuck me, but his lips cover mine, stifling my words.

He plunges deeper into my pussy, a pussy that can never

have enough of him. He moves faster and faster, pacing me so I don't climax too soon.

He lets his hand fall away, releasing mine. I cling to him with both hands as I spread my legs for him, and he gains more traction. I grab the headboard with one hand to anchor myself and keep the other on him. His thrusts are so powerful we're both off the bed when we finally come together.

He falls on his back, catching his breath. My wrists hurt as he held them so tight, but I don't mind.

"Today will be a great day." He turns on his side to take me in, running a finger down my face as if he's making a sculpture of me.

I wonder if he will be going on a trip that I don't know about, and inwardly I wonder if I should be concerned.

"Yes, it is."

I love him but he's never come close to saying those words, and I don't know if he's capable of it.

"We've got to get going," I remind him. "We're to meet at the restaurant for brunch today."

"Yeah." He looks at his watch as he throws back the covers. "We're running late."

I wish we had more time together. He's been consumed by work.

"So, what was all that talk last night of murders?"

"Right, shit." He pulls on his pants. "We have to tell Dante about Gambino."

"Right." I tear through my suitcase as there's a knock on the door.

"Yes?" Massimo answers without opening the door.

"Just checking to see if you're alright," Savio answers.

"Yep, out in a few."

I find my jeans and a t-shirt I put on before pulling a

thick sweater over it. I grab thin socks and slip on the leather boots that go to my knees before zipping them.

Massimo is wearing the jeans I love that show off his ass and a designer long-sleeved shirt that repels the wind and a pullover sweater.

"What?" He catches me eyeing him.

"Nothing." I continue with my makeup.

"We need to go," he pushes.

"Okay." I quickly outline my lips and apply lipstick. No real Italian from Sicily is worth her salt without lipstick and heels.

My phone dings. Laura wants to know how I am. I text I'm busy and I'll check in later. She tries to keep me on, but I don't respond again. I have bigger issues on my mind.

Our guards walk us to the same place we were last night and it's a reunion as the men hug each other, and we sit at tables filled with tons of breakfast foods. Juliet is radiant.

"When are you getting engaged, Sal?" Dante teases.

"Wouldn't you like to know?" he quips.

"Marriage, who says I want marriage? Who has time? I have to run my business."

"What's your business?" I ask and everyone breaks out in a laugh.

"She's actually the daughter of Conti, and she took over after he died. Her brothers didn't have the head for it," Sal explains, but I notice that the Micheli men and Riccardo exchange a private look when he says it.

"I have my syndicate in Rome, so it's a lot of work for Sal and me. He runs bars and numbers up here. I have my base down there."

"That would be tough."

"We do have some information for you," Massimo

speaks in between his sips of juice and loading up on carbs and bacon.

"What's that?" Dante asks. "We've got to leave soon as we're going on an undisclosed honeymoon after this."

"I had Besnik email me pictures from his trip to the Alps and Valentina recognizes one of her dad's underbosses is in it, a man by the name of Gambino. Does that mean anything?"

"We know his name and he might have a wife named Ignazio," Francesca adds.

"No, that's his daughter. She's a weird one; our dog doesn't even like her," I add.

All eyes are on me again. "What? She's not a nice person."

"What does she do, who is she?" Francesca asks.

"She's his daughter. She's been gone for years. She only recently showed up, and I have no clue where she is; she's much older than me. There was some reason she left, like in Switzerland, and we have lots of our money there as their penalties for money laundering aren't as stringent as Italy."

"Daughter? What would Gambino's daughter be doing in our business?" Dante asks.

"No clue. Her father was close to mine, in fact, he'd be in line to be the next don."

"That's motive," Sal murmurs.

"Can you get a picture of her and maybe find out where she is so we can question her?" Dante asks.

"I can try."

"Great." Dante picks up the bill for everyone's breakfast, and then we all exchange phone numbers and say our good-byes as we head back with our men. They pack the SUV for our trip into Pranzano that's further inland. The sports car doesn't have much trunk space.

In the car, I text Laura and ask her if she's heard about Ignazio.

*No, why do you ask?*

*No reason, just wondering if Uncle Federico is okay. How was he with the funeral?*

*Fine. You should have been here.*

*I know, it couldn't be helped. You know how it is with an Italian man when he sets his foot down.*

*Well, you were missed.*

I know Papa's associates would note my absence, but more importantly, all the bosses showed up and pledged to my brother.

We're on the road, and the radio plays softly as we're still tired.

"It was a very nice wedding, even if Juliet had something big planned."

"I never imagined meeting my brothers like this."

"How was that for you?"

"Good, strange, but overall, I felt at home with them."

"I guess so. I mean, your family got bigger. How will your mother take it?"

"Speaking of her, I spoke to her the other day. I need to take you by to meet her."

"Oh." I'm surprised as he's never mentioned meeting his family before.

"I'm taking you to where the famous butcher of all of Italy is, he has his home restaurant, and butcher shop in Pranzano."

"Really?"

"Yes, in fact, he knows about everyone. Very Italian, and loves to wear the colors of our flag. As old as he is, he's on social media. Go figure." He chuckles.

"And his beef is amazing?"

"You've heard of him."

"Of course, he's traveled extensively, and he had a TV show. Mama loved to see him cook."

"Well, that's the surprise."

"Did I ruin it?"

"No."

"We're almost there."

"Are Savio and Micro behind us?"

Massimo looks in the mirror, "Yes, two cars behind."

"Okay."

"You okay?"

"I'm on edge. I feel we should be helping my brother."

"We're all working on it the best we can; if we win the war for him, he'll never be respected. That's how it goes."

"It doesn't mean I have to like it."

"True."

Massimo parks on a narrow side street in Pranzano with narrow streets and only local residents are out and about. We walk towards the butcher shop, and it's in the early afternoon when we arrive.

Motorcycles are racing through the hills as the motors hum in down shift and whine in high gear. A row of them come through the town, slower due to the pedestrians, and then they rev the engines into high gear as they roll out of town.

Walking through the center we pass by a monument of a blue cow and then the butcher shop with a charcuterie board out and tiny cups of wine for sampling.

Massimo waves at Dario, who is always talking to someone as he wears his apron and oversees his workers. We walk through the store to the restaurant that is equipped for lunch. We get the last table on the rooftop with plexiglass to break the wind coming in from the hills.

The view is amazing. We order wine and calamari before our beef burgers arrive, the ones he's famous for aside from his upscale restaurant across the street.

"This is divine," I mumble after my first bite.

"Yes, it is, so are you."

I can't trust my ears. He tells me I'm beautiful, but he never mentions love.

"Mm." I pretend I'm occupied with my food.

We drink wine and finish our burgers when he suggests we take a walk. He slips his hand in mine and we make our way through the town to the church at the end of the street. On the way back, we pause to overlook the scenic view down into a valley below us that is a vineyard in winter and the sun peaks out as if on cue.

I look at Massimo, who is holding a small box in his hand.

"I should have given this to you before." He pulls out a ring and takes my hand to slide it on.

I want to pull my hand away however, that would be rude. I don't want to piss him off.

"Why bother? I don't need a ring."

"You're mine. I even had it inscribed inside the band with our names."

"You bought me, but you can't buy my heart, Massimo."

The ring is on my finger, gorgeous, matching the necklace he gave me. But the magic is broken. I was a fool to think he'd fall in love with me. I might be a Principessa, and someone can pay for me, but it doesn't mean he owns me. He needs to learn the difference even if it comes at the cost of my lonely heart.

We return to the car, and I storm past him and climb into the SUV with Savio and Micro. They look confused but don't ask any questions other than what music I want and if I need anything.

WE ARRIVE HOME and it's late I drink plenty of water and go to bed with the TV on. Massimo arrives late and smells of alcohol. I pretend to sleep.

"Remember, you have your interview at the hospital tomorrow, and Micro will take you. Savio and I have work to do."

"Fine."

It's the first time we haven't touched since we first slept together.

## 27

## VALENTINA

Massimo left early this morning. The vacuum is running downstairs, so Samira must be here. She'll be mopping next. I have her routine down. It's hard to believe I've been here close to a month, and although Massimo might not love me, maybe I can use my mind and degree for something worthwhile.

I pull out a pantsuit. It's chic these days. Rain hits the bedroom windows and I wonder how Massimo and I will make up. If Samira's stories are true, I'm sure he's been through worse breakups.

He seemed upset enough to go out drinking, no doubt Savio took good care of him after we got home. Those two are inseparable.

Laura calls.

"I haven't heard from you; I wanted to make sure you're okay," she says.

I put the phone on speaker so I could dress.

"Yes, yes. Massimo planned a romantic side trip for us, then ruined it. I do have a nice engagement ring, though."

I pull on my undergarments and slip into the pantsuit, looking at my watch to make sure I'm not late and I'm good. I'm sure one of the guys has the car ready for me this morning. Massimo is always on top of my security.

"I have an interview today at the hospital in Florence. I think I can work with kids and be safe."

"Oh, that's so exciting. Good luck."

I plop down on the seat at my makeup table in the bathroom. Before I lift a brush, I look at the ring on my finger and pull it off. I turn it to see inside the band and there, it is, Valentina & Massimo. What the fuck does that mean?

I slip it back on. I can't deny I love the bling. God help me for being in love with my future husband, who seems to only love me for my body. Why buy me when he could have anyone? Sure, he helped Papa out, but look where that left Papa in the end. *Would he still be here if he didn't make a deal with the devil?* The devil with a heart of black lava like Mt. Etna.

Laura called him the devil. How did she know he was so dark? I found him to be different and interesting, and as the days together pass, I realized we bumped into each other, and his eyes drew me in. The fact is that I saw the same loneliness in themas I have in mine.

"Thanks, and how is Marco?" I ask as I apply foundation to my face.

"Fantastic, we're getting married in June, but it will be hot."

"June is good." I'm going through the motions as yesterday weighs heavily on my mind. Talking to Laura is good because I've been too occupied to be a good friend since I moved here.

"He rented a place a town over, not far from the water."

This strikes me as odd; he doesn't make that kind of money. Most Italians live in condos that are on top of each other. The area she's describing is individual units, not high rises. They've been refurbished and sold for lots of euros.

"That's quite the area."

"It's close enough to Mama and Papa, you know."

"Yes, I do."

"How are your folks?" Her father, Paulo, was one of Papa's bosses, it's how Laura and I got to be such good friends. Our fathers always got together when we were kids for family nights—the ones where 'the family' had a different connotation. We were kids. What did we know?

"Great, why do you ask?"

"I haven't seen them in forever."

"Yeah, but really, your brother is doing good, things are running like they should."

"Mm, no problems with my brother running operations?"

"Not that I know of. Papa goes to work like usual."

"Great, well, I'm heading out. Wish me luck."

"Luck."

I hang up and finish my handiwork with lipstick.

I pick up my dress pumps and slide them on my feet. Funny, Laura didn't mention any disturbances in the streets.

My phone buzzes; Micro is waiting in the car.

I grab my purse which has too many items in it and should be considered a health risk. I don't have time to change it, so I head down the gorgeous staircase like I'm the woman of the house.

"Samira, good morning."

She greets me. "Where are you going so early?"

"I have an interview at the hospital to work."

"Work? Massimo takes care of you."

"Yes, but I want something other than charity work, not that it's bad, I just need to feel needed." I choke back on tears that threaten to spill over my cheeks that my husband can be many things, but being a heartbreaker is his number one skill. Well, next to killing, obviously.

Damn it. I love him so much my heart breaks that he can't say it. Sure, he loves my body, but I'm more than a sex object.

"Well, good luck."

"Thank you. I'll see you in a few hours."

She closes the door behind me.

It's still raining, and Micro has an umbrella for me as he opens the car door.

"Thank you."

"No problem," he says in Italian and gets in to drive me downtown. He gives me the approximate time it will take and I'm golden. Now if I can nail the interview, I should have a job helping kids.

Micro drives with patience. If I weren't driven around most of my life, it would be a bit annoying.. Maybe it's just that I'm in a pissy mood due to Massimo. I wonder what he had going on today.

Micro parks at the hospital, and we enter, giving our identification and getting a pass in the form of a sticker on our shirt.

"I can't remember what floor," I flip through text from Massimo, looking for the information.

"Third floor is children," Micro hits the button.

"Thanks, how do I look?"

"Fantastic as usual." He smiles.

We get off the elevator. "I'll stand here, as the door is there," he points down the hallway.

"Great. I really think I'm fine. Massimo is a stickler for security."

"It's good to be that way," Micro agrees.

"Great, another soldier toeing the line." I head towards the doorway for my meeting as I look at the note in my phone, Mrs. Valeti.

When I get through the double wooden doors and see a handicap button to open them it makes me pause. This is a children's wing. Why do they need handicapped doors?

I push on through, and I'm in the middle of a children's play area. There are air hockey tables, an area for smaller kids with a pretend kitchen, and floor games. It hits home that aside from living in my mansion that was a prison. These kids have their own prison, which doesn't resemble mine.

I've been so thoughtless all these years, thinking about myself and what gala to go to that I've forgotten what real life is like for others. Others aren't healthy or wealthy.

These kids aren't privileged; they have health issues, and this is their world. These are their four walls, just like my room in Sicily was my four walls.

"You must be Valentina." A woman in her forties enters the room and shakes my hand I didn't even put out.

"Yes, I am." I finally realize she's my connection. "I'm here for the job as a counselor."

"Great, we need you. The kids can't use the playroom without a counselor here."

"Oh?"

She smiles and walks me around the open area. "This is the area for the toddlers, all age groups have their allotted time slot. The video games are on a cart, and it goes room to room for the kids in isolation, that's mostly popular with teenagers to seven-year-olds. Right now, we need someone with your early childhood development and counseling background to open the playroom and listen to the kids. Our policy is that the kids will talk and play, and you can give feedback to the parents that might help their quality of life."

It's gut-wrenching to imagine being sick at such a young age. How can I say no?

"The kids and their parents haven't been able to use this facility very much as we can't keep dependable staff with the required degrees for what we pay."

"Wow, so if a counselor doesn't show up, the kids can't play?" I'm still playing catch-up.

"Correct." Her face shows concern and I'm unsure if she thinks she scared me off or I generally grasp what she's saying. It's tragic that the kids don't get to have the equivalent of recess time that healthy kids get every day at school.

Everyone needs time to hit the reset button and just be. Just be free and carefree. A place to forget what needs to be forgotten and a place that makes them smile.

Isn't that what I'm doing here in Florence? I've escaped my room in Sicily and thought the mansion with Massimo was an even swap. But it's not. It's so much more.

I have a man who wants to make love to me at night, he even laughs at a funny movie with me as he holds my hand. Massimo took me on a road trip even though it might be dangerous and incidentally met his new family. So many of my family members are called that but aren't my family. I long to belong and have real family.

"That's a shame," I reply with shallow breathing. I can only imagine kids of all ages have been cooped up in their bedrooms on the floor for days on end due to staffing issues.

If I was a mother, I'd be livid. It's not fair to the kids. I know what being caged up feels like, and days when I watch life pass me by as Laura moves on and gets her happy ending with Marco, I'm sold to save my family.

These kids don't get half of what I've been given, or even a fraction of what I have now. And yet I still want more. Yet, these kids have something I don't.

Love. I want to be loved.

That's why Massimo's ring hurts. It's expensive and gorgeous, but I wouldn't care if it was a tab from a soda can. I want to hear him say he loves me. I want to know that he can return my love for him.

"Are you okay?" Mrs. Valeti asks.

"Oh, yes, I have a feeling the kids and I will get along very well."

"You came from a prestigious school, the salary isn't much, but we need you. Are you willing to be a part of the staff?"

"Yes, I'd like that very much."

As if it was planned, the door bursts open and in come mothers carrying toddlers in their arms. Some are in the arms of nurses.

"Wow." I smile, they are all so cute, some have IV poles being wheeled in and others are in their mother's arms, wearing caps on their bald heads. Most are in pajamas, but they all have a smile on their face coming into the room.

"Mrs. V, can we play now?" a boy of approximately four asks as he tugs on her skirt.

"Yes, Matteo, you can, I'll be here for a few hours. I'll play blocks with you in a minute."

"Thanks," he replies in Italian and darts off to the thick mats on the floor with roadways on them for their tiny cars to use.

"He's been in and out of the floor for a year. I can't say 'no'."

"Of course not." I smile.

"I'd like to meet with you again and get you started with the protocols we have to follow. Call it a formal orientation. Are you up to it?"

"Oh, I'm up to it, alright," I reply.

"Great, I'll have human resources call you and set up a day and time."

"Perfect." I take her hand in mine, and our eyes meet. "Thank you."

"I look forward to seeing you soon," she says and walks off to find Matteo, who's been patiently waiting for her.

I'm an emotional mess. Why wasn't the ring from Massimo enough? Maybe that's how he shows love. Did I screw it all up wanting too much from him? Is it over or can we work through it?

I wipe a tiny bud of moisture from the corner of my eye as I exit the playroom and bump into a large person.

I mumble excuse me, but he doesn't seem to hear, and he doesn't move.

"Follow me, and no one gets hurt," the voice sounds familiar.

I look up. "Ridolfo!"

"Your family needs you, it's urgent." He grabs me by the elbow that's holding my purse.

"What are you doing here? It's called a phone call, Ridolfo. I'm sure if Giovi needed me, he'd call."

"He wants me to bring you back. He doesn't know who he can trust."

I believe him. Although it's strange he knew I was here. "My brother doesn't know I'm here. And he didn't message me."

"I know, come with me." His grip tightens on my elbow. I

can't cry out and scare the kids. I move my arm in an attempt to get away, but it's futile.

He reaches for my purse, but I pull back, knowing I must protect my phone. I try to trick him by stepping back and sliding my purse down my arm.

"How did you know I was here?"

"Your phone, GPS."

"You're not on my GPS tracking anymore."

He shrugs. I wind up the purse, hitting him in the face, which catches him off guard for a second. I run towards my meeting spot with Micro at the elevator. My hopes are dashed as I see his feet as he's being dragged into a tiny room. The signage on the wall says blankets and sheets.

He's incapacitated, and his captor is none other than the infamous man with the neck tattoos. He lets Micro slump to the tiled floor before he pushes his feet in and closes the door.

"We don't want that to be you, do we?" His menacing voice strikes fear and anger in me.

There are times to fight, and there are times to go along with their plan and hope that the outcome will end in my favor. This is one of those times. I'm not armed, we've been caught off guard. I only hope Massimo can save me one more time.

"Tell me you didn't hurt him."

"He'll wake up with a bad headache." His snide smile makes my skin crawl. "I'm surprised a princess like you cares."

"You, who are you?"

"Your worst nightmare. Let's get going." His gruff Sicilian accent comes through like an unleashed Marvel villain on a surfboard.

"I'm not going anywhere with you."

Ridolfo moves behind me and my worst nightmare lunges towards me, and even though I kick and hit, I'm not strong enough to save myself. A cloth slips over my mouth and nose before I have a glimpse of the stairwell door opening.

"Ridolf..."

## 28

## MASSIMO

"**W**hat's up with you? What was the last thing you drank? You need to drink a beer or something."

Savio drives me to a store and buys Birra Moretti.

"I was thinking more along the lines of scotch, bourbon, hell if I know, but my head is killing me."

"This should help." My trusted friend hands me the cold beer, which, to my surprise, hydrates me immediately.

"Fuck, I forgot we used to do that in high school."

"Some habits never die. Which is more than I can say for you, man, you look like shit. What happened yesterday? You gave her the ring?"

"Yeah, thought she'd be happy."

"How can you fuck that up?"

"I don't know. Maybe she's too good for me. I thought I could buy her the world, like she's always wanted. She lived in luxury. I have more, I don't understand."

We get back in his black Mercedes.

"But what does she want?"

"A job, which I got for her, by the way, she should be

there now." I glance at my watch. "I expect she'll come around once she gets it. She wants freedom, this job will do that for her, and keep her under my roof."

Savio makes a short slap against my hurting head before we get in the SUV.

"What is she to you?"

"She's everything, or I wouldn't be so fucked up right now. What do you think?"

I buckle the seatbelt and lean my head against the door frame.

"Well, I think you should tell her that, do something that conveys that sentiment, don't you think?"

"I don't know how."

"Well, if you can run the organization, you can damn well keep a wife."

He's got a point.

"Italians, we're all supposed to be so romantic. Tuscany was great, and the reunion with my family, great."

"Your grandfather might not see it that way. By the way, your mother checked in with me as you've been absent."

"Thanks, yeah, I need to take Valentina there after we fix things."

"She has to want something you can't buy her possibly?" Savio is driving, and I think he's onto something as a single guy.

"Maybe, but I can't say it, I'm a hardened criminal, I can't love. The two don't go together."

"Everyone falls in love at some point."

"She's already a target. Do you know how many enemies I've made? My family?"

"It's how it goes. Where are we going?"

"I need to visit some contacts. We're working on a big deal of drugs, and it's a new seller. I'm leery."

"Makes sense. Maybe we should stick with who we know until we get this Gabriella you talk of."

"Oh, that bitch is so dead. Valentina's father didn't deserve to be taken out, and what a gutless shit, poison."

"I have the word out with our contacts and have her names flagged the best I can; we don't have control at all the borders, but we'll see if she surfaces. I have a hacker who's trying to track her bank accounts."

"Great."

I glance at my watch, surely it mocks me as Valentina should be home now. And yet, there's no word.

I hit a button, and her phone goes to voicemail, so maybe she's still mad at me.

"What's up?"

"She's never not returned a message to me, it's a rule. I'm calling Micro." Micro's phone goes to voicemail. "Fuck. Turn around, we have to go to the hospital, step on it."

"Okay, what happened?"

"Something is wrong. No one is picking up. This can't be good."

"Maybe she's being leveraged by the men who are trying to overthrow her brother. That's what I'd do. It's obvious she's the family's weakness. However, they don't know who they are dealing with now. Gambino is behind this. We don't know who works for him and his plan."

"We'll be there in twenty." Savio tries to placate me, but traffic is at a standstill. It always is this time of day.

*Fuck, fuck, fuck.*

"Running would be faster than this traffic—these damn trains and trams. My God, I guess this is why I live up the hill," I say, pushing my right foot to the floorboard even though I'm not driving. I put my right hand on the grip area in the door's panel, clinching it with my hand so I don't pound the dashboard.

"Easy there, Massimo."

"Yeah, I don't want to fuck up your vehicle, it's a nice Mercedes."

Savio gives me a wry smile. It's a bad situation. I'm ready to lose my shit, and we need to break up the anger welling inside me.

Savio makes an illegal pass on a car ahead of us. It's risky, considering we have weapons, and the polizia have the uncanny ability to give out way too many tickets for shit like this. They add more and more officers every year and don't get me started on the criminal investigations. Pretty soon, we're going to Switzerland with our bank accounts and making inroads north.

I'm a visual person, and the roadmap to work with Grandfather is mapped in my head. Even if I piss him off, I'm worth more to him alive than dead, plus I'm family. That would be a huge no-no, as the rest of the guys wouldn't trust him if anything happened to me.

Hell, the Pope could kill me, and my grandfather would be in the hot seat to account for it. That's how respected I am, but today I feel like a jilted lover. And I hate the feeling.

"There, the sign is ahead." Savio swerves to the right and presses the gas pedal, making us take an exit faster than what's deemed safe, judging by the sign posted by the road. We're on two wheels when we come to a screeching halt in front of the hospital. Savio drops me off in front of the tall new building with a wing the Michelis built, and now I'm not as pissed about it. It's not like the day we discovered we didn't win the bid to build it.

I run up to the elevator and bump into Micro coming

out, and my phone rings. He's calling me, only I'm here already.

"Fuck, that motherfucking man with the ugly as fuck neck tattoo of a skull and needles."

"He's Russian, Ivan is his name. Bad motherfucker if I say so myself. Where is Valentina?"

"They jabbed me with a sedative, and she's gone. I found this." He hands me her phone.

"Fuck, can't even ping her. Not that they'd be that stupid."

"Right, what now?" Micro asks. "I'm sorry, Massimo, she's fantastic, I'd take a bullet for her any day."

"You bet your ass you would." I clap him on the back.

Savio circles around and comes back to get me.

I'm so twisted up over the fact that I love her, I can't think straight.

"We know the Gambinos have a motive, he's the underboss, he has to have help, and now we have a Russian. This is larger than just an internal Sicilian takeover. Giovi can't beat this himself with that kind of money, men, and firepower."

"I'm sure Dante wants his name cleared. And it appears they aren't safe with Gabriella waltzing around killing at will." Savio makes a good point. "Gabriella is still in the wind. Good God, I hope she doesn't have her."

"There was another man with Ivan, tall, a bit round, I've seen him at the house in passing when Valentina first arrived."

"That might be her guard, Ridolfo."

"Sounds to me like they have a lead time longer than my arm," Micro comments.

I call Dante, filling him in, and he agrees it's time for a family meeting.

We drive to Sal's home as Dante is still on his honeymoon.

Marchello looks at Prende, his look is showing more concern than he should in front of her.

"Blood is blood," Dante says through the speakerphone in the middle of the table. We're all sitting around the round table and it's eerie how quickly it's turned into a war room.

"Sorry to interrupt your honeymoon," I say.

"Blood is blood, Prende's father was killed, now Valentina's, and we're not safe until we know what Gabriella wants. We can't live with this hanging over us."

"I have to reserve a larger jet, I think we need a tour of Sicily."

"I'll check the airports," Francesca adds, and her fingers fly across the laptop she pulls from her bag. "I can see if a plane flew there."

"Sal, hook them up with supplies. Sorry, I'm not able to help on this run. Marchello, you stay here, run the business, and be our liaison."

"Got it."

"They flew out over an hour ago," Francesca announces.

"That's well-timed," I muse.

"Well planned for sure." Sal nods to Francesca.

Even though it's battle time, I get a taste of the chemistry between the two of them, and it reminds me that these coward holding Valentina could be cutting or raping her as we play catch up.

We head to warehouses I didn't know about before and gather tons of C-4, tranquilizer darts, AR-15s, AK-47s, knives, and flash bombs.

"Jesus, Francesca, you guys can take over the world from here."

She smiles, the light in her eyes only rivals that which she carries for Sal.

"You know it, I bet we could. We'll get her back, Massimo."

"Yeah, blood for blood." Sal packs items similar to power bars and refillable water containers in a bag. He even has bulletproof vests and camouflage wear.

I'm fucking impressed. My day is starting to look up as I have some control now that we're pooling our resources.

It is a quick flight to Sicily, and we've got bags of gear packed, and we booked a house to rent that's not in Palermo. Francesca and Sal booked it online. We know the streets are crawling with adversaries, and we have no clue who is on who's side or the fate of Giovi, or his mother. We need to get eyes on the De Luca castle to find out if he's under siege.

We assume telecommunications are limited or monitored. Francesca and I head out, having changed into clothing more typical of tourists with a backpack filled with snacks to cover our contraband. I have an idea of the setup of the home from that and what she's told me over the past months.

We don't think Giovi is hurt, otherwise, there would be no use for Valentina, she's only important if they need her to get what they want. A new don can't take over unless he's dead.

I lead Francesca down a narrow path by the beach, and we use the scope in her backpack to obtain visuals if we can. I hope Ridolfo isn't inside the home, he could open the door and let the enemy walk in without warning.

It just so happens we find Giovi making a hot spot on his

computer and using his phone, but Francesca is on top of it and intercepts the call with her encrypted laptop.

"Giovi, are you okay?"

"Yes, but they have my sister, I don't know where. They want to exchange us." He pauses. What does one say in light of the grim situation?

"Gambino is one of the main players behind this, who else?"

"I'm not sure, but he must have a lot of my bosses to have me holed up here like a rat."

"So, who else can be involved, and what are their addresses?" Francesca has her hair up in a ponytail that is wrapped around a baseball cap that has *Italia* on it.

She pulls a pen out and a small notepad, writes down names and addresses, and then keys them into the dark web to get the few details the intranet ironically doesn't have.

"Who is Laura's father? I see there are numerous pings off cell towers to a Paulo."

"Son of a bitch, that's Valentina's best friend. Her father must be in on it as his future son-in-law just bought a house he can't afford unless he had some ill-gotten gains.

"Okay, anyone else you can think of? Do you have any ideas where they might be holding Valentina?"

"It has to be a warehouse at the port where those bosses move contraband or one of their homes. I don't know. I can't think of any other place they could be."

"Okay, sit tight. Do you need anything?"

"We're fine now, but the sooner, the better, as they say."

"Of course. Trust me, no one wants your sister back more than me."

"Thanks, I'll wait to hear from you. I'd offer you more men, but I don't know who is on my side. Some will wait it out until it's over."

"Of course, we're on it." I hang up the cell phone.

Francesca writes down addresses as she goes and runs checks on the businesses and holding companies in the area.

"Are we sure she's in the area?"

"Let's hope we also have ships here, too. I know you're upset, but they want her alive," Francesca takes a second to reassure me.

"Well, I have a list, and we can tail Gambino and Laura, and I have Ridolfo's address. I'm thinking we can take his daughter Laura and we can play kidnap roulette," Francesca shrugs as she takes a sandwich out of a decent-sized plastic bag, shakes the crumbs out, and then stuffs the bag into her backpack.

"So it's a possibility. Let's meet with Sal and Micro to see if they have made any progress on tracking down the addresses under surveillance.

"Sounds good. Dibs on that fuck Ridolfo," I state. "I'm killing his ass."

"You got it." Francesca closes her laptop, unbothered. I'm still trying to figure out how she fits in with the group of us men, but her mad hacking skills are impressive. I never figured a woman would be inclined to do that, but then again, I grew up and worked in a business dominated by men.

We walk along the beach, and Savio picks us up at the road.

"I have the locations, but Sal said we need Francesca to hack into the video feeds. We found an old storeroom at the back of Gambino's seafood shell company, and it could be a place to hold someone."

"Great, let's go." Francesca climbs in first and launches programs on her phone.

By the time this is accomplished, it's late in the after-noon, but we manage to get his place of 'business' done, and we go to a place that's not close to where we're staying to grab pizzas and beer.

"I'm concerned that Valentina has been gone a day."

"In a usual kidnapping situation, I'd say that's a huge concern, but we know what we're dealing with here, more or less. And we're here. Faster than any other team could be, and we'll find her," Sal says.

I order pizzas to go, so we have food back at the house we're renting. We grab wine, vodka, and limoncello from a grocery store.

Francesca sits at the dining room table and monitors her hacked system.

"Looks like we have activity." We all crowd around her and see Gambino, as Valentina ID'd him for me from the Alps pictures.

"Yeah, that's him. If we follow him, we'll eventually track his people and find her. A hostage needs to eat and be taken care of." I state the obvious. There is no way I can sleep tonight, or any night until I find her alive and well.

"We'll find her," Savio murmurs, pouring himself vodka and cranberry.

"Hell, forget the juice, Savio," I tease. It's been a long and complicated day.

I flip on the TV and find the local news channel to keep my mind occupied, and there is live coverage of a restaurant on fire, and they mention the address.

"Oh shit," Francesca announces.

"What?" I ask, turning it up.

"That's Luciano's restaurant. It's an address I know, it came up under De Luca's name today. I ran it for additional places to watch."

"Now we don't have to, that eliminates one place, though it would have been stupid to use it, although it has food and a bathroom." Micro shrugs, and I hit him on the back to tell him he's an ass.

Meanwhile, Gambino is in his storeroom on the camera I watch with Francesca, and he's on the phone; he gets money from a safe and leaves.

"We need to trail him. He's paying someone for dirty deeds."

"Yeah, let's go, Francesca, you can stay here," Sal suggests.

"Like hell, I'm not missing out on any action," she says and closes her laptop, grabs a jacket, and is the first to the door.

Micro drives, passing the building and observing Gambino meeting with a man in the alley.

"That looks like—" Francesca pulls up social media accounts. "Yes, that's Marco, Laura's fiancé. Damn, Valentina is one popular woman. She's been the target all along."

I clear my throat, although I know she doesn't mean any disrespect by it.

We drive by like we live on the street and wait until Marco leaves. Gambino goes back inside; he's alone, but we don't know who might show up next. There could be more than one person milling around. Chances are higher he's not alone, not when a war to take over the island is at stake.

"What do we do?" I ask.

"Let's take our weapons and find out. We'll get more information kicking in doors than knocking on them. I'll disable their cameras so they don't see us coming."

"I'm so in love with you," Sal says to her, giving her a sensual kiss.

She pulls her tiny backpack on over her jacket, puts her

Beretta in a holster covered by her jacket, and we all arm ourselves.

I pack some C-4 just in case shit goes sideways. We're not on our home turf, and I'm not leaving anything to chance. The fire going on down the street will take up valuable resources from the town. I doubt there will be any police driving by, besides, they're all on someone's payroll, and there are no others who would come here to do what we're doing.

Sicily keeps to themselves unless it involves crimes that are tried in Rome and are huge cases that could gut them.

We line up and carefully walk down the alleyway to the back door Federico Gambino just walked through.

There are two new arrivals in the alley going to the same door.

Francesca sneaks around the cars like a cat, jumps, and kicks the largest man in the chest knocking him to the ground.

I'm behind her and take the next goon, throwing a punch at him and connecting with his jaw. His head turns and I throw up an opposing elbow to swing his head back towards me as he puts his arms up to defend himself.

I use the taser on the ring I collected, it tases him and he falls to the ground where I pistol whip him unconscious.

I turn to see how Francesca is doing and she is punching the shit out of the man's face. Sal is by her side, telling the man to give up the location of Valentina.

"Fuck you," he spits.

Francesca whips out a knife and runs it through his shoulder, separating it from the bone, and the man cries out in excruciating pain.

"Wanna try that again?" she asks in Italian.

"Ahh," is all the man can get out.

"You useless piece of shit," she mumbles, stabbing him through his boat shoes and the meat of his foot.

God, she's amazing to watch. I'm so happy she's not pissed at me.

"Boat," he manages to get out as she slits his throat. The alley falls silent.

We check our surroundings again and approach the door.

I turn the handle, it's open. I look at Francesca, and she nods. She's got me covered. Sal is armed behind her, and Micro is in the rear.

We enter. I scope out the top part of the building, which is mostly old rafters with a walkway, it's dimly lit. The sound of a man speaking draws our attention to the back room.

He hangs up the phone.

"Who are you?"

Just our luck, an asshole walks out of the bathroom.

Francesca doesn't even look at him and raises her right fist, breaking his nose, then she turns to face him.

His hands are on his nose as he tries to scream, she stuffs a rag from the floor in his mouth to buy a few seconds. Sal hands her a wire, and she strangles him like she is slicing bread.

We arrive at the doorway and find Federico in the stuffy office sitting at his chair, drinking amber liquor in an old swivel chair that squeaks.

"That's great. Wow, what a fire that is, that will piss Giovi off."

I raise my finger for everyone to be quiet and still, our guns raised.

"I don't know. Just hold her, Marco, no one is going to be by the fishing boats, and she has a bathroom. Is it asking too much for what I paid you? Don't make me regret having you move up in rank." His phone beeps when he hangs up.

Francesca puts two fingers up, she's going first. She looks kinda kick ass in the jacket, ball cap, and boots to her ankles that are more military looking than anything. She's no little woman either, she's built.

I nod.

We both enter the room, one on each side of Gambino.

"What the fuck do you want?" The big man sits, but I know he must have a gun under his desk.

"Carefully move your chair away from the desk, nothing too quick," I say.

"Ay, you have the wrong guy. I don't know what you want, but I have men coming, and you're going to be fucked."

He's not moving.

Francesca nods to me, we had discussed my background on the flight down and decided to take the lead roles of shooting assholes. It seems it brings us both pleasure.

I have him covered in his chair as Francesca moves around to knock his chair backward. He kicks his legs up to try to kick the gun out of her hand, but she's too quick. She tips the chair with great force as he's a big man, and he goes over face-first into the concrete floor.

He moans as he hurts. As if we care.

I hold a gun on him, and Sal moves to zip-tie him and gets him into a sitting position on the floor.

"Please put him in the chair, sweetie," she says to Sal.

Sal makes him stand, although as stupid as the Sicilian is, I'm sure he knows what's coming.

"Normally, I'd let Valentina's fiancé knock you off, but I'll let him have Marco." She hostlers her gun and pulls out that large sandwich bag she had earlier. The one in her backpack. She wraps it around his head and tightens it as he kicks and flails around as Sal, Micro, and I hold his extremities.

When he's lifeless, Micro says, "One down, more to go."

"Let's go," I signal the door. We want to get in and out before anyone else shows up.

Someone might check the cameras that are offline and come to check things out. There are men on every street corner, and who knows what side they are on. We still have danger ahead as we creep back to the van and pull out of the alley, waiting until we get to the road to turn the headlights on.

The streets are crowded with people watching the smoke in the air and the wail of sirens from fire trucks.

## 29

## VALENTINA

I am sitting in an old fishing shack on the docks where the ships come in with fresh fish. It's one of the family's fronts to pay men to work that go out and get what they can, and we make sure they stay in business. That I do know, as I like being by the water and have seen funny business down here occasionally.

The shack stinks of fish guts even though it's been hosed off, and I'm tied to a chair. The rope they used is the one for boats, and it scratches my skin and feels like a wire brush.

I'm wondering how far out they thought these plans through. Sure, I loved Laura like a sister, and it hurts that her fiancé is in with the bad guys, and I assume her father is probably behind this too. It's fitting that all the rats in this nest are closely tied by familiar ties.

Since I've been here most of the day after I woke up, I've had time to think, and once I saw the Russian with the neck tattoo, who I didn't know was Russian as I never spoke to him at the gala. But, just the same, he's a big-time mafia, and now I think the Russians are behind this takeover as much as my father's traitors.

The tell for me was that Laura, Samira, and Massimo were the only ones outside Micro and Savio who knew I was at the hospital this morning. I can't believe Ridolfo served us my entire life and turned on us.

I hope Giovi and Mama are okay. I'm stiff from sitting, the fast food he gave me hurt my stomach. I'm the daughter of the Goddamn don, and I'm pissed off that this was so easy for them.

But mostly I want to see Massimo and make sure things are okay with us. I grew up today. Now, I want to get the hell out of here and get on with the next chapter of my life.

"I have to pee," I say.

"You can wait," he mumbles.

Even though Laura loves Marco, I never knew him well. I just wanted to be loved and happy with a man like he was with Laura. Now that the veil has been removed and I see him for himself, I wonder if Laura was in on this. She was a last-minute addition to the gala, and it's not like her to be mooning over a man if she really loved Marco. I think she purposely pretended to be distracted that night.

I'm trying to remember what Papa said in this situation. I'm supposed to make friends with Marco and make it harder for him to kill me. I hate to give him the satisfaction of sucking up to him. I don't think he has the stones for it, but I don't want to find out. If it comes down to it, I'll delay him by offering him a blowjob. He seems to think with his dick anyway.

I'm cut off from the world. The shack is old, and the night's cold wind blows through it. I'm glad I wore pants today. I don't know how I will stay awake, but I have to look for an opportunity to get out.

Something exploded thirty minutes ago. Marco taunted me with the news. Papa's first self-made restaurant burned to the ground. It seems this was like a kickoff event for the evening. It seemed to be significant to Marco, but who knows?

Dolts.

It's dark. Only an old light bulb is hanging from the ceiling, and it looks like it could fall off the electrical cord at any minute. I can't believe men work in these conditions. Maybe the men under Papa were pissed at him.

My body is stiff as a corpse. I've seen one of those now. I don't want to be the next one. No. Gambino and Gabriella need to go. There's no doubt in my mind she and her dad were in this together. Why did she leave all those years ago and suddenly return, and this master plan unfolds?

What are the odds of that? I've had time to contemplate that as well.

Our dog hates her. They are good judges of character. She was at both events where the murders occurred, and no one else I've been in contact with has shown me any other evidence. Well, sure the Micheli family were at their own wedding, and their family was there as well.

Even if they wanted Argon dead, we didn't know them. We have no beef with them. We have our own pipelines to move anything we want. Papa never met Massimo before the gala, he dealt with his grandfather, but we were in debt. And Papa was old school and didn't like debt, so that makes no sense. Plus, selling me cleared the slate. I hope it's not Massimo's grandfather.

All this time in my room on the island, I've had time to put together the 'family' Papa had, and from my window, I could see the drugs being brought in here with the fish. I'm sure every joint the family owns launders money, and no one on the island can say a peep, or they disappear.

I'm not sure who does that part. I don't want to know. I

hope I get out of here soon. I'm nauseous from the smell and want a shower. I know Massimo will find me. He has to. He's done it before. He can do it again. He has enough money to buy all the help he needs.

Then it dawns on me. Maybe these guys want money from him for me.

Fuck, I didn't even consider that.

If that's the case, the sky's the limit. I hope they don't know how wealthy my fiancé is.

Marco left briefly and returned with a few paninis. He gives me one, and I'm so hungry I scarf it down. He gives me water to drink, and now we wait as night falls, and I wonder how long I'll be here.

I'm not going to think about any other alternative. Marco lets me use the bathroom with a gun on me. As if I'm capable of taking him. I had to pee so badly. I'm sleepy, and I force myself to stay awake. The wind blowing in the weathered slats in the wall continues to wake me.

I must have drifted off. I hear a bang.

I jolt in my chair, but I hurt and can't move very far.

Massimo? Is it him, or am I imagining it?

There are words, then Massimo pistol whips Marco upside the head before he shoots him like a dog, and he and Francesca wrap him in fishing nets and hook his body on a boat anchor before they send him out to sea.

Sal cuts through the ropes holding me. I try to move and can't. I'm in pain. I try to stand. Sal catches me when I slump forward.

"Breathe." His voice comforts me, and he puts his jacket around my shoulders.

"I'm thirsty," I whisper.

"Just a minute, Massimo will be here in a minute."

My eyes close, I'm tired.

"Valentina." It's Massimio and his strong and capable arms wrap around me as I lean into him, safe at last.

"I'm so sorry. I love you. I was crazy without you. I'd never stop looking for you," he promises as he squeezes me to him like he'll never let me leave his sight again.

"I love you too. I'm sorry about the ring. I was afraid I might not be able to tell you that. I'm so sorry. I was full of stubborn pride."

"No, I judged you on your background and upbringing, never realizing you wanted something different." He's kissing my dry lips, and I don't know why. I smell, I'm tired, I have no idea what time it is.

"Giovi?"

"He's fine. We knew where you were, and he just had to sit tight. It seems some of your father's men set him up and were going to take over. We changed that, and they realized that you were the person they could use against your brother."

"And Laura?"

"She worked with Marco, but we're not going after her. I don't do women and children. But she'll pay. They'll be broke because her father was a part of this, too."

I would have cried knowing them my entire life, but I just want to get back home with my family. All of my family.

Massimo helps me in the van, and minutes later, we arrive at my brother's house. Giovi and Mama run out and hug me. I'm sobbing. I'm so relieved to see them and know the worst is over for me.

Or so I think.

Massimo helps me take a shower. I'm so exhausted I fall asleep in my old bed and in his arms. I swear he's going to watch me all night to make sure I'm okay.

## 30

---

## MASSIMO

I can't believe I found Valentina, and holding her in my arms wasn't enough to reassure me she is okay. I can't let her out of my sight. She sleeps so peacefully, and I can't believe I almost screwed up the most important relationship in my life.

I'm never taking her for granted and can't wait to get her home. I fell asleep next to her hugging tight enough to smother her with my love. I never want to be apart from her again.

Breakfast was a feast, and the gang showed up. Everyone hugged Valentina and she cried when she heard of what all transpired to save her. She grew up with these men, and it was all about money.

Dante called Sal to make sure we were all fine and that he'd see us in another week. They are on a Mediterranean cruise and enjoying themselves, but they mostly sat on the phone until we resolved the issues in Sicily.

"I never doubted you guys for a minute," he said.

Yeah, well, it appears we're all tenacious sons of bitches,

and even though we're in a criminal organization, there is code amongst us, and we take care of business.

As word got to my grandfather and our friends in high places, it seems our mission isn't done until we find Gabriella.

Micro passes behind me and whispers that Francesca went out last night and took care of Rifolfo. I nodded. It's a fitting end for him, too.

"So, what is the deal with Ignazio, Mama?" Giovi asks.

"She got pregnant, gave the baby up, and disappeared. She was involved with a man that beat her and she knew he'd never let her, or the child, have a minute of peace. So she made the ultimate sacrifice, and she must have given the baby up for adoption. She visited once here and there over the years, but when Don Conti died, she was home more and was close to her father."

"You're not kidding about that. Like father, like daughter, I guess. I heard Conti wasn't a treat to deal with either," Valentina said.

"He wasn't a good person at all," Sal says, "Dante tried to negotiate with him and found Juliet to use as a pawn. Things went south after they met, and it was dicey for a while. I'm so glad that's behind us, but really, how much more do we have to go through to be safe?" Sal asks.

"We won't be safe until Gabriella is dead," Francesca murmurs in a low voice. "I know my father and if Gabriella is anything like him, we'll have to be on top of our game."

"Really? She's that bad?" Valentina asks as she sits between her brother and me. It seems the two have returned to the closeness they had when they were younger.

She's smiling and happy to be here. I wonder for a minute if she wants to stay in Sicily.

"We have to track her down. I have contacts, and

Massimo has some, too. We're watching the borders. I doubt she'll be in Switzerland. It appears that she's fluent in so many languages it makes sense she'll be in France or Russia," Francesca says.

"Russia? Really?" Valentina's mother, Emilie, asks.

"Oh, she's quite accomplished. She has a few fake IDs that pass as real. She's highly financed, and she'll probably be on the move now. She'll be questioned for the murder of Argon and your husband. Both were killed the same way, and she was at both places. We're going to turn over all our evidence as soon as we get home," Sal states. I've hear he's good with numbers, logistics, and putting things together like this.

"Yeah, one of my guys had a picture of him from the ski trip, and Valentina recognized Gambino. I'm pretty sure the woman with her back to the camera is Ignazio, as we now know her," Massimo reiterates. "I'm sure we'll find more now that we know who we're looking for."

Valentina puts her hand on my leg under the table and squeezes it as she leans into my shoulder as I wrap my arm around her.

"I don't know how to thank you all for all that you've done." Giovi takes a sip of coffee.

"You're family Giovi, don't forget that." I smile a genuine smile. I've found a great family.

"We're all family. When are you two setting the date?" Giovi asks.

"I don't know. I got a job at the children's hospital as a child life specialist, so we'll be busy."

"Really?" I ask. I never got to hear the outcome of that.

"Congratulations, Valentina," Micro says. "I'm so sorry I lost you."

"It's okay. They were determined. It has a happy ending."

"Yes, it does," I say that because I won't rest until Gabriella has paid for killing Valentina's father. Her entire mission was to set Dante up to take the fall for two murders, prevented Juliet's first attempt at her wedded bliss, and sullied the Micheli name. She'll get her due.

Champagne pops, and Valentina gives a start as Sal pulls glasses from the cupboards in the kitchen and pours champagne.

"Papa always has good alcohol," Valentina snickers, taking a glass of bubbly.

Sal hands us all a filled glass. I look across the table to Francesca who is calm, but Micro, and I have no ideas of what's going on. Giovi and his mother look on, waiting for his next move. I exchange a questioning look with Valentina.

"I wish Dante and Juliet and Marchello were here for this because I wanted to share this moment with everyone. With that being said, I can't wait any longer." He turns to Francesca. "Francesca, you're my world, my life. I love you. I can't imagine a life without so much excitement in it."

And yes, we all snickered at that. Now that I'm in on the secret of her being quite the femme fatal.

Francesca listens, giving the calm appearance of a gentlewoman as her hair cascades over her shoulders and down her back. She's radiant. Her ears hold large diamond earrings, and there's a sparkle in her eye. She's a far cry from the woman who wore a ball cap and baggie that suffocated a man to death yesterday.

"Will you marry me?" Sal kneels, taking her hand in his.

I haven't known them very long, but the amount of love in this kitchen is warmer than numerous suns. I find it cathartic with my dark past and it reminds me that life can change on a dime. In my darkness, I'm accumulating these incredible moments of light.

"Yes, I will," Francesca smiles as Sal kisses her properly on her perfect lips to seal the deal.

"Great, because I need you to pick out your ring." Sal chuckles, and we all laugh.

She smiles and nods, "Smart man, so pragmatic. I love that about you," she says, giving him another lingering kiss.

We finished with the congratulations, we all pitch in to clean the kitchen, and just as we gather in the living room to talk about Luciano and happier times, I got a phone call. I don't want to talk to my grandfather now. I want to enjoy this moment get Valentina home, and install more safety protocols.

"Answer, it might be important," Valentina urges me.

"You do have a way about you. You are the only person who gets to tell me to do anything." I'm smiling when I say it.

I answer the phone and the room falls silent.

I listen, say thank you, and hang up. I take a deep breath and let out a sigh.

"What, Massimo?" Valentina asks.

"Gabriella crossed the border, and she's in Belarus."

"Russia?" Francesca asks.

"In winter? Is she crazy?" Giovi asks, and I understand it's more of a rhetorical question.

"That's below-freezing temperatures now," I note.

I look at Sal, Micro, and Francesca. "I guess we can wait till March. We'll need time to prepare. This is a huge undertaking, and I'm so happy we will have a stockpile of toys for every occasion," I flash my cocky grin.

"Um, do we know anything about this situation? I just got you back," Valentina softly spoke into my ear.

"Oh, you've got nothing to worry about my little bluebird. We're getting married before I finish this." I kiss her in front of her entire family.

I hope you enjoyed Dirty Born! If you want more, download the bonus scene here Dirty Born Bonus Scene or https://dl.bookfunnel.com/lvtd3lymvs. The hunt for a killer is on, and you can grab the exciting conclusion to the series as well as Riccardo's love story in Dirty Deals. https://www.amazon.com/gp/product/Bo9NMMPTN2

# FREE SAMPLE OF ITALIAN KING

Italian King Sample Chapters
https://geni.us/ItalianKingBookLink

Dante is the head of the family and he has his challenges

cut out for him when his plan to gain access to a port with a rival mafia family backfires.

Kidnapping

Close Proximity

Suspense

Thriller

# ALSO BY ZOE BETH GELLER

Dirty: A Dark Mafia Romance Series

Dirty: A Dark Mafia Romance Series (Micheli Mafia) Series of 5 books

Italian King: A Dark Mafia Romance (Micheli Mafia) Book 1

Dirty Vengeance: A Dark Mafia Romance (Micheli Mafia) Book 2

Dirty Bargain: A Dark Mafia Romance (Micheli Mafia) Book 3

Dirty Born: A Dark Mafia Romance (Micheli Mafia) Book 4

Dirty Deals: A Dark Mafia Romance (Michell Mafia) Book 5

Dirty Series Dark Mafia Fan Group

Volkov Brava

King's Promise: An Arranged Marriage Romance

Maine Megalodons

Faking it with the Football Star

Maine Maulers Hockey Series

Series 2

Maine Maulers Hockey Series

Rookie in Love

Jagged Ice

Hotter than Puck

Benched by the Nanny

Puck in the Oven

Sin Bin Hockey Series

Series 1

Tyler: Hooked (Free prequel to the series)

The Sin Bin Hockey Series

Jackson: Against the Boards

Alan: Between the Pipes

Erik: Fire and Ice

Blayze: Slap Shot

Paavo: The Defender

Spencer:Penalty Box

Isak: Coach

Kaden: Game Time

Liam: The Enforcer

Jake: Roughing

The Sin Bin Hockey Series Box Sets

The Sin Bin Hockey Series Box Set Books 1-4

The Sin Bin Hockey Series Box Set Books 5-7

The Sin Bin Hockey Series Box Set Books 8-10

Zoe Beth Geller's Hockey Pond Fan Group

# ACKNOWLEDGMENTS

Thank you to everyone who is following me on this journey. I hope you are enjoying this series. Special thanks to my hubby for his support.

# ABOUT THE AUTHOR

I live in SWFL Florida with my grown kids and grandkids. When not writing I enjoy swimming, cooking, family nights and watching my son play ice hockey. I've kinda become the team mom which is cute because my kids aren't 'kids', they are adults!

I am the author The Sin Bin Hockey Series which is a collection of 10 standalone novels. There is a bit of continuity across books and they do not need to be read in order.

My second series, Maine Mauler Hockey Series, is a pro team series based, obviously, in Maine! These are interconnecting romances that can be read as standalone, but due to the interaction between players and a series arc it is best if you read it in order.

Other works include my dark mafia -The Dirty Series: A Dark Mafia Romance (Micheli Mafia). This was inspired by my love of Italy and I've visited family there many times. It's my home away from home. This series starts off with Italian King. These books should be read in order as the plots and romances are involved and carry through with the murder, mystery and suspense plot. This is a 5 book series. Book one is not as dark as it gets, it all builds. Book 2 is femme fatale because Francesca spoke to me and took off. If you know my books you'll know it's like a rollercoaster. Set up, get to the peak and then the Whoosh to the end. But this romantic suspense series builds as a murder mystery! I consider this a Steamy Contemporary romance where the mafia aspect grows and grows, and some characters, and scenes, are darker than others.

Want to sign up for the low down on my progress on the next book? Send me feedback? Want to join contests and enter for giveaways? If mafia is your jam, you can sign up for here for the Mafia Newsletter

Hockey fans can sign up here and get Tyler free. If you just want to sign end not get the free prequel, up you can do so here.

What to be an ARC reader? Sign-up for my ARC! You can do hockey or mafia or both. It's like shopping, tons of options!

Fan Groups


Zoe Beth Geller's Hockey Pond
The Dirty Series: Dark Mafia Romances


Follow me on TT at zoebethgellerauthor1


ZBG Website

www.ingramcontent.com/pod-product-compliance
Lightning Source LLC
Chambersburg PA
CBHW070535310726

48976CB00002BA/630